★ "Smith's fast-paced and compelling historical novel would be a valued addition to any collection."
—*SCHOOL LIBRARY JOURNAL*, STARRED REVIEW

★ "Through meticulous research, Smith immerses her readers in a war narrative not often told to American readers, as well as a conflict-filled love story."
—*THE HORN BOOK*, STARRED REVIEW

"Smith's beautifully written book examines the strength and limits of patriotism, while also being a quiet portrait of deep love . . . This is the kind of high-stakes love story that will leave readers stressed and sighing in equal measure, yet grateful to have seen the portrait of these two lives."
—*BOOKLIST*

"This absorbing historical novel, set in Japan during eight days in 1945, thrusts two teens in the midst of war into a charged romance."
—*PUBLISHERS WEEKLY*

"A pensive depiction of young love and endurance amid wartime uncertainty."
—*KIRKUS REVIEWS*

"[Hana and Taro's] short time together easily lends the story the sighs and swoons of a doomed romance, but their relationship is not so much star-crossed as it is a genuine depiction of two terrified kids finding a respite, however brief, from the hopelessness of war."
—*THE BULLETIN OF THE CENTER FOR CHILDREN'S BOOKS*

THE
BLOSSOM
AND THE
FIREFLY

Also by

SHERRI L. SMITH

Flygirl

Orleans

Pasadena

The Toymaker's Apprentice

THE
BLOSSOM
AND THE
FIREFLY

SHERRI L. SMITH

PENGUIN BOOKS

PENGUIN BOOKS
An imprint of Penguin Random House LLC, New York

First published in the United States of America by G. P. Putnam's Sons, 2020
Published by Penguin Books, an imprint of Penguin Random House LLC, 2021

Visit us online at penguinrandomhouse.com

THE LIBRARY OF CONGRESS HAS CATALOGED THE G. P. PUTNAM'S SONS EDITION AS FOLLOWS:
Names: Smith, Sherri L., author.
Title: The blossom and the firefly / Sherri L. Smith.
Description: New York: G. P. Putnam's Sons, [2020]
Summary: Told in two voices, seventeen-year-old kamikaze pilot
Taro and fifteen-year-old war worker Hana meet
in 1945 Japan, he with no future and she haunted by the past.
Identifiers: LCCN 2019005509 | ISBN 9781524737900 (hc) |
ISBN 9781524737917 (ebook)
Subjects: LCSH: World War, 1939–1945—Japan—Juvenile fiction. | CYAC: World War,
1939–1945—Japan—Fiction. | Kamikaze pilots—Fiction. | Musicians—Fiction. |
Family life—Japan—Fiction. | Japan—History—1926–1945—Fiction.
Classification: LCC PZ7.S65932 Blo 2020 | DDC [Fic]—dc23
LC record available at https://lccn.loc.gov/2019005509

Penguin Books ISBN 9781524737924

Printed in the United States of America

Design by Maggie Edkins
Text set in Sabon LT Pro

1 3 5 7 9 10 8 6 4 2

FOR PEACE

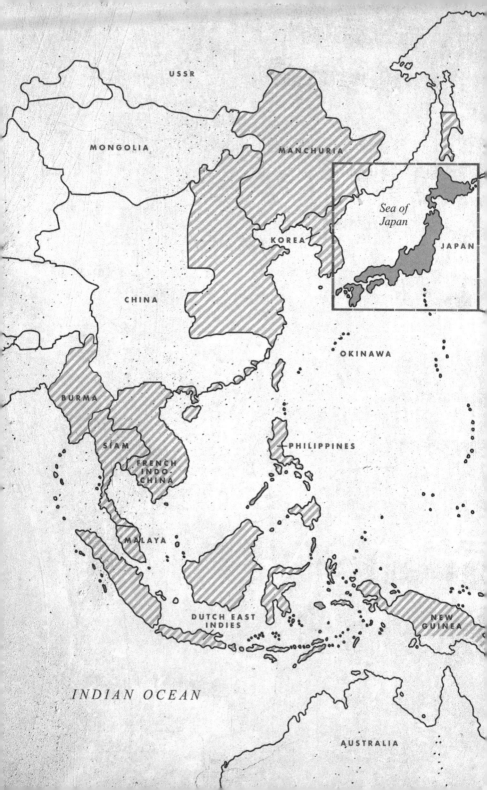

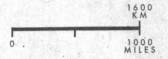

THE
EMPIRE
OF JAPAN

PACIFIC OCEAN

THE
HOME
ISLANDS
OF
JAPAN

*Sea of
Japan*

HOKKAIDO

HONSHU

HIROSHIMA

OITA
TACHIARAI

TOKYO

AKENO

SHIKOKU
KYUSHU

NAGASAKI
KAGOSHIMA BAY
CHIRAN

PACIFIC OCEAN

1945

CHAPTER 1

HANA

My father's voice wakes me—thick as wool, slightly scratchy. "Get up, Hana. It's time to get going." Music fills the room in a cresting wave. He must be playing the koto again.

Then a hand rocks my shoulder gently. I roll onto my back, flat on my futon, and open my eyes. There is no music. And I remember: my father has gone off to war.

My mother is there, kneeling beside me. She pours hot water from a kettle onto a fresh towel in the washbasin.

"Quickly now. Don't make Sensei wait."

She slips out of the room, and I lie there staring at the ceiling. Wooden slats, darkness. The sun will rise soon.

I get up. I roll my futon into a bundle, then push it into the closet. I kneel by the basin and unravel the hot towel with burning fingertips. Steam rises off of it like a sail in the wind. I drape it over my face, carefully wiping the corners of my eyes, my mouth. I breathe. Rinse the towel. Slide the cotton yukata from my shoulders to my waist and wipe my chest, my arms. They said the bruising would go away in a week or two. It's been three. What was once black and purple is now yellow and green, almost gone, but not quite. There is a stiffness that has not left me. But I no longer limp. I should be pleased.

I finish my towel bath and pull my uniform from the closet. Baggy monpé pants, deep blue, gathered at the ankles and at the waist. I push aside my work shirt and retrieve the rest of my school uniform. Blue jacket. Middy blouse with rounded collar—a bit loose lately. My mother has taken it in twice already, as food has grown less plentiful, folding in the seams without cutting the cloth, tacking the excess fabric down with optimistically loose stitches. As if food and peace are on the horizon and I will need those extra inches back. For now, the cotton bunches uncomfortably beneath my arms, but we must make do. This is a season of emergencies. As was the last season. And the one before.

I pull on white tabi socks, split between the big and second toe. Brush my hair in quick, long strokes and tie it into a knot at the back of my neck.

In the kitchen, a rice ball and a weak cup of hot tea await me. I use the tea to wash the taste of ash and dirt from my mouth. It's there every morning now, these past three weeks, no matter how I scrape my tongue or rinse with water. The rice sticks in my throat, but I know my duty. For a week I would not eat, and I fainted on my first day back with my classmates. Now I do not faint. I swallow the rice, drink the tea.

"Okā-san, I'm leaving," I call to my mother.

She is in the front room, the one that contains my father's tailoring business. The morning is dim outside, the house darker still. She sits at a low cutting table, sorting through scraps of fabric too small to be of use on their own. When the sun comes up fully, she will pull back the shutters and sew the scraps together by the light of day. Something can always be made of what remains, she says. I hope she is right.

"Have a good day, Hana. Give Kaori-sensei my best. And see if your farmer has any onions to trade. This patchwork would make decent pants for children."

"I will, Okā-san."

My mother believes I still work in the fields with my classmates, that I help the farmers indoors with their tallies, their bookkeeping—hence my clean collar, my school uniform instead of work clothes. She believes this because it is what I have told her. It's what we have been instructed to say to protect our families from worry. And the first lie I've ever told my mother.

I bow, slip my feet onto my platform geta, the cloth thong tucked snugly in the notch of my tabi, and slide open the front door.

There are both Western and Japanese houses here in Chiran. On the main street around the corner, many buildings have hinged doorways; some even have display windows. Covered in blackout cloth now, of course. The whole world has become darker in recent years. Lanterns at night are targets for the enemy.

Mariko is waiting for me across the wide road. I avoid the splashing stream that runs along the gutter. A gray-and-white carp glides by, headed for the river. Mariko is shivering. It's chilly today. April is always unpredictable. By noon, we will be sweating, no doubt.

Soon, Sachiko joins us, and Hisako, Kazuko. One by one, or

in twos and threes, the eighteen girls in my unit gather on the corner. We are the girls of Chiran Junior High School. Almost identical in our dark blue uniforms, white collars tucked in to make us less visible from the air. We wear our hair in braids or ponytails to keep it off our faces as we work.

Sensei arrives and claps us to attention. The sky is turning pearly gray. Shops are beginning to open their windows. Chiran is waking up. Everyone needs to take advantage of the daylight while it lasts.

And then we hear the rumble of the truck. And our workday begins.

The brakes argue with the road as the truck stops in front of my class. One by one, we climb into the back. They no longer pick us up at the junior high. The school is a hospital now. Our teacher enters last, pausing to catch her slipping geta so it doesn't fall into the road, and shuts the truck gate with both hands. We slide down the wooden bench and she sits. The truck complains an old man's gripe of grinding bones and dry joints, and lurches forward.

It runs up the rutted road, squeak-jostling at every bump, our young bodies flying up and down, as though on horseback. Mariko huddles against me for warmth, though the humidity is slowly rising. The road dwindles, leaving behind the roar of the river, the old samurai houses with their stone walls topped by high green hedges and tidy gardens framing the rolling peak of Hahagatake. The low-slung village homes built of disapproving wood, stained dark with age and rain. The countryside is ripe with the familiar scent of kuromatsu pine and cherry trees— with fewer blossoms now. We have to harvest at the shrine these days. We pass tea and sweet potato fields, climbing the gentle slope to Chiran Army Air Force Base. The sun is about to rise.

We arrive at the base and tumble out of the truck bed, clap our palms twice on the back door to let the driver know we are free of the wheels. The truck grumbles forward, pulling for home. We pause a moment, chattering like birds, like acolytes calling down a blessing of normalcy for the day. And then we begin.

We pinch each other's cheeks for color, comb the dust and leaves from our black hair. Only our youth keeps our cheeks plump and glowing. Beneath our thirteen, fourteen, fifteen years, we are old women with youthful, useful bones.

Sensei claps for our attention. We don our best smiles and clip-clop like trained ponies to the runway. We scoop our arms full of cherry blossoms, the branches showing like black bones through the creamy pink flesh, like starving women, once great beauties, with some beauty still. The pink-and-white petals fall like sighs, like hopeless love in a movie, in a song.

We line the pitted runway, treacherous in our wooden shoes, their raised soles marking the dusty gravel with soft equal signs. We are equal to the task. We are Japan.

The Tokkō Tai appear, olive uniforms sharply creased, flight jackets left behind. They won't need them where they are going. Their duty keeps them warm.

Saké is poured. Toasts raised. The generals give their speeches; the boys say their prayers. We accept their offerings. Gifts and letters. We offer courage in return.

We are the future of Japan.

These are our warriors.

They will save us.

The boys mount the steps to their aeroplanes, climbing toward heaven.

The girls wave goodbye.

The girls wave goodbye.

The girls wave goodbye.

Until there is no one left.

CHAPTER 2

HANA

Once I was a schoolgirl carrying books and giggling behind my hand with my friends. War was a thing for foreign places. But there has been no school in Chiran for a year now. Last April, even students were mobilized for the war effort. At first it almost seemed like a holiday. We went from studying books to weeding the sweet potato fields outside of town with the old farmers. It was hard work, but we all felt like we were doing something useful. Only we never guessed it would last so long. By summer, we were missing our lessons. By winter, it was as if our school days had been a dream. At least working in the fields assured we had food to eat. We were serving our country, and glad to do so.

And then one day, there were aeroplanes overhead, painted with large white stars. Bombs fell from the sky like overripe melons. Such a raid had never happened before so far from the base. I could not comprehend it, and stared at them in wonder.

And then everyone was screaming. I was screaming. An old woman digging potatoes beside me grabbed my hand. We ran and hid in silt trenches they'd had us dig alongside the road, where the dirt was clear of crops.

The melons burst like thunderclaps, throwing earth into the sky. My trench collapsed. I was buried alive.

Kaori-sensei knows this. My teacher was there, leading the charge to dig me out. It took a long time to find me. When they did, it was as though I had been dead a long time. My face was white with dust, my black hair gray. My monpé were caked with blood and soil, hardened into mud. I was a brick unbaked in an oven, waiting to dry.

"We've got her! She's here! She's here!" the old men cried, and they pulled me into the world like rough midwives, slapping my back to get me breathing clearly again. The other trenches had held, I learned later. We had been lucky, everyone said. My classmates were safe, and I was alive. But the old lady who had urged me to take cover was dead.

That was three weeks ago.

I was carried home on a plank of wood while everyone watched the skies overhead. Some stayed to retrieve the bodies, unburying the dead so they could cremate them properly. My mother was waiting in our doorway. She is often afraid to leave the house unattended, lest word of my father come while she is out. When she heard the news, she sent the neighbor's boy instead.

His geta slapped along the roadway as he ran ahead of us, echoing out a tattoo to which he shouted, "She's alive! Hana is alive!"

How I'd wished he'd shut up. Hadn't anyone told him? I was a ghost. I was like the others. I was dead, too.

Kaori-sensei does not know this. Nor my mother. Nor my friends. No one seems to know I am dead but me.

CHAPTER 3

TARO

Spring 1928

"Taro . . . Taro!"

The wings of the crane drifted overhead, white as snow, bright as his mother's smile.

"Taro . . . Taro!" The jingle of the paper bird on its string, the jounce of the stick over his head, the lilting voice singsonging his name.

Shōji walls, white ceiling, wall panel open to the burning blue sky.

"Taro!"

The little bird dipped and jostled, swooping and swinging through the air, white and crisp against the curve of a cheek, the corner of a smile.

Reaching fat hands, baby fists clutched, grasping at the sky.

CHAPTER 4

HANA

Our fathers have all gone to war. Or nearly all of them. Those that were able-bodied and strong. Otō-san left a year after the war with the West began. But Japan has been at war even longer. When I was barely two years old, the Emperor set his sights on China. A great depression had spread across the world. Japan was going hungry. Expanding into Manchukuo meant food and resources that the home islands could not provide. But Manchukuo was not enough. When I was eight, the Empire spread west and south across China, into Nanking, Beijing, and beyond, soldiers and aeroplanes carving the way. Some of the men in our village went to the mainland and came back with tales of adventure.

Japan had been hungry; now it feasted, and still its belly growled.

As our Empire grew, the long-reaching hands of the West tangled with our own across Asia. The British, the Americans, the French—everywhere the Emperor wished to be in the East, the West was also.

What the West forgets is that our Emperor is descended from

the sun. The sun shines where it wishes; it shines where it must so that the people may prosper.

And so, when I was twelve, our Emperor struck a mighty blow against the too-greedy Americans. The silver planes that had practiced over the bay in nearby Kagoshima flew straight and true to Hawaii and surprised the lazy Americans. Pearl Harbor was the site of that battle, and it began a new sort of war. One that has grown to swallow the world.

When my otō-san went away, he said, "It is an honor to serve the Emperor." But I knew he did not want to go. At night, I could hear him whisper through the shōji screens to my mother that America was too mighty. That determination could not feed and fuel an army. That Japan might not win this war.

But history tells us it is not the way of men to be satisfied. It is not the way of empires.

And so he went. Mother walked two steps behind him, holding my hand. We bowed together as he boarded the train. There was music and a whole crowd of people from the neighborhood. We waved flags and sang bright songs about the Emperor. Father reminded me to be brave.

"It is for you that we fight, Hana-chan. My little flower." But he did not say this in front of everyone. He left it in a note where only I would find it, tucked inside the strings of his prized instrument, his koto. A koto has thirteen strings, and they held the note tenderly as a butterfly. I still remember the pressure of his callused hands, strong from pulling and measuring fabric, thick-skinned from being pierced with needles, maneuvering my own soft fingers to learn the shape of the songs. Tailor's hands, musician's hands.

My father's koto lies silent now, alongside the wall of our second room, just as his shoes stay by the door and his photo rests near the butsudan altar, as if he is already an ancestor instead of a soldier. As if he is dead. His koto's wooden body lies on the tatami mat like a weeping woman who misses her true love. At least that's what my mother says. I suspect she is talking about herself. Okā-san should have been a poet. Instead, she is a tailor's wife, now a tailor herself. And, when I am not in service to the Emperor with my classmates, I am a tailor too. I lie silent as well, my voice stilled. I used to play the koto and sing. "Like a nightingale," Otō-san would say. He is a poet, too. But my classmates only sing in the service of the Emperor, and the songs they sing are of war.

Okā-san knows nothing of the waving, of the saying good-bye. What would she think—her little girl surrounded by rough soldiers, her daughter watching men go to die? We lie to keep our mothers happy. To do our duty well. We are good little citizens. Whatever we do, it is good.

CHAPTER 5

TARO

Spring 1933

"Taro, do you hear that?"

Little Taro tilted his head and listened. A sound like two boards slapping together, like geta clogs stamping on wood. The *click-clack* call of the kamishibai man! Taro's father hustled him into his shoes and a warm cotton jacket, and they were off—running up the street, turning the corner, hoping to beat the crowd. But it was too late, as always. Every child in the neighborhood was already there—and more than a few adults, too. They crowded around old Uncle Kamishibai—this uncle was a new one to Taro, with long hanging earlobes and a shiny golden tooth. He smiled and waved the children closer to his bicycle booth. The wooden kamishibai box on the back was open at the bottom—a drawer full of sweets! Taro's father elbowed the way forward and hoisted Taro into his arms to look inside the drawer. Taro chose two barley rice treats. His father clucked his tongue and handed over a coin.

"Thank you, Oji-san," Father said respectfully.

"Arigatō gozaimasu, Oji-san," Taro said.

His father held out his hand. "Give me one for later, Taro. Mother will say we've spoiled your dinner."

Taro handed the rice-paper-wrapped treat to his father, sadly watching it disappear into the gray suit pocket. Another hoist, and Taro was on his father's shoulders. They joined the back of the crowd as the old man set up his theater. The drawer slipped back inside the bottom of the box, and the top lifted up until the dark wood became a picture frame. The sides slid open like curtains in a movie theater, and suddenly it grew as quiet as the cinema when the lights go down.

Uncle lifted a thick yellowed paper card from the back of the box and slid it into place. The wooden frame was suddenly a window onto a forest. And Uncle said in a kindly voice that carried across the crowd, "There once was a very old couple who were not blessed with children of their own. Every day, the old man would go into the forest to gather twigs and sticks to sell as firewood, and the old woman would go down to the river to wash clothes . . ."

Taro made a low sound in his throat and clutched his father's shoulder. He knew this story! It was "Momotaro, the Peach Boy." He was a Taro, too—and a hero!

The kamishibai man shifted his voice to that of a little old woman. "Grandfather, Grandfather, look what I have found floating in the river!" The window frame showed the little couple inside their house, marveling at a giant momo, a peach.

"Let us cut it up and eat it together," said Uncle in the voice of an old man. But before they could cut the peach, it split open, revealing a beautiful little boy with shiny black hair and bright brown eyes.

"Your prayers have been answered. I have been sent from Heaven to be your loving son!" Uncle said in a strong young voice.

All of the children cheered, Taro included. His father patted his leg, bouncing him a little.

In the next illustration, the couple rejoiced and named their new son after the peach in which they had found him. Momotaro grew big and strong on Grandmother's millet dumplings.

"But then one day they heard of terrible doings. An island of demons was threatening the villages on the shore!" Uncle continued.

The children hissed and booed. The slides grew darker. Taro hid his face behind his fingers. Blood-red oni—demons with gnashing yellow teeth and rolling white eyes—filled the window, laughing and screaming as they stole food and money from the poor innocent villagers.

Then came the part Taro loved. Momotaro announced he would go to punish the demons. His mother made him a sack of dumplings, and his father wished him luck. He struck out across the countryside. Along the way, he met a dog.

"Momotaro, where are you going?" the kamishibai man howled.

And all the kids shouted, "I am going to fight the demons!"

"I am hungry," Uncle howled. "Give me a dumpling, and I will go with you!"

In the picture window, Momotaro tossed a delicious millet dumpling into the dog's open, smiling mouth. Then the two friends set off together, until they met a monkey. The monkey and dog fought terribly until Momotaro called out for them to stop.

"Momotaro, where are you going?" the kamishibai man yowled in his funny monkey voice.

And all the children cried, "We are going to fight the demons!"

"I am hungry. Give me a dumpling, and I will join you!" Uncle revealed a slide of the monkey hanging from a tree above Momotaro, reaching for the offered treat. Then the three friends traveled down the road until they met a pheasant.

"Momotaro, where are you going?" the kamishibai man asked, this time in a whistling cheeping voice.

"We are going to fight the demons!" Taro shouted.

His father laughed. "Good boy, Taro!"

The pheasant requested a dumpling and joined the little party.

When they finally reached the ocean, they found a boat and sailed across to the terrifying island of the demons. The pheasant flew up over the demons' castle and returned with advice on how to get in. Momotaro and his three friends stormed the castle and battled the demons in picture after picture, both frightening and funny.

The kamishibai man's demon voice sent shivers up Taro's back. He clutched his father's hair and held on, trying to be brave.

Finally, Momotaro was triumphant! He tied up the demon king, loaded the boat with all the stolen treasure, and returned it to the people to whom it rightfully belonged. At last he headed home with his friends to where his worried mother and father were waiting. Momotaro had great wealth now, thanks to the ancient treasures of the demons, who were forever forced to do his bidding. He set them to work washing clothes and gathering wood, so his parents never had to work so hard again.

The children cheered and clapped. Taro clapped so hard he almost fell off his father's shoulders.

"Okay, Taro," Father said. "I am going to watch the news slides, and then we must get home, okay? Can you play quietly?"

Taro nodded, but on the ground he was just a little person in a sea of big legs as the adults moved in to see the stories they liked most, the ones about problems like money and war. These slides were boring—marching soldiers, gray tanks, and aeroplanes. Father made aeroplanes like the ones in the news. But there was never a single giant demon in sight.

Now Uncle's voice sounded like the ones on the radio, commanding and fast, nowhere near as funny or perfect as his monkey and pheasant. Taro sighed as the kamishibai man rattled off news of a victory in China, securing more land near the Great Wall. A terrible earthquake and tsunami in Honshu in the far north of Japan. Momotaro would have stopped the tsunami, Taro decided. He'd have had the pheasant flap its wings until the waves turned the other way. Or maybe he and his friends could build another wall, like the one in China, to hold back waves from the sea.

The other kids wandered off to play games at home. Taro stood alone, unable to see past the wall of kimono and suit pants. The candy was still sweet in his mouth, but lonely—he was sure—for the candy in his father's pocket. He wondered if he could find it without bothering Father, but Momotaro would never do something without asking his parents first. Taro wouldn't either.

At long last, the news story ended. Some of the grown-ups cheered, but others grumbled about the war. Father, looking satisfied, said it was time to go home. Taro was so tired, he dragged his feet on the cobblestones, his legs heavy.

And then he heard something—a voice like a singing woman, like a bird, calling to him. Like the pheasant in Momotaro's story. With a gasp, he dropped his father's hand and set off to find it.

Trip-clop! Trip-clop! He ran up the street as fast as his short legs would carry him.

"Taro! Taro! Where are you going?" his father cried.

Taro smiled. He was going to catch the demons! But first he would need new friends!

Trip-clop! Trip-clop! He ran as fast as his new clogs would allow. The geta were slippery and loud, drowning out the sound he was trying to follow, that high sweet voice singing to him.

Trip-clop! Trip-clop!

He could hear his father coming after him, catching up on longer legs. And now, something else. The straining plings of music. The blind man on the corner nodded to Taro's wake. Father was more appropriate. He stopped and paid the koto player a small coin.

Trip-clop! Dash!

Taro skidded to a stop on the corner. He closed his eyes and listened.

There—above the music of the blind man, a woman was singing. No, a bird! A nightingale, but such a long, sad sound.

"Taro! What's gotten into you?" His father was breathless.

"The bird!" Taro said, pointing.

In a window above them, in the narrow lane, a man was drawing one arm across the other. Petting the bird, Taro guessed, for that must have been the source of the singing. And when it sang, Taro went flying up into the clouds, like the bird itself. Better than an aeroplane with its rattle and hum. Better even than make-believe, because it was real.

But then his father was laughing, like falling rocks, bringing Taro back to earth.

"That's not a bird," his father said. "It's an instrument, like the shamisen, from the West. It's called a *violin*."

CHAPTER 6

HANA

This afternoon, we will not be waving goodbye. It is a resting half day while our elder brothers wait for orders. The radio says we have made another great victory over the British and American forces in the Sea of Japan. Three of our elder brothers wept at the news. Their old commander body-crashed during the battle, taking many enemy sailors with him. They would have crashed with him, but their aeroplanes are in need of repair before they can fly the distance to the American fleet. More than one plane had limped in for a landing when they arrived, some trailing oily black smoke. Not all of them could be fixed in time. No one can blame the pilots for not being able to fly, but still they blame themselves and are eager to complete their mission.

While the tokkō do exercises in their bunks, we carry their sheets and clothes to the river for washing. They've promised to come sit with us while we do our work and sing songs from the places they are from.

"Don't dawdle," Mariko says to me, even though her back is

turned and she cannot see that I am falling behind. It's become a habit of mine, reluctance. I don't wish to go forward to the river, nor back to the barracks. I am an in-between girl since the day I died beneath the sweet potato field. I am a moment in time, trapped like an ant in sap.

"Hana! I'm serious! We need to hurry or the best rocks will be taken."

She rushes through the trees, and I follow her, hauling my basket on my hip. The best rocks. We are at war with half the world, and the most important thing to Mariko is a good pounding rock.

"I can see that look," she says, although she has still not turned around. I quicken my pace.

Poor Mariko. Her hair is in two spry pigtails that stick out like the ears of a young black rabbit. Her little brothers came home with head lice and, in a panic, her mother cut all their hair. She thinks it's too short, but I like the way the pigtails bounce as she hurries along. My own hair is twice as long and gathered at my neck, heavy and hot.

The trees give way to the field, then the riverbank, and sure enough, most of the other girls are already there. Mariko hisses in annoyance. "I told you so. You have legs like sticks, going so slow. Come on."

Mariko's pink face transforms, her cheeks dimpling as she smiles and nods to the other girls, gently bullying her way to a good spot.

"There! See how good this is? Now we can make our brothers' clothing spotless, and they can be proud of their uniforms."

"Thank you, Mariko-san." I hang my head. She is right.

Whether I am here, there, or nowhere, what matters is that we do our duty to the pilots.

We step out of our geta, tie the balloon-like legs of our monpé up around our thighs, choose a piece of clothing from the pile, and get to work.

"This one has holes in it. I will be up half the night darning when we are done," Mariko says. "And I am happy to do it!" she confirms, lest it sound like she is complaining.

"Hakata-san has teeth for toes!" Sachiko says, giggling into her hand. Sachiko is the same age as me, but she plays at being younger or older, depending on her audience. A natural airhead, my mother says. But with her heart-shaped face and easy laughter, she can make even a goose feel handsome by batting her lashes. "Look!" she says, brandishing a tattered cloth. "He chews through his socks in his sleep!"

Even I can't help but laugh at that one. But, as the girls move on to wondering if he clips his teeth and brushes his toenails, I find the bubble of laughter fading. What must it be like to toss and turn so much that your feet turn to grinders, that your body is eating its way out of your clothing?

"Daydreamer!" Kazuko cries.

A moment later, a wet sock hits me in the back. I spin around and catch Kazuko grinning at me. If Sachiko is a heart, Kazuko is a square—broad and solidly built, and as steadfast as the other is flighty.

"Troublemaker!" Mariko returns, launching her own sock back at Kazuko.

"Careful, girls, or we'll get their clothes mixed up!" Kaori-sensei says. Our teacher is not always with us when we do laundry, but today she is keeping an eye on things. In her own drab work clothes, she reminds me of a closed flower waiting for spring to arrive. She's kind-hearted and doesn't mind that we sometimes splash each other or do silly things. She knows it's necessary.

We are the future of Japan. They are always telling us so. But if we don't laugh sometimes, we will become brittle and break. So much shattered porcelain already litters the world. It would not do if we were to join it.

"Oh!" Sachiko exclaims, dropping her sheet into the water. "Did you see that woman this morning who fainted on the runway? I hear that was Second Lieutenant Kawasaki-san's wife! Do you remember him? The one who turned out to be Korean by birth? Reiko's mother told me so, right, Reiko? Anyway, he's older than the other pilots, so it's no surprise he is newly married! His wife came hoping to get pregnant. Isn't that romantic? And how sad! If it worked, he will never know his son. Reiko, didn't he visit her at your restaurant?"

"I mind my own business, Sachiko," Reiko says, eyes on her laundry. When Mrs. Kawasaki fainted today, it was Reiko's mother, Tomihara-san, who caught her. Tomihara-san runs Tomiya Shokudo, a small restaurant next door to my house, but she finds time to come to every farewell ceremony. She loves the boy pilots like her own sons. She also knows that we girls tend to them, but she approves, so she keeps our presence to herself.

"Oh!" Sachiko gasps. "This *is* our business! We are Nadeshiko Tai. We should know what is going on with our brave pilots."

Nadeshiko Tai is our official unit name. Every youth war group has one. Girl units are often named for flowers. A nadeshiko is a delicate pink blossom that grows even in difficult climates. It also gives its name to the old Japanese feminine ideal, *Yamato nadeshiko*—humble and pious, cheerful and innocent, loyal and kind, hardworking yet delicate and pure. We are far from being such ideal females, but we try.

"Let's sing a song!" Kaori-sensei suggests, clapping her hands for attention. Soon she has started singing "Umi Yukaba," the ballad of young sailors and soldiers dying for the Emperor without regret. I bend my back to the laundry, my lips moving to the words, but I do not sing—another thing that's gone missing since the day I died. I no longer have a voice for song.

One patriotic tune leads into another, and then we are joined by male voices as the pilots, done with their exercises, come to join us at the river.

They follow us as we hang the laundry to dry beneath the cover of trees. It will take longer this way, but the sheets must not be visible to the enemy overhead. Then it is time for the midday meal. We walk with the pilots, still singing, and make our way to the triangle barracks, where a soldier with a hand truck of dishes is waiting. From the outside, the barracks look like little more than A-shaped roofs resting on the ground. That's because they are dug six steps into the earth. The wooden doorway is rain-stained and green with new moss. Inside, the short sunken walls support the roof so that the ceiling is high in the middle, but barely tall enough to stand with your head ducked at the edges. Two sleeping platforms line either side of the barracks, with feet facing the wall so no one hits their head upon rising in the morning. Shelves on the wall hold footlockers and helmets, in case of air raid.

The boys go inside to roll up their futon and we girls line up at the "kitchen," carrying back trays of rice, pickled plum, and seaweed. The boys sit cross-legged on the sleeping platforms, backs hunched against the slant of the roof as they devour their meals. I stand by the hand truck, doling out portions and loading the girls' trays. Mariko carries cups of miso soup. The salty scent of the broth makes my mouth water, but we do not eat until the boys are done. We bow our thanks to them and clear their trays. Then it is our turn to sit on the grass outside with bowls of rice. It is so good and fresh, this spring rice, I could cry. At home, we only have rationed rice—old and dusty—and not much of it. But here on the base, they offer the best. Still, Sensei cautions us to eat only our share. A little food can go a long way, if we are not greedy. And my appetite has dwindled since March.

After lunch, we check the sheets drying beneath the tall, naked pine trunks. If they are still damp, we redistribute them to catch the wind. The ones that are ready we carry back to the barracks. Mariko knows I don't like to go inside since I died. So she makes my pilot's bed for me, while I sit on a nearby rock, sewing the holes in a still-damp sock.

"Hana, you will have to go in and help someday," Kaori-sensei says. But she does not say it unkindly. After the bombing, I did not leave my bed. For one week, I lay on the futon, sore and afraid. Okā-san tended my bruises and stayed by my side. Each night, she sat beside a single lantern shuttered but for a thin rail of light on my face because I could not bear the darkness. But

27

duty called. My limp lessened, my bruises hidden behind clothing, I went back to my unit and discovered we'd been reassigned to serve the tokkō. I had died in the bombing, and now I would be a handmaiden to the dead.

But on my first day at the base, when I stepped down into the barracks, a great stone hand reached out to squeeze my throat, crack my chest, and blind me. For the second time in two weeks, I was dragged back into the light, given water and a towel for my sweating face, fresh air for my constricting lungs. Sensei says it is just nerves, but I know the truth. The earth has swallowed me once. Only a foolish person would give it a second taste.

"I will do my best, Sensei," I murmur. The other girls talk about me behind their hands. They think I am afraid. It is not fear that keeps me aboveground. It's common sense. I will stay above the dirt, not in it, until it is time for me to leave this earth once and for all.

I must continue. I am Japan.

CHAPTER 7

TARO

Winter 1936

"The spider climbs up the ladder, the spider climbs down." Taro followed his sensei's instructions, plucking a rising and falling scale on the violin.

"And now we are ready to play."

Taro stood in the center of the room. His parents were watching. They had invited his aunt and a neighbor.

"All this talk of war is trying," his mother had said to his father this morning as he mulled over the news of a pact between Germany and Japan to counter a treaty between China and Russia. "What we need is a little pleasantness."

Now they all sat patiently over cups of hot tea as Taro tried to ignore them, focusing on Ayugai-sensei's hands as they directed the flow of the music.

"Haru no Umi"—"The Sea in Spring"—began with gentle plucking, imitating the sound of the koto. Then Taro laid the bow across the strings, and the ocean swelled.

Miyagi Michio's famous piece was written in memory of the water by his home, last seen as a child before he lost his sight. Meant as a duet for traditional instruments, Ayugai-sensei had adapted it for violin. Taro played it like a child. Joyfully. It brought smiles to his parents' faces, but Sensei was not happy.

"Of course he lacks the *mono no aware* Miyagi-sama intended for this piece. But Taro is only eight. Perhaps, in time, he will learn to play the melancholy beneath the joy," his sensei said apologetically to his parents.

"We are sorry he has not yet found the ear for it," Taro's father replied quickly. Taro's cheeks burned. He would do better.

But later, when his mother put him to bed, she whispered into his ear, "Time enough for sorrow later, Taro. Today, play like it's spring."

CHAPTER 8

HANA

This is Chiran, in the south of Kagoshima on the island of Kyushu, the last in the chain of home islands above Okinawa. This is my home.

Before the war with the West, we were known for our tea, our dolls, for the nearby hot springs, and the black beaches where one can be buried up to one's chin in healing volcanic sand. We were known for some silk and for our sweet potatoes. We were a stop on the way from the beaches to the city, from beautiful Kaimondake, Mount Fuji's twin, to Kagoshima city, with its shining bay and view of smoldering Sakurajima. Now we are known for our army and navy air bases, our strategic proximity to the enemy.

Seven hundred years ago, a mighty man lived in our prefect, lord to more than five hundred samurai families, whose houses dot the sand streets at the end of our town. Samurai were warriors, loyal and brave, who pledged allegiance to their lords and lived by Bushido, a code of honor until death. The yards still boast perfect gardens—smooth stones, pure green moss, and a long wall to keep out invaders.

But there is no stone wall large enough to keep the Western invaders out. Today, we no longer have samurai. We build our walls with men. Soldiers keep filling the gaps where others have fallen, and the men have given way to boys, and this is Chiran—the last line of defense. If Okinawa falls to the Americans, we are next. If we fall, then so will Tokyo, and all the rest of Japan.

We must not fall.

———

Tonight there is a meeting of the women in the tonari-gumi, our neighborhood association. My mother has asked me to come serve tea.

Every week they gather to discuss all village business, big and small, from organizing ration delivery to gathering money for the war effort. They meet at alternating houses, a different one each week, and sit drinking tea and eating sweet potato stems or azuki beans. They gripe over who can afford to buy ocean fish these days, not just the river carp available in town. My mother will bring some salted plums to offer the hostess, Mrs. Higashi, as a thank-you gift. I will make the tea go as far as possible with leaves scavenged from the old plants behind our house. I'll pick some extra to bring to the base tomorrow. They have plenty of tea, but none tastes as pure. Perhaps I can give it to the kitchen staff. The boys have all the ocha they need and then some, but the people working in the kitchen have to make do like the rest of us.

This week's meeting is at Hisako's house. Hers is an old noble family. Their land is gone, but they keep a fine house in the walled samurai district up the road from our home. The boy she loved was also from a samurai family. They were wealthy before the war. But Okā-san says such a family's greatest wealth is in their son. In this way, the war has made them paupers.

I follow my mother along the road, glad to be in monpé rather than a kimono that might trail and dip into the stream that runs along the same path. The sun has gone down, but the sky is still light. The carp in the water are rising to catch evening bugs, kissing the surface as they search for their meals. The fish are the only ones to not go hungry in a war, I suspect. The less food we have, the more bugs seem to thrive.

"Hurry up, Hana!" Okā-san urges. I pull my eyes from the cool flow of water in time to see her disappear through the entrance to the samurai district.

Eight feet tall on the outside, the sturdy gray wall is rough but tightly mortared. Inside, all is silent but for the chirping of birds and the susurration of the wind. Our geta break the natural silence, crunching softly on the sandy road. I try to match my steps to Okā-san's so that we sound like one person interrupting the quiet avenue. Far ahead, the walls stretch like a long, eloquent maze, broken by a gate here, a doorway there, and the occasional step up into the gardens of the samurai.

Hisako's house is several turns away. We reach it, and my mother gestures with her chin for me to pull the gate wide. The old men of the house have scurried off into town, to Tomiya Shokudo or some other place, no doubt. The young men reported for duty long ago. But Hisako is there, and Mariko, waiting on the wide veranda, kneeling to help guests remove their shoes, or rising to carry their packages inside.

"Go on, then!" Okā-san insists. She slips off her own geta, nodding a quick hello to my friends. Taking the sack of plums from my hands, she hurries inside. Cries of greeting ring out as she disappears through the sliding door. I settle in beside Mariko and wait.

"Are we the last?" I ask.

"No, we are expecting three more," Hisako says in her low, distant voice. She reminds me of thunder over the mountain, a storm moving away across the sky.

"Kaori-sensei says she will not make it tonight," Mariko announces. "She is working at the hospital. Can you imagine! After a full day at the base, she is helping there, too?"

The hospital that was our school is just up the hill from my house. It's strange to think of sick people, wounded soldiers, propped up in our old classrooms.

"My mother says it's because she knows the filing system," Hisako says softly. "Before she became a teacher, she worked in the office there. I suppose they need people who are good at such things."

"I would be terrible at it!" Mariko decides. "My handwriting is too messy, and I'm not good at remembering where things are."

All of this is nonsense, of course. "Mariko, there are no men here tonight. No need to act silly."

Mariko blushes. She's not a flirt like Sachiko is, but she thinks too little of herself out of habit. I've never understood why.

"Well, maybe I could do it," she admits slowly. Any further revelation is interrupted by the arrival of two more women. We rise and take their packages, help them inside. The last member to arrive is old Mrs. Hirano. We can hear her tapping her cane as she climbs the stairs. We rise to our feet.

"Ah, Hana-san!" she calls out, too loudly for the quiet night. "How is your health today?"

I bow and thank her. "All is well," I say.

"Good! Good! Such a terrible thing, that bombing. I was glad to see your pretty face went unscarred. And the rest of you too, neh? It won't do to lose all our pretty ones to this terrible fighting. A soldier deserves an attractive wife. And we need you young people to make more Japanese! We've lost too many by my count, neh?"

She pauses and jabs her cane toward Mariko and Hisako. "You three pay attention! This is your duty in the war. And help your mothers, neh? Such hard times make everyone ugly. Look at me! I've lived through three wars in my time. No wonder my face is so full of wrinkles!"

She cackles loudly as Hisako and Mariko each bend to help her slip out of her shoes. I offer to take the sack swinging from her wrist, but she shoos me away. "I'm old, but sturdy. Leave it be. But make my tea extra hot, will you? A pretty night, but these bones feel a chill. They always do when the seasons change."

We follow her indoors at a respectful distance, sliding the shōji screens shut behind us to keep out the cool April air.

Inside it is warm, and the air smells of tea and roasted soybeans. The screens have been pushed back to join two rooms together, and still there is quite a crowd. Mariko and I move between the women, filling teacups and offering plates of savory snacks provided by Hisako's mother, while Hisako carries the gifts brought by the tonari-gumi members into another room. She will sort and store them later. Most likely, several of the small cookies and other things on the trays tonight are from the last time her mother hosted. If they are stale, no one comments. It's a treat to have them at all. Salted peanuts and preserved items are a favorite gift because they will last without losing flavor and reduce the burden of hosting the next time. Occasionally, there are oranges or other fresh fruit—a luxury this early in the season, but possible because there are farms nearby. The cities are not so lucky. Even here, in the midst of war, there is a subtle or not-so-subtle tug and pull between the women, showing off with gestures of abundance and largesse, attempting to appear better-off than they are. Than any of us are.

At last, every plate is full, every cup steaming, and we retire to the back veranda, one ear open in case we are needed. The water is on for more tea. When it boils, we will do another round. Once upon a time, we longed to attend these meetings, to hear what secret things the older women spoke of when no men were around. Aside from a few off-color jokes, it was mostly complaints about husbands and sons. That has faded with the war. There is no one left to complain about but grandfathers and boys too young to cause much trouble at home.

"Today, they will discuss recipes for the new rationing," Hisako confides. "They are strange. So much frying."

"Yes!" Mariko agrees, tugging her short hair. "My grandmother says the government is trying to fatten us up and disguise the poor flavor of canned goods."

I doubt Okā-san will give in to the new frying fad. We make

do with very little. Rice, a bit of vegetable, an egg if we are lucky—that is enough for us. The rarer treats, like salted plums, are saved for guests, or evenings such as this.

With such dull talk inside, we are glad it's warm enough to sit outside where we can sip our own cups of tea and look at the stars, while Mariko wonders what life will be like if we are ever tonari-gumi women, wives and mothers eating salted nuts and boiled beans, counting up coins and donations for the war effort. It feels like make-believe, pretending there will ever be peace again.

"I could do it," Mariko says suddenly. We are swinging our socked feet off the edge of the veranda. Hisako's family's garden surrounds us. Soft slopes shaped by unseen earth and covered with fine moss rise like frozen lavascapes turned tender and green. Maple trees and evergreens are pruned into delicate poses, like dancers frozen in time. It's a lovely place. The rush of water from a little fountain. The twinkle of moonlight off the basin where koi swim in long, lazy strokes back and forth. We could be living two hundred years in the past, courtiers writing poetry in the gardens of our samurai lords. Or perhaps it will still look like this in another two hundred years. The future will still come to Chiran, despite the war.

"A clerk. I think I will ask Sensei what it entails. Don't you think? It would be good to have a career," Mariko says.

"Yes," Hisako replies, plucking the leaves off a strip of bamboo growing in a pot at the veranda's edge. Bamboo is a greedy plant. It will take over a garden if left unattended. Pots are the best way to contain it. "It's wise to have a way to support yourself. When we graduate, I must find a job, too."

37

"You will both have to," I say. "Okā-san says there will not be enough men for every job needed after the war."

I wish I had not said it. *Not enough men.* That means our fathers, brothers, friends, may not be coming home. But that has been the truth since we were little girls. Since we were born, I realize now. I have never known a time when Japan was not at war.

"The kettle will run dry," Hisako comments, and rises to her feet. She brews a new pot of tea, and we follow her, this time with a bowl of sweets.

In the front rooms, the women are nodding vigorously as Hisako's mother counts the donations. "Enough to provide new firefighting hoods!" she announces. There is polite clapping. Since the Americans began firebombing Tokyo, there has been a great fear the same will happen in other cities and military towns like Chiran. The women have organized a fire brigade. Last week, we saw an example of a civil defense hood—heavy drab cotton lined with wool, shaped to cover the head, neck, and shoulders and tie across the front. Wool and good cotton are fire-resistant. Such hoods are valuable against burning ash.

That is one thing to be grateful for—on the day I was buried alive, the bombs that fell were not incendiaries, filled with long-burning fuel. No one in the fields could have survived that.

We return to the veranda while the women complain about the fabric rations and question Okā-san on her next delivery. In a few days, they will line up with their tickets, elbowing each other for a chance at new pants, a new shirt. Now that the warm weather approaches, everyone will need lighter workwear.

"Hana," Mariko says, drawing my eyes from the star-studded sky. She takes my hand in hers. I reach across to Hisako, and we swing our feet again, like we used to when we were children. Tomorrow will come soon enough.

CHAPTER 9

TARO

Spring 1938

"Taro! Come say goodbye to your father!"

Taro finished buttoning his shirt and ran to the door. His parents were already outside.

It was a bright May morning. Irises were just beginning to bloom at the edge of the yard. Their purple softened everything. Father looked handsome in his uniform—a drab khaki tunic with bright brass buttons, jodhpur pants wrapped ankle to knee with leather straps Father called puttees, golden epaulets, and sky-blue collar patches that indicated the Army Air Force. He made Taro want to stand straighter.

Taro slipped on his shoes to join his mother in the yard. Together, they clasped their hands to their sides and bowed from the waist. Taro bowed so low he could feel his cheeks hanging off his bones like heavy laundry wet from the wash. He swallowed, afraid of drooling onto the cobblestones. A rustle of cloth, and his mother was rising. He followed a split second later.

Four months earlier, the military had initiated a national mobilization law. Men and women were being called into

CHAPTER 10

HANA

When I was little, my mother tried to teach me how to sew. I did not have the fingers for it. They were too soft and tender. Every time I made a stitch, I pricked my skin. My blood would stain the cloth, and I would cry and cry, partly from the pain and partly from the trouble I had caused. It would take a day of soaking and scrubbing to clean up my mistakes.

Today, I am mending uniforms with Mariko. We are sitting on a rock behind the barracks at the edge of the trees for more sunlight. When we are finished here, we will go deeper into the woods and cut tree boughs to cover the barracks roof. This way, planes passing overhead will only see more forest and drop their bombs elsewhere. There are eighteen of us girls again today. Plenty of help. But for now, it's just me and Mariko, sitting quietly in the shade.

I stab myself with the needle, but my callused fingers do not bleed. I don't wince. It has been like this since the day I died.

"I hope we have some fish with dinner at home tonight," Mariko says. "Omaru-san was saying just this morning how he misses all of the fish he and his brothers used to catch from the mountain stream where he lives."

"Has he tried Tomihara-san? I bet she has a rod he could use in the river. She has a way of finding treats for her favorites," I say.

"They are all her favorites," Mariko says, and smiles. "Do you know they call her Mama-chan? I asked Reiko if it makes her jealous, but she just smiled. I think Reiko is a favorite of all the pilots, too. They give her little gifts, so it's only right that her mother treats them so well."

"It's the other way around, Mariko," I say. "They are kind to Reiko because she is like a little sister to them."

Mariko sighs. "To think, if this war was not on, we would be going to dances and parties with these same boys. We could wear dresses instead of monpé. Our cheeks would be pink and fat, and the boys would call us pretty instead of 'the future mothers of Japan,'" she says, dropping her voice to mimic a man's. "Ugh! There is nothing worse than being called a mother by a cute boy, especially when they are all older than us! It makes me feel ancient." She sighs and picks up the thread for a new sock. "This war is making us all so skinny and old! Feel my hair. It used to be glossy. Now it's short *and* brittle. I don't dare try to brush it too much for fear it will break off. Even lice wouldn't live in it now!"

"You're exaggerating," I say. "Don't let old Hirano-san frighten you."

I am sewing a button onto a shirt. The rock that makes my seat is cold, the damp seeping into my monpé. Thick clouds drift across the sun. It is a hot/cold day, sunny one moment, gloomy the next. I understand how the weather feels. Next, I will mend the pocket on a pair of pants and lower the hem. These boys are still growing. Their uniforms cannot keep up.

"I am not!" Mariko drops the sock in her lap and grabs my hand. "Feel this! Like straw! I wish I could have some ocean fish. My mother says the oils in deep sea fish are good for our hair and skin. It seems silly to me that all of our young men are willing to die for us, but we are getting uglier by the instant! When we cut branches later, let's look for berries in the woods. Maybe we can find something to stain our lips and cheeks. I feel so dull all of the time!"

I nod and knot the thread, biting the tail off with my teeth. I fold the shirt carefully into the basket of repaired clothes and drag the pants out of the mending basket. "Pass the thread," I say.

"You're not listening. But why should you? You've never been vain about your looks. But I have to be, Hana! I'm not talented and clever like you. You can sing and dance—boys always like good dancers. Or you can take over your father's tailoring business. But me? I will marry a farmer, most likely."

"I thought you had decided to find a career," I reply.

"Be serious, Hana! Even with a job, there still will be fewer men to choose from and all these pretty women! I have to look my best so I can be picky. I don't want to marry a dolt."

It's been a long time since my family performed at the festival, Otō-san on koto, me and Okā-san singing and dancing. Playing the koto myself when I was old enough to do so without getting tangled up in the strings. We were like songbirds back then, Otō-san, Okā-san, and me. Now we are a broken set. Mariko knows I haven't danced or played koto since Otō-san went away. And though I mouth the words, she knows I no longer sing. Like her hair, I, too, have lost my sheen.

I sew a straight line across the edge of the pocket, doubling back to make sure it's secure. "How can you even think about marriage, Mariko? Will we even live long enough to get married?"

Mariko's eyes fly wide. "What? Of course we will! With such magnificent men fighting for us, why shouldn't we?"

"There is little enough fish, Mariko," I say softly. "There is less rice. We both know the tonari-gumi meetings are more bravado than a sign of plenty. And you see the boys here. Younger and younger. We used to have grown men, real pilots. Now we have boys who dream of being pilots one day. And the aeroplanes are terrible. Two more boys had to force a landing yesterday because their engines failed."

Perhaps it is cruel to say this. I know to keep such thoughts to myself. Perhaps kindness is another thing I've left behind. Or hope.

Mariko is silent for a long time. Her needle is not moving. The wind lifts our hair, carrying the scent of dry pine needles.

"Well . . . I don't want to marry a dolt. But if I have to, I want to do it well. You should want the same. We are the future mothers—"

"Of Japan!" we say together. I press my lips into a smile. Mariko giggles. It turns into a snort. And more laughter.

"Oh, Hana," she gasps, "this is Jiro-san's small clothes! I don't want to sew underwear!" She hands me the torn underpants. "Here, you won't blush like I will."

"You wanted pink cheeks," I remind her, and drop the underwear on her head.

She is still shrieking when the pilots arrive. A new group. We do not know them. We swallow our embarrassment, stuff the clothes into whichever basket is closest, and bow our heads.

"These are your Nadeshiko Tai girls. They'll mend your clothes, do your laundry, and bring your meals until your day of victory," Lieutenant Maeda instructs the boys. Maeda is not a bad sort. He has worked at the base in Chiran since before the war, so he is familiar to us all. Still, I keep my eyes on their shoes. We will shine them, too, and they need it. The dust of the fields has turned them a dusky brown. A fat beetle makes its way across the spring grass, stumbling over the rise and fall of the land. I watch it disappear into the weeds. I disappear, too, until the boys are gone.

Soon, we will learn their names.

And then we will wave goodbye.

CHAPTER 11

TARO

Summer 1940

Taro was a butterfly skimming the tops of flowers. He was an eagle diving from great heights. A mighty warrior, storming into battle. He hit a sour note, grimaced. Adjusted his position on the smooth black chin rest, took a deep breath, and reset the bow at the beginning.

He was playing Mozart.

He stood at the open window of the family room hoping some little kid would hear him and want to play too, as he had so long ago. Except for when he made mistakes. Then he stayed by the window because he didn't want to hear the conversation going on in the next room. The walls were thin, and his father was home on leave from the war.

"Doesn't he know any Japanese songs?" he heard his father ask. Taro flushed. Sensei had said Western music was no longer in favor with the Emperor, nor Western sports, clothing, ideas. But didn't Mozart transcend nations? Not the way he was playing it, perhaps. He redoubled his efforts.

"You forget," his mother said. "Mozart was said to be German."

Taro smiled. Germany was allied with Japan. But he could hear his father's noncommittal grunt.

"He is working very hard," his mother said. "We can be proud of that."

Taro closed his eyes and played. Careful to avoid the same mistakes.

"And I am not saying he should stop. But music school! What kind of living can a musician make? He should be an engineer, or an officer. Half the world is at war! With France fallen to the Germans, Indochina is ripe for the taking. The country needs men who contribute to the real world."

Taro squeezed his eyes tighter, drawing the bow back and forth, pausing to pluck the pizzicato notes, sawing deeply into the darker tones. He was a submariner, diving beneath the waves. *This* was the real world, shadowy, deep, and blue.

"Pilots. Now, there's an opportunity! A boy who goes to Army Youth Pilot School and applies himself will have his choice of assignments in the Imperial Military Academy."

"You would have two soldiers in this house."

Taro's mother said it so quietly he almost couldn't hear her, but this was the soft moment, pianissimo. She was pianissimo, too. She had not questioned, merely stated. But it was enough for his father to hesitate. Then, piano, soft but not as softly as his mother, his father said, "When he is old enough . . . The Emperor needs men, not music."

And Taro's heart sank deep into his stomach, farther than the submariner in the depths. He would become a soldier, an officer, a pilot. There was glory in it—the broad skies over the mountains, the oceans, everything in one clean glance, like a concerto, a symphony. Something bubbled, crackling inside of him. He didn't know if it was excitement or fear, disappointment or joy. But it leaked over into his music. The violin skipped, jumping like a startled horse.

Taro grimaced.

Took a deep breath.

And started again.

Shōnen Hikōhei. Youth Pilot School. To enter meant giving fifteen years of his life to the army. Fifteen! That was three more years than he'd been alive. Of course, the boys at his grade school would be jealous. Not everyone loved Mozart, but they all wanted to fly. The biggest heroes of the war in China were pilots—daredevils like Kashimura Kanichi, who once landed his plane with only one wing.

No one ever called a musician a hero.

Taro leaned into the music, trying to focus on the piece. He could be a pilot. He would do well in school and make his parents proud.

But he would never stop playing the violin.

Out in the street, he heard a clatter. Someone was outside listening. He wouldn't stop to look, nor let it distract him. Instead, he poured himself into the music, hoping the listener would understand.

CHAPTER 12

HANA

Laundry. Always laundry, hanging in the wind to dry. Mariko, the others, and I gathered the clothing from the lines first thing today. We've had no new boys since yesterday afternoon, but the staff is always busy. So now, with our arms still aching from hauling and tugging and tucking this morning's bedsheets, Mariko and I sit in one of the base offices, sewing and patching staff uniforms, pretending not to listen when news comes in on the wire next door.

"Do you remember Hakata-san and how his toes had teeth?" Mariko asks me. She holds up an olive green sock, bald at the heel, the ball of the foot missing completely. "Corporal Sanyo's entire foot is a mouth. He must eat dirt and rocks to chew a sock so badly!"

I smile, but it fades as I remember nervous little Hakata-san. Some of the Nadeshiko tried to give him courage in his final days. They spoke of cherry blossoms and sunrise, the temple where he played as a child, and the dark forces coming to wipe it all away. And he, bright as the sun, was the only one to stop it. They'd painted him a hero, and he became one, for a few shining moments, when he bowed to us and mounted the wing to his plane.

His toes had teeth.

His plane did, too.

Hakata-san body-crashed gloriously into an American ship.

At least, we think he did. There were many enemy fighters in the air. The escort planes did not stay long enough to confirm his end. But a ship went down the day he flew out, so we consider it our elder brother's work. His and his comrades.

"Don't look now," I say to Mariko, and hold up a pair of underwear. "Sergeant Ito has teeth somewhere else!"

That is when the radio crackles: a flotilla of American ships has been spotted heading north toward Okinawa. With them they bring fighter planes and bombers, fire, blood, and death ever closer to home. Through the wall we hear the men exclaim, "At once!" and orders are given down the line.

Mariko and I stop our stitching, eyes only on each other, waiting, trembling on the branch of uncertainty.

"There you are!" The commandant turns the corner, startling us. "Eavesdropping, no doubt." We lower our eyes rather than deny it, and bow our heads in deference.

"Just as well," he says. Commandant Asama is a bulldog. He rumbles and growls deep in his chest, and it raises the hairs on the backs of our necks. But it takes a strong man to run an army base. It takes a bulldog to run a war. "Tell the other girls to get ready. We have a new flight coming this afternoon. A big action in the works."

My cheeks are suddenly damp. I don't dare look up. I am a

ghost. It is better to be a ghost. From the corner of my eye, I see a tear drop onto Mariko's half-mended sock.

"Well? What are you waiting for? Get going!"

"Yes, Sensei!" We leap to our feet, tossing our mending back into the basket. The staff men will understand. Pilots always take precedence.

The other girls are dragging new branches onto the roofs of the barracks when we arrive out of breath. Half the group drag the dried-out boughs to the woodpile. The rest wipe sweat from their foreheads, surveying their handiwork. They look proud, for the moment. Capable and strong.

"Attention! Attention!" Mariko cries. "We must make ready for a new flight!"

Shoulders drop. Heads turn. We never know when a new unit will arrive, or when they will leave for their final attacks. The pilots tell us it has to do with weather, ship locations, and strategy. Most depart at dawn, using the dim light as an element of surprise. But the army's decisions are mysterious to us Nadeshiko. Sometimes I imagine the Emperor as a great bird flying over the ocean, able to see the enemy, to direct his might against them. But then I see flight after flight take off, with few reports of success, and I wonder if we are merely throwing lives away like pebbles into the dark.

Of course, Sachiko is smiling. "I wonder if there will be any cute ones this time," she whispers loudly to Kazuko, who has the good sense to shush her. Sachiko wrinkles her button of a nose, but her tongue stops revolving for once.

"Has something happened?" Poor sensitive Hisako has read our faces as clearly as headlines.

"The Americans are nearing Okinawa," Mariko says. Every Nadeshiko goes still. In the silence, I think of my father. His voice, his hands. Are they both raised in fear now? Or righteous anger, as they kill? Okinawa is so close to home . . .

———

I am the Philippine Sea, the waters of East China.

I am the Sea of Japan.

I feel the ships on the water like gnats on my skin, biting, nipping, tearing me raw.

I feel my dead beneath me. *Taihō, Shōkaku, Hiyō*—great warships, now gone, along with the sailors they carried, sunk in battle as the winds of war swept through the Philippines last June.

The newspapers spoke of ships and aircraft loss—not of fathers, of sons. We all heard the whispers—less than half of our aeroplanes returned. It is why our tokkō are so young. Final replacements for what has been squandered.

Such a scandal! How could our great military have been so wrong? How could they have thrown so many lives away? The prime minister of Japan and his government resigned, so great was their shame.

And now another American flotilla marches on my back, my waters no longer a barrier, but a road, crawling up the spine of our defenses, moving closer and closer to the heart of my world. What will happen when they arrive?

CHAPTER 13

TARO

Winter 1941

"Taro! Taro, come down!"

In 1778, Wolfgang Amadeus Mozart wrote the Violin Sonata in E Minor. He was twenty-two years old, and his mother had just died. Taro was proficient in several of Mozart's other works, but this sonata—the most sublime piece of music he'd ever heard, the very song that dragged him up the street and into the life of a musician—eluded him. And so he was practicing.

A pebble hit the window. Taro had grown. At almost fourteen, he could now see outside without leaning forward. Two of his friends stood in the street, trying to get his attention. Bundled up against the weather, they shifted from foot to foot, trying to stay warm. They held up two half-finished model aeroplanes— Zero fighters meticulously carved from lightweight wood. Taro smiled and waved them away with a shake of his head, continuing his practice. But the time for such toys was over. He didn't know if they would let him keep his violin at Shōnen Hikōhei. What if he wasn't allowed to play for a whole year? Ayugai-sensei had tried to tell Taro he'd be able to start over when the war ended, but that was not how music usually worked. If you left it, it left you. Practice was everything.

So Taro practiced.

He could see Mrs. Tanaka across the street humming along as she hung out her clothes on the laundry line. It was a cold day in early December. The futon sheets and yukata she hung would have a thin coat of ice before they ever dried.

A stray dog, a black-and-white-spotted mutt with brown ears and a shaggy coat, slept in a fading patch of sunlight on the side of the road, the only spot of warmth to be had today. The dog's back was pressed to the worn wooden planks of the Tanaka house. Its chest rose and fell in metronomic sympathy, but its ears still twitched, alert, following the dip and flow of the music.

Taro played for Mrs. Tanaka. He played for the dog. The music swelled, filling the room, spilling out of the window.

"Taro! Come quick!"

He lowered the bow, resting the violin carefully on the floor, and pushed the sliding shōji screen aside.

His mother was in the front room listening to the radio. She motioned for him to kneel beside her on the tatami mats. She wore her simple cotton yukata, the robe tied tight across her waist. Her hands rested like nesting birds, one inside the other, on her lap. She sat listening to the radio as she would an honored guest, ready at a moment's notice to rise and offer it something, an adjustment of the antennae or the dials instead of tea. "There is to be an announcement from the Imperial Palace!"

They'd bought the radio when his father first went to Manchukuo, so they could follow the path of the war in China. Since then, it had brought them news—first of victories on the mainland, then of the Americans' attempt to stem the tide of the Emperor's success by blocking the flow of oil to Japan. Then came news of a pact between Japan, Germany, and Italy—the three nations would join together against the United States, should it ever enter the war.

At first, Taro had found it confusing. After the Great Depression, everyone knew the United States had no interest in foreign affairs. And hadn't Italy and Germany been enemies of Japan during the Great War? But, as Taro's teacher explained it, the United States would never risk a war with all three nations. They would have to give Japan the oil it needed and cease to meddle in its affairs. Then, all of Asia could prosper in the Emperor's hands.

Or so he'd been taught.

And then Taro's mother leaned forward to turn up the volume.

On the radio, a man with a clipped Tokyo accent read an announcement from the Emperor:

"We, by the grace of Heaven, Emperor of Japan, seated on the Throne of a line unbroken for ages eternal, enjoin upon ye, Our loyal and brave subjects: We hereby declare war on the United States of America and the British Empire."

Taro's mother gasped. His stomach clenched as she grabbed his hands. Until now, the enemy had been Chinese, Russian, French. Now they had awakened the sleeping giant of the West. But surely the Americans would not strike back. To do so would risk war with not one, but three great nations. Japan would prevail. It should have been exciting. And yet, with his father away . . .

"Mother . . ." Taro said, but her eyes were closed. "Please, you mustn't worry. Everyone knows the Americans are indolent. They do not have the discipline of the Japanese."

The radio crackled, continuing to play exaltations of the might of Japan. The announcer described a predawn attack in a voice tense with excitement. Foreign names like "Pearl Harbor" and "Hawaii" filled the air.

Taro's mother opened her eyes. She turned the radio dial off with a silencing click. Outside, the rousing shouts of "Banzai! Banzai!" rose from the street, exhorting the Emperor to live ten thousand years. But inside their home, all was silent.

"Get the incense, Taro. We must pray for our soldiers, for your father . . ." She trailed off, leaving her last words unspoken. But he heard what she would not say: *And for you.*

———

The next day at school had the feeling of a holiday. In the schoolyard and hallways, students jostled and joked with each other. In all of the excitement, Taro forgot his mother's worry. Every boy in his class was going to be a soldier. A pilot! They were all going to be heroes in this new war.

"Silence!" Taro's teacher called for attention. The class fell still, all eyes on Sensei as he donned white gloves and removed the framed photograph of His Majesty, the Emperor, from the cupboard where it was stored. Silence reigned as he held it up before the students. It was an impressive portrait. The Emperor was young and distinguished-looking, in white gloves and a medal-covered military jacket, complete with sash and sword. He wore glasses, which made him look smart, and a serious expression that suited a person of such importance. The Emperor was the 124th descendant of the sun goddess, Amaterasu Ōmikami. Upon assuming the throne in 1926, he had declared his reign to be the Shōwa Era, or the "Period of Bright Peace." Perhaps, Taro thought, the Bright Peace would come when the war was won.

At the front of the classroom, Sensei cleared his throat and began to recite the Imperial Rescript for Education. Taro and his classmates joined him in unison, as they did every morning. But today was different. Today they were not just good students— they were citizens of the greatest country on Earth.

"Ye, Our subjects, be filial to your parents, affectionate to your brothers and sisters, as husbands and wives be harmonious, as friends true . . ." Taro fell into the singsong response of long-remembered words, vowing modesty, moderation, and benevolence, but today he truly listened to the words. He had no brothers or sisters, but Sensei had explained that his fellow countrymen were his family. Taro straightened up and spoke extra loud at the part about cultivating the arts. It meant the Emperor approved of his violin playing, no matter what his father said. The words of the rescript painted the picture of a perfect world, one that he was proud to live in. His chest swelled with thoughts of Bushido as he crowed the next lines, "And, should emergency arise, offer yourselves courageously to the State; and thus guard and maintain the prosperity of Our Imperial Throne coeval with heaven and earth!" The archaic language was both commanding and comforting. The Emperor cared for every child in this room.

"Very good, class," Sensei said when they were done. "We are in a new war, and the rescript requires each of us to bravely offer ourselves to the nation. That is why we recite the rescript every day. It is only in times of great striving that we truly show our worth. Some of you are worried. Father is at war in China; Mother is part of the National Defense. But do not be concerned. Our Emperor's actions are necessary for Japan to grow. This war against America will be brief because of the decisive actions of our military. But also because of the fortitude of our people! The Americans will sue for peace. But first we must set an example for these outsiders, these gaijin. Show them what it is to be Japanese! Be worthy!"

"Hai, Sensei!" Taro and his classmates promised, pride swelling in every young chest. "Hai!"

CHAPTER 14

HANA

Sensei has us line up at the top of the hill on the path to the barracks to meet the new pilots. "They will be part of a new decisive action," she says. There is tension in the air, as if the entire base is bracing for a blow. But who will strike first?

We wait beneath the shadowed pines, listening for the sounds of approaching aeroplanes, of marching men. We are far from the nearest runway, out of sight behind low hills and tall trees. Once upon a time, the barracks were regular buildings in neat rows closer to the main gate. Air raids have forced them to go undercover, spread out—along with kitchens and grounded aeroplanes—scattered throughout the forest. The landing fields are the exception, great black Xs crisscrossing the open land to the north.

A honeybee-like drone rises on the wind, becomes a roar. I close my eyes.

I am the airfield. The smooth, dark runway glides down my back. The planes descend one by one, silver combs tucking my hair into place. They adorn my paved tresses, and the men inside hop down, marching into view.

Eight of them this afternoon, each no more than two or three years older than the eldest of us, who has just turned sixteen. A flying officer leads them up the hill to the barracks, shouting orders and instructions. They follow along like proud young roosters.

My geta catches on a stone in the path as we turn to follow. By the time I catch up to the group, my tabi sock is smudged with earth, and there is a slight ache in my knee—the stiff one that never seems to mend. I stand outside the barracks, slip my foot out of my shoe and rub the smudge off on the back of my pant leg.

Through the open doorway, I watch the boys inspect their new home, gazing up at the dark wooden ceiling, choosing futon by some arcane order only they know. Once they are settled, we introduce ourselves. They are set to fly out tomorrow, so there is no point in remembering their names. Instead, I stand in the doorway, making note of uniforms, of needs. I avoid reading tabs marked with their names. After the evening meal, we will ask them for their home addresses and promise to send letters to their families, telling of their time here and how brave they were on their last day.

I used to think I would remember every pilot I met, that I would never forget them. But even in these few weeks, there have been so many faces, I wonder what I will remember in another month, in a year. Will this war still be going on? Will I still be Nadeshiko, darning socks and serving rice at the air base when I turn sixteen?

The answer lies with these boys, and how well they die.

To die for the Emperor is the greatest honor, as everyone knows. But when I died, I was not noble. I was afraid. I knew it was coming, but only for moments, not hours, not days. What would it be to premeditate your death and fly out deliberately to meet it?

A chill falls over me. Clouds skid across the sky, pushed by the rising wind.

"This one is a daydreamer," one of the pilots says, emerging from the barracks. He's a square-jawed brute whose name starts with N. Mariko has done a better job than I have, learning their names. What I do know is he likes egg custard. He declared it loudly just a moment ago. They always talk about favorite foods here, what they wish they could have. I understand. When I was dying, I lay still for so long, I thought of everything. Of the rain, of my father. How I would never hear him play again. And how I would never eat my mother's kurobuta-tonkotsu. Perhaps that's why I have lost my appetite for such things now. Such delectable pork is not possible on war rations. And the dead do not eat.

"What are you dreaming about, Little Flower?" the pilot whose name begins with N is asking. I feel a chill. He has learned my name is Hana, which means "flower," and in mocking me has stumbled on the nickname used by my father. Or perhaps he is only thinking of the nadeshiko blossom that gives our unit its name.

"I am wondering if it will rain," I say without thinking, and point to the clouds in the sky.

The girls fall silent, and the boys frown. Only Sachiko, fool that she is, bubbles happily, "She means if it rains, you do not have to fly tomorrow! No one body-crashes in the rain!"

She treats these boys as new pets, each a delight to be coddled as long as possible. No one else sees it that way.

My cheeks burn with shame, and I bow my head. My heavy knot of hair slips sideways over my left ear. Would that it could cover my face.

"Forgive me," I say, my voice harsh with embarrassment. "I was careless."

But he is laughing and declaring tomorrow a perfect day for sunshine. "Besides, battleships don't fear the rainstorm, so why should we?" he asks.

Of course. The Americans are coming. Nothing can prevent that now.

"Reiko's mother serves egg custard," I offer by way of apology. "Not as good as your mother's, no doubt, but it might help you remember her custard better."

He smiles, as if already thinking of scooping the creamy dessert into his watering mouth, and I know I have done my job today. We Nadeshiko Tai are here to help these boys do their duty. If they are smiling when they leave, we have done well.

By now, most of our new pilots are done unpacking. They emerge into the sunlight.

"Taro, will you come to Tomiya Shokudo tonight?" N asks. "This one says they have egg custard maybe. You could bring your fiddle and play."

"Oh, are you a musician?" Sachiko chimes in, twining her hair with excitable fingers. "We have a very musical group here! Not long ago, two of the pilots walked three miles to play a piano again before their flight. It was so romantic! And you're a fiddle player!"

The boy called Taro does not look up from his bag. He's still inside the barracks, perched on the middle futon. I peer into the gloom. His hair is neatly trimmed, and his attention is focused on his task—carefully decanting something precious from his duffel. A black case for holding an instrument.

He looks up. Large dark eyes in a serious face. Then a smile plays across his lips. "It's not a fiddle," he says, and N laughs and laughs. It's an old joke perhaps, with only a day or two left to be told.

Sachiko laughs merrily, without understanding the jest, and proposes we walk to the river. The pilots are free until their orders are confirmed, and it is a beautiful day. Taking Kazuko by the hand, Sachiko leads the way.

This is what I see by the river: ten girls sitting in the grass in the dappled sunlight, eight boys standing, leaning, sitting on rocks. One boy lies on his back, watching the clouds. Sachiko is next to him, laughing as he tells her the shapes he sees. Mariko is writing down everyone's addresses and bowing her gratitude. I should be doing the same, but I am frozen in the shadow of a tsuburajii tree, watching the scene like a painting come to life. If I was the artist, I would call this *Last Spring*. It is the perfect picture of beauty, but the knowledge behind it makes it exquisite.

This is what I see when I look at a tokkō pilot: the condition of his clothes—loose buttons, frayed collar—and the shape of his shoes, well-polished or worn and ill-fitting, which betrays the condition of the socks beneath. I look at his hair, clipped and brushed, as it should be, or going shaggy, which indicates a state of mind that no longer cares for appearances. This can be good—he may have already detached from this life—or it can be bad, indicating he has no self-control. The most important thing in the short life of a tokkō special-attack pilot is self-control. Strength of character is the greatest weapon we have against the enemy. After all, doesn't the Imperial Rescript decree that every citizen of Japan be filial, modest, moral, and courageous? We learn this from the first days of school. We recite it in class and transcribe it into our school journals. Pilots even write of spiritual fortitude in their letters home. If it fails him on his final flight, how will he body-crash successfully?

These boys' uniforms are impeccable. They have not hop-scotched around from base to base without anyone to care for them. Their hair is trimmed and smooth. Their shoes are pristine. These are the perfect tokkō pilots. The government should take pictures of them, smiling, apple-cheeked boys.

"Hey, Little Flower, we hear you sing well. Will you sing for us?"

I startle out of my reverie. Sachiko and the cloud watcher are calling to me. It seems my nickname has spread. And someone is telling tales out of school.

"Come on, Hana, sing us a song!" Sachiko cries, clapping her hands. "You used to be so good at the cherry blossom festivals!"

"Why don't we all sing?" I say. She doesn't know I've lost my voice for singing. It's still buried on the mountainside in a ditch.

N looks like he's about to protest, but the other girls come to my rescue. Mariko claps her hands, and they all launch into "Dōki no Sakura." The boys throw their arms over their friends' shoulders as they sing—two cherry blossoms of the same season, doomed to fall, brothers-in-arms vowing to meet in the afterlife at Yasukuni Shrine. What should be a somber song seems almost joyful the way they sing it, like a festival drinking song.

I should like to see the great Yasukuni in Tokyo, the Shinto shrine of our gunshin—war gods—where the spirits of our honored war dead dwell. With no bodies to bury, families pay their respects at the shrine. Perhaps when this is all over, we Nadeshiko Tai will make a pilgrimage, too.

"Nakamura, you sing like a bullfrog!" one of the boys says to N. Nakamura. That was the name I couldn't remember. Nakamura barks out a laugh.

"I know! That's why I asked the girls to sing instead!"

They launch into another song, and I move my lips but stay silent, trying to distinguish each voice from the next. There is Mariko, with her high, sweet vibrato, a better singer than she thinks herself to be. And Sachiko, with her little-girl voice, earnest and off-key. Hisako sings in a breathy alto, as if she has spent the night in sorrow. And Kazuko sings the song exactly as we learned it in school. Even when the others stumble on the lyrics, or fail to reach a note, she is there, a baseline strumming through the entire composition. These are the girls of my unit. We are sisters here.

The boys are a different story. There is Nakamura, with his toneless, deep voice, much deeper than when he speaks. I suspect he took singing lessons in a swamp, as his friend suggested. That same friend has a lovely baritone, like a wooden flute. But he is uncertain of it at times. And then there is the boy with the violin case. He does not sing, only listens, like me. Although, the way his fingers tap, I suspect he hears music just the same. The rest of the boys bellow as if shouting out of a passing train, not caring who hears them or how foolish they might seem. These are the ones who make me smile. I suppose that is a benefit of dying soon, not caring how one looks. All that matters is that they crash well.

"Look! The sun!" Nakamura says, pointing my way. His finger chases away my brief smile. "Did you see it? A *sun* flower!"

Sachiko giggles, and even Mariko laughs. I smile again because it pleases them, but my cheeks are red.

A messenger arrives from the main office. The boys will have exercise and briefings soon, but it appears their flight has been delayed a day. Not by weather, but by strategy. The tokkō will fly out in waves, to crush the enemy with constant attacks.

The boys cheer each other on with bravado, resetting their courage for the new date. Later, they will go over their aeroplanes together to assure their readiness. Then tonight they will visit the comfort girls or drink saké at Tomihara-san's and eat egg custard until it is time to say goodbye.

The messenger departs, and I, still blushing, excuse myself to see about their next meal. I hurry across the pebbled path, annoyed with myself, clutching at the sides of my monpé. Nakamura is a name I have learned, and now I will not forget it. Things will be harder now. But, I tell myself, it is only one more day.

CHAPTER 15

TARO

Spring 1943

Taro pressed a hand to the sun-warmed window as the bus came to a stop. This was it. Oita Air Cadet School sprawled before him in a series of low wooden buildings and a few more modern ones. It looked like a school, not a military base.

"Where are the airfields?" the boy beside him demanded. Nakamura was his name.

"Kenji Nakamura," he'd introduced himself earlier using the Western name order—given name first—and with a Western handshake that clipped Taro in the forehead mid-bow. He'd confided he thought it made him sound more sophisticated. It didn't, really. "I'm going to be a fighter pilot, like Kashimura Kanichi. How about you?"

"Why are you shouting?" Taro had asked. Nakamura's voice was forte, as Taro's violin teacher would say. The loudest of the loud. Or was it the strongest of the strong? That would suit Nakamura, too, Taro had decided, rubbing his forehead. Nakamura had given him a lopsided grin.

"Sorry." He had dropped from a bellow to a husky voice, as

if he'd just woken from a nap, reminding Taro of a grumbling frog. "I've got two brothers, and we live by the train tracks."

Now he was pushing his way to the window, inside voice forgotten. "Maybe behind those buildings?"

"What?" Taro was lost.

"The airfield. You know, aeroplanes. Flying?" Nakamura made a propeller sound and flew his hand through the air. "They must be behind those buildings."

"No, you ninny," a boy said from the seat in front of theirs. From his air of authority, Taro guessed he could be as old as seventeen. "This is cadet school. No different than high school, except we get to wear uniforms and learn the military way. We won't see any planes for a full year, assuming we don't screw up here. Flunk, and you're infantry for sure."

Nakamura laughed. "Flunk? Not me. I was born to fly. Right, Taro? Fighter pilots all the way."

"Only birds are born to fly," Taro replied, gazing out at the school grounds. A worm of worry burrowed in his belly. "The rest of us have to learn it."

———

"Inhale . . . breathe out."

Taro exhaled in a sigh.

"Open your eyes wider. Look left. Right. Up. Down. Good."

The base doctor made notes on a chart. He thunked Taro's knee with a small rubber reflex hammer, making the leg jump, and had a nurse draw some blood. "For tuberculosis and other ailments," the doctor explained.

"All right. I'm going to have you run in place for five minutes and then take your pulse. Do you know how to do this?" The doctor placed a finger on Taro's neck, explaining pulse points. Taro did as he was told. It must have been satisfactory. He was given new clothing and assigned to a barracks that held almost a hundred other boys. Nakamura was waiting when he got there.

"How did you finish before me?" Taro asked. They'd been called in alphabetically, and Inoguchi Taro came well before Nakamura Kenji.

"Extra healthy, I guess. Maybe when they took my heart rate, I ran faster than you." Nakamura waggled his ears and lay back on the bottom bunk.

Taro laughed. "Did you show them that trick?"

"You bet. The nurses loved it. Only great warriors can control their ear muscles. Hey, I saved you a spot." He pointed to the upper bunk bed. "We can share this one," he said in his husky indoor voice. The other boys were already unpacking. Taro looked at the footlocker at the base of the bed. It would hold his shoes, but little else.

"Do you mind if I take the bottom bunk?" he asked.

"Not at all. Us pilots need to get used to heights," Nakamura said with a grin.

"Are you afraid of them?" Taro asked, surprised, as Nakamura moved his things to the top bunk.

"Afraid? No. Unacquainted with, yes. The tallest thing I've ever been on is a mountain, but both my feet were on the ground, so it doesn't count. What about you?"

"My father is a pilot. He was an aircraft engineer before the war."

"He ever let you fly?"

"No, but I've been up. I was little, though, and sitting on my mother's lap. Then the war in China started, and there were no more pleasure flights."

"I know what you mean. We used to go on picnics down to the sea, my whole family—brothers, cousins, aunties and uncles, grandparents, too. But that many people out in the open is a bad idea these days. Not to mention picnics are a lot less fun with rationed food."

Both boys sighed. Taro slid his violin under his bunk.

"What do you suppose the food will be like here?" Nakamura asked. "My brother says in the army they have all the fish and saké they can handle."

Taro tugged at his new uniform. It was thick olive-drab cotton in a Western style. He liked the cut of the jacket. He should find a way to send a photograph to his mother. "I hear they save the good stuff for officers and pilots."

"Yeah, probably," Nakamura said, leaning on an elbow to look down at Taro. "But we're going to be pilots soon. It wouldn't do to starve us. We need our strength! What's that you're hiding away there?"

"It's not hidden. Just trying to keep it safe."

"Is it a shamisen?"

"No. A violin. I've been playing since I was a kid."

"A fiddle, eh? Do you know any jazz?"

"It's a violin, not a trumpet. Or a fiddle."

Nakamura shrugged and lay back on his bed. "Well, let me know if you learn some jazz. That would be worth listening to."

The older boy had been right. Life at Oita was not much different from Taro's junior high school. Except, instead of regular teachers, they had a mix of civilian and military instructors. And instead of going home at the end of the day, they convened in a dining hall like private-school kids. They slept in cots or hammocks in the barracks, instead of on clean white futon at home. And, of course, there were the uniforms and rifles.

"Have you ever fired one before?" Nakamura asked him the first day they were assigned their weapons. They stood in line, waiting for the rest of their class to retrieve a gun from the weapons master.

"Never," Taro replied. He was bleary-eyed from the six a.m. wake-up reveille and burst of morning exercises. Now that they were gunkoku-shōnen, or military youth, the boys were expected to run everywhere in unison. At first it was fun, but as the days grew warmer, it just left him sweaty and sore. The lieutenant in charge promised they would soon become hardened to the discomfort. The Emperor needed fit soldiers, not soft schoolboys. Still, Taro would have given a lot for more than a two-minute dip in a hot furo bath—preferably one not crammed with ten other boys.

To make matters worse, he wasn't even sure he had buttoned every hole properly on his shirt. His jacket hid any mistakes for now, but there would be a uniform inspection in a couple of hours, before classes started. He'd have to figure it out somewhere between breakfast and study period.

And now he had a rifle to worry about. He held it gingerly

against his chest as they waited for the rest of the weapons to be assigned. "I'm a city kid. What would I be shooting at?"

Nakamura shrugged. "Rabbits? My father hunted rabbits, but I guess he used snares, not guns. Boy, would he like to get his hands on something like this!"

Taro laughed but quickly turned it into a cough when he caught their commanding officer glaring at him. Laughing was not the military way, especially not in formation. Transgressions were punished. Severely. Two boys had been punched by the inspection officer their second day for not having polished their boots properly. Laughing would earn him a hard slap at the very least.

Nakamura had straightened, his rifle held over his shoulder, the perfect specimen of an army man. Taro mimicked him until they were sure the CO wasn't looking.

"What was that for?" Nakamura frog-whispered.

"Your dad's a soldier now, Nakamura. He's got a rifle twice this size."

Nakamura's eyes widened. "That's right! Boy, I'd like to get my hands on something like that!"

Taro snorted, but managed not to laugh. The rifles were impressive, but everything about the military life was making an impression on Taro. He had been used to reciting the Imperial Rescript for Education at the start of each school day, but now they had a Rescript for Soldiers and Sailors to memorize. His days were filled with lessons and inspections and drills in the yard. He sparred with Nakamura and the others in kendo, fighting each other with sticks the length of his body, as the samurai had once fought with swords. He learned about military planning and mentality. And now he would learn to clean and care for his firearm.

The last rifle assigned, the boys came to attention and paraded across the grounds to the firing range, where two lieutenants ran them through the workings of their new weapons. Taro's fingers shook a little as he loaded his first bullets. At the lieutenant's command, he took aim and squeezed. The trigger was stiff and slow to respond. When it did, the recoil slammed the butt of the gun into Taro's shoulder. His ears rang and, most surprising of all, tears came to his eyes. He blinked them away, blaming them on the dull ache in his arm.

"Quite a kick, eh?" the lieutenant shouted. Taro rolled his shoulder, wondering if it would affect his playing. Violinists needed strong arms for proper positioning. Not that he had played much since arriving at the school. Once he had his routine down, he would make time, he told himself. For now, he lifted the rifle—*his* rifle—and took aim once more.

Beside him, Nakamura was grinning. "Aw, worried about your precious violin arm? Don't look so sad. Rifles are infantry stuff. We're gonna be pilots. Eagles don't use rifles—they have claws!"

———

Taro missed both of his parents, but his mother most of all. She would have been proud of his grades. He scored well in math and in history. He learned the ranks of officers from privates to generals, and was only beaten once, for tracking dirt into the barracks.

For all his mother's worry, Taro believed the war was going well for Japan. Not a day went by that their teachers didn't crow about the bravery and fortitude of the Emperor's soldiers. And if the officers' faces sometimes grew shadowed as they huddled around the command office and their voices dropped when the cadets marched by, Taro took comfort in knowing his superiors were so actively working toward victory.

Sundays were home days, when local families would open their doors to the cadets. Taro and Nakamura became favorites of the Oshita family. Mrs. Oshita lived with her elderly father-in-law and two little boys, who clung to Nakamura like monkeys on a tree. Taro would bring his violin some days and play for the family. The boys would dance and Oshita-san would smile and clap slowly, sometimes even singing if it was a folk tune and she could remember the words. On those days, Taro would feel close to his mother and worry less about having signed on to fight a war. But the worry only returned twice as heavily on Sunday nights, and he would try not to make a sound as he cried into his pillow, knowing from the heavy sighs throughout the barracks that he was not the only one.

CHAPTER 16

TARO

Fall 1943

"Taro, did you hear?" Nakamura frog-whispered one day as they ran to the auditorium with the rest of their group. While he didn't think he was as hardened as the lieutenant had promised, Taro was getting used to all of the running, especially now that autumn had made the air crisp and cool. Nakamura said it was to prepare them for emergencies, but Taro thought it was to tire them out so they wouldn't fidget in class.

Taro's hair was newly cut, and the clippings made the back of his neck itch. But a soldier wasn't allowed to scratch like a flea-bitten dog. Fortunately, Nakamura ignored his scowling. "Great news," he said. "Hiroshi got a jazz record from his sister. Sent to his home-day family! She's brilliant. I'd marry her if she'd have me."

Taro had to agree, it was impressive. Jazz was contraband, as were most Western things these days. They were un-Japanese. Yet somehow military uniforms were still based on British designs, and even mess-hall rations were more Western in style, with meat-heavy dishes to build muscle.

"Hiroshi's sister *is* married," Taro reminded him. "And twice your age."

Nakamura sighed. "Some women like a younger man."

Taro laughed, drawing a frown from their CO. He cleared his throat and stood straighter. Sunlight gave way to a narrow door, then a high-ceilinged room lined with chairs. The boys filed in, heading to the end of each row and taking their seats until every chair was full.

"Anyway, I was thinking we could go check it out later, after dinner. You can pick up some jazz riffs for that fiddle of yours. That way, even if they confiscate Hiroshi's contraband Western tunes, we'll still have you."

"You already have me," Taro said. "And Mozart. And Beethoven—"

"And a pain in the neck. Fine. Be a stodge. I'm going tonight anyway. Got a line on some unsupervised shōchū. We're gonna have a fine time with or without you."

Taro shook his head. He knew he'd end up going along, but not for the pilfered booze or the jazz—which he liked well enough, and knew how to play a little—but to watch Nakamura dance. His voice wasn't the only thing that reminded everyone of a frog.

"I wish to remind each of you boys," the base commander was saying, "of the importance of what we do. What does our beloved Emperor wish for us?"

Taro rose to his feet, along with the other cadets. Hands at his sides, he recited the virtues of the Imperial Rescript for Soldiers and Sailors.

"The soldier and sailor should consider loyalty their essential duty—"

"Loyal to jazz," Nakamura whispered.

"The soldier and sailor should esteem true valor." Taro pinched Nakamura on the leg.

"The soldier and the sailor should highly value faithfulness"—Nakamura pinched back—"and *righteousness*—" The pinching had become anything but righteous.

"And make simplicity their aim."

"I'm simple," Nakamura whispered. Taro bit his lip to keep from snorting out loud.

"If the heart be not sincere, words and deeds, however good, are all mere outward show and can avail nothing. If only the heart be *sincere*," Taro said firmly, "anything can be accomplished."

At this point, Nakamura pinched him mercilessly. Taro's voice rose in a yelp on the word *accomplished*, and he lost track of the Emperor's wisdom until the vow to fulfill his duty of grateful service to the country and be a source of joy, not only to the Emperor, "but to all the people of Japan!" The cadets all said this last line as loud as thunder. They bowed sharply in unison and broke into clapping afterward. In the front of the room, their commanders beamed at them.

Taro felt flushed with pride. Almost enough to ease the pain in his thigh.

"Try that again, Nakamura, and tomorrow I'll bring a stick-pin with me," he murmured.

"Try *that*, and I'll wear iron underpants."

"Now," the CO said, "we have a treat for you boys. The commandant has procured some entertainment for tonight. After dinner, we'll be showing a movie. Report back here at nineteen hundred hours. Dismissed."

Nakamura groaned as they filed out into the open air. "A mooovie! What are the chances it'll be something good, like *The 47 Ronin?*"

"Next to none," Taro said. They were much more likely to show newsreels and training films than samurai epics.

"Whatever it is, I hope it's short. We don't want to keep that record waiting. Hey, why the long face?"

Long face was a good way to put it. Reciting the virtues of the rescript had weighed Taro down. "You should try to be more serious," he told Nakamura as they followed the flow of cadets toward the mess hall. "You heard the rescript. It's through moral fortitude that we'll defeat the enemy."

"Oooh, did you write that down in class today?" Nakamura joked.

Taro stopped in the middle of the walkway. "Kenji, I'm not like you. I can't laugh at everything. Aren't you ever afraid of failure?"

Nakamura looked at him, his broad face growing serious. "Taro, why do you think I make a joke of everything? We're fifteen! If I don't laugh, I'll cry. Or worse, I'll throw up. Sure, it's all mathematics and calisthenics now, but we're going to be fighter pilots! It's the best worst thing that's ever happened to me. To any of us. Don't make me get all sober about it now. It'll ruin the fun."

Nakamura shook his head and jogged away. "Catch you inside," he called over his shoulder.

Taro sighed. He would make it up to Nakamura. Learn some of this new jazz record later tonight. But the worry would not leave him. Nakamura was a grasshopper, always bouncing around. But Taro must learn to be fearless like the dragonfly, whose wings did not allow it to travel backward. He would not shame his mother and father. As his old music teacher, Ayugai-sensei, had said in his last letter, "To play great music, one must practice every day. Why would moral strength be any different?"

Taro would need a role model, someone to imitate until he was ready to perform on his own.

Over dinner, Taro scanned the faces of the boys at his table and the sergeants overseeing the room. But most were just like him—uncertain bodies wearing uniforms they did not yet know how to fill. He closed his eyes and recalled the moment, years ago, when Taro's father had decided Shōnen Hikōhei would be his destiny.

"Okā-san," Taro whispered. His mother had borne the news with dignity, sending off first her husband, then her son into the arms of war. Like the samurai women of old, she put country before all else. He would learn to do the same. With his mother as a moral role model, not even Nakamura's hijinks could steer him wrong.

Decision made, he flicked a bit of rice down the table at Nakamura. His friend brushed it aside like a gnat, but soon a bit of rice came flying back. Taro smiled. Nakamura never stayed mad for long.

———

Back in the auditorium, some of the boys popped sesame candies in their mouths and stared into the dark, waiting for the movie to start.

"Mmmm. Just like the kamishibai man back home," Taro whispered to Nakamura under the *clack-clack* of the film projector warming up. He slurped to keep from drooling as the honeyed bittersweetness of the candy filled his mouth.

Nakamura opened his own mouth to reply, but just then the screen came to life. Ominous clouds filled the screen. From the speakers, the wind whistled and screamed. The boys fell silent. A title card announced this was a navy film, but they were army. Some of the boys booed, only to be shushed by the teachers in the room.

And then the title appeared over violently crashing waves: *Momotaro's Sea Eagles*.

"Hey!" Nakamura grabbed Taro's wrist. "It's you!"

Taro grinned. He was on his father's shoulders, peering over the heads of the crowd, hands sticky with candy, watching the old kamishibai uncle tell his tale. Only this was 1943, and he was a military youth now. The story unfolded in glorious moving pictures—animations not so different from the kamishibai man's slideshow, but full of action, sound, and life.

Trumpets swelled and rolled into a bright military anthem. Plucky xylophones tapped high notes, brass brayed, and the song resolved into a marching version of the familiar folk song "Momotaro." The boys sang along as a realistic aircraft carrier cut through cartoon waves. "Momotaro-san, Momotaro-san, where are you going, Momotaro-san? I'm going to fight the demons. Will you come with me?" The boys around Taro nudged him as they sang. He wasn't the only Taro in the group, though. He was glad it was a popular name, or he'd never hear the end of it.

On-screen, shadowed figures with streaming ears unfolded the clever wings of aeroplanes. Rabbits! The boys cheered as the rabbits fueled the planes. The animal was the zodiac sign for many of the cadets in Taro's cohort.

"Flight check!" someone shouted, and everyone laughed.

A high-pitched whistle summoned the animal crew to the deck of the carrier, and there they were—a battalion of monkeys in boots and headbands, dogs in overalls, and pheasants in flight suits. Taro grinned until his eyes stung.

"That's you," he said, pointing to a proud monkey.

"No way," Nakamura said, "I'm the dog with the jaunty circle around one eye. Very stylish!"

And then he was there, large as life in black and white on the screen. Momotaro was a round-cheeked boy with a strip of cloth around his forehead emblazoned with a rising sun—the hachimaki band of a true samurai.

The room filled with cheers as Momotaro's troops piled into their Zero aeroplanes to attack Demon Island.

"Hey, it's Pearl Harbor!" Nakamura crowed as the telltale slide guitar music of the islands began to play—full of yearning, dreamy glissandos and deep vibratos that brought to mind warm winds and waving palm trees.

Momotaro's pilots bombed row after row of towering battleships, sending pale-faced, piggish sailors and one particularly oafish bearded drunk scurrying for their lives.

Soon Taro was roaring along with the others as the victory unfolded. They grew sober when the monkey's torpedo missed its target and raucous when the brave little monkey dived out of the aeroplane to catch the torpedo and ride it into the enemy ship.

"Not sure that's regulation," Nakamura joked. Fortunately, the resulting explosion blew the little monkey right back up into his badly damaged aeroplane, in which he, the dog, and the pheasant pilot limped home. Try as they might, they could not keep the bird in the air. Fortunately, this was a cartoon, and some friendly pheasants came to the rescue, flying the crew safely home on their feathery backs.

At least, that's what Taro thought happened. He never saw them actually land. Only the aircraft carrier waiting for the missing aeroplane, and the small figures carried high on birdback into the sky.

The movie ended to much applause and bravado. Someone started the shout, and they all joined in, "Banzai! Banzai! Banzai!" They bowed three times to the screen. A moment later, they were dismissed.

"Not bad, eh, Momotaro?" Nakamura said as they headed out into the night. "Almost makes a man feel like he can fight!"

Nakamura threw an arm around Taro's shoulder and steered him away from their barracks. "Now where you going, Momotaro-san?" he croaked horribly, trying to mimic the song.

"I was going to—oh," Taro said, catching on. "I'm going to listen to ja-aazz," he sang off-key. "Will you come with me?"

Nakamura scratched his chin. "Give me a dumpling, and I'll think about it."

And off they went into the night.

CHAPTER 17

TARO

Spring 1944

Twelve months marched by, and then it was time to graduate. Taro's mother made the long journey to see him, arriving on a damp spring morning when the cherry blossoms were in bloom. He looked sharp in his air cadet uniform—the blue silk sash that showed he was a graduate, the graceful military sword at his side with its tassel and cord, the pin that said he was destined for flight school. When she saw him, she pressed a handkerchief to her eyes.

"Taro! You look so like your father. For a minute I forgot where I was!" She smiled, and Taro grinned. "You've grown! Sixteen, and you look like a man."

"It's Corporal Inoguchi now, Okā-san," he joked. "And, you know, I think I'm even taller than Father now!"

His mother squinted up at him in the morning sunlight. He inhaled the familiar warm scent that came from her kimono, perfumed by the cedar chest her father had brought back from Tokyo years ago. He breathed it in, stepping closer. His mother tilted her chin.

"I think you're right. As much as he would want to be here, thank goodness he's not here to see that! A man always likes to think he is taller than his little boy."

They both laughed, and Taro found himself reaching for his own handkerchief.

Then he brought his mother around to meet Nakamura and a few of the other cadets.

"We're off to Tachiarai Army Flying School in Fukuoka next," Taro explained. Tachiarai was 130 or so kilometers northwest of Oita. Not far, really, but it seemed worlds away. No more classrooms and lectures—they would be on a real air base, learning how to fly. He couldn't help but smile. "Nakamura and I will be part of the same squad, I hope. Some of the other boys will be studying navigation and gunnery at a different base. If we do well, we will be there until December, and then on to Advanced Flight Training and then . . ."

"The war," his mother said softly. "My son, the Imperial Army Air Force pilot." She smiled again, but slowly. There was *mono no aware* in this new smile. Taro seized her hand and squeezed it. He was surprised to feel calluses on her once-soft skin. The war was hardening everyone, but he had hoped—stupidly, he realized now—that she would somehow be spared.

"I have something for you," she said. She reached into her bag and pulled out a folded piece of white cloth.

"A senninbari!" Nakamura breathed—a thousand-person-stitch belt. It was the closest to a whisper that Taro had ever heard from him.

Taro soberly accepted the belt. Senninbari were traditionally given to soldiers to protect them in battle. He unfolded it—three, then four feet of cloth. The sash ended in strings, allowing it to be tied around the waist. And every inch was covered in neat little rows of red knotted stitches. One thousand in all. Each one made by a different woman. It took his breath away.

"I stood by the train station at first. But when the trains became less frequent, I went to the temple and even the market," his mother explained. "Everyone was so kind."

Taro folded the senninbari back up, as reverently as he would a flag, and placed it inside his uniform jacket, against his heart. When he bowed, it was almost to the floor. "Domo arigatō gozaimasu, Haha-ue," he said, using the most formal term for *mother* to show his deepest respect.

When he straightened again, she looked pleased. Even Nakamura was impressed into silence. Taro took a breath and smiled.

"It's useless to say 'don't worry,' but I will say it anyway. Don't worry about us, Okā-san. Nakamura has my back, isn't that right, Kenji?"

"And Taro has mine!" Nakamura said in his bullfrog voice, the outdoor voice that made him sound like three boys instead of one.

"Momotaro always comes back to his parents, doesn't he?" Taro said.

"Momotaro-san, Momotaro-san, where are you going, Momotaro-san?" Nakamura bellowed the children's song.

Taro tried to read his mother's face. She was smiling softly, but it did not reach her eyes.

"I'm going to fight the demons!" Taro sang back. He turned

to Nakamura, who rolled his eyes and wagged his butt like the dog in the story. "Will you come with me?"

"If you'll give me a dumpling, I will go with you!" Nakamura crowed.

"That's great! Here you go! It's nice to have friends!"

They danced around, Nakamura playing the dog and the monkey and the pheasant, all of Momotaro's faithful friends, until Taro's mother was laughing, and the handkerchief came out again to wipe a different kind of tear from her eyes.

CHAPTER 18

HANA

Laundry again. I suppose pilots should not have to sleep on day-old sheets, but I wish just once they would want to. Wet sheets on a windy day can chill you to the bone. I rub my fingers to warm them and pick up another clothespin.

"Oh!" Sachiko chimes in. "Did you hear the sad news? Lieutenant Fuji'i will finally body-crash today! He has written the commandant so many times, even in his own blood! And they always refused him because of his wife and children."

"He is a very good instructor," Mariko says.

"Yes! That's what I thought! But now they say he's had a letter from home. His dear wife has drowned herself and their children, to wait for him on the other side! Isn't that romantic? How like a heroine in a novel! A true samurai wife! He must be very proud. You will see how happy he is when he finally joins his men. We should sing a good song for him."

"We should light incense at the temple for his family," I say. The thought of that woman, with two young daughters tied to her body, terrifies me. Is it brave to be so obedient? Perhaps.

"Did he ask her to do this?" I wonder out loud. I should not let Sachiko's gossip drag me in, but I do. I can't even guess what my mother would do in this situation. What I would do.

"No! That's what's so wonderful!" Sachiko cries. "He didn't ask! She knew he was unhappy and that they were the cause. That's true love. She died to set him free!"

"I would have lied and had a neighbor send the letter. Then he could die, but his daughters would live," Mariko says gravely.

"Mariko!" Sachiko gasps. "That is so selfish!"

"It's practical." Kazuko steps in. "Those girls were future mothers of Japan, weren't they? Just like us."

That silences Sachiko for a while, and we all return to the heavy work at hand. The sheets are cumbersome this morning, and my fingers are red and raw. My stomach grumbles beneath my middy blouse. I pat the buttons to soothe it.

"We can make tea next," I tell Mariko, who has fallen into a dour mood. She nods, but does not smile, and I see that it's happened. The war has finally worn her down. Now she will become the old woman she so feared. The wind has made her pigtails unruly. I pin the last corner of the sheet to the line and reach to brush a stray hair from her cheek.

"Mariko?"

She smiles wistfully at me, and I see there are tears in her eyes.

"Hana, I don't think I can be a samurai wife."

I return her small smile. "Just be Nadeshiko, then. Your dolt of a farmer husband won't know the difference."

"Hana!" She swats me with the corner of one of the hanging sheets, and like that, the old woman disappears, and we carry on like we've been told to do.

When the last sheet is hung, Kaori-sensei gathers all the Nadeshiko in the field behind the barracks. A stack of bamboo rods lie on the grass beside her. Mariko makes a disgusted sound. "Time for drills," she moans. "I thought we'd left those things behind."

"Line up, girls!" Kaori-sensei says brightly. "There are no farewell ceremonies until this afternoon, so we have time to do our exercises. Each of you, take a stave from the pile. Sergeant Kawahara was kind enough to drive them over from the school. He thinks we might consider keeping them nearby so we may practice whenever we have time. That's a wonderful idea. Are you ready?"

"Lucky for you." I nudge Mariko.

"Splinters every day!" she cries.

Kaori-sensei stands in front of us, looking fresh and cheerful as always. I don't know how she does it. If Sergeant Kawahara had told me it was a good idea to be armed and ready every day, I would take it poorly, but she seems to believe he is only being practical. That it's not a veiled warning of an invasion to come. But I cannot forget, if the enemy lands on our shore, honor and the Emperor demand we fight to the last woman and child—gyokusai, the shattering of the jewel that is Japan. I think of Lieutenant Fuji'i's wife, wading into the river, stoic, obedient. This is different, I tell myself. This is the way of a warrior.

Mariko and I each grip our bamboo staves in both hands. We've been drilling with them since we were twelve years old. Some find the weight in their hands comforting. Mariko calls them a health hazard—no matter how tough her hands get, she always catches a splinter when we spar. I think they will not be hazardous enough. The staves are as long as we are tall, and two or three inches around—small enough for us to grip, but thick enough so that they will not easily break. One end is cut at an angle, creating a sharp point, like a hollow needle. The other end is blunt so we may lean our weight into it if necessary.

I hope it will not be necessary.

"I promise to take the life of at least one enemy soldier!" we cry in unison.

"Ichi!" Sensei shouts, and we hoist our staves onto our shoulders.

"Ni!" she shouts, and we stab the air in front of us.

"San!" she shouts, and we shift our grips, thrusting and dancing forward one step, then two, like swordsmen. We pair off and spar with each other then, staves clashing and clocking together like poorly played drums. I don't think the Americans will have bamboo staves when they land. I don't know how well our maneuvers will perform against men with guns.

But bamboo is plentiful here; guns and bullets are not. It is the story of our war in Chiran, and perhaps all across Japan. We use what we have, and we do what we must to survive.

"Itai! Another splinter!" Mariko exclaims. We pause in our sparring to tend to her hand. The splinter is easily removed. Our fingers are not as soft as they once were.

Nothing about us is.

———

In the afternoon, we all file down to the runway to say goodbye. "We are running low on cherry blossoms," Mariko comments.

Kazuko points ahead. "Ah, that's why."

Two of the girls have covered one of the aeroplanes in flowers. "It must be Fuji'i-san's plane," she tells me.

It turns out we are still soft on the inside. Otherwise the sight would not be such a splinter in our hearts. Many of the girls are weeping openly today, even as they smile and say they are happy. Fuji'i-san is not smiling. Nor is he sad. He is ready. The boys from yesterday's picnic are here to see the other pilots off. The one called Nakamura looks more solemn than I'd have thought possible. The laughing boys of yesterday's picnic stand like soldiers now. They bow deeply as the pilots give their farewells. They have heard the tale of Fuji'i-san—from Sachiko, no doubt—and must have been deeply impressed. I am surprised to find my cheeks are damp. Beside me, Mariko wipes her eyes.

The officers drink a toast with saké. White funeral boxes are set aside containing hair and nail clippings from each tokkō. Without bodies to bury, their families will be given these keepsakes to cremate at their local Buddhist temples. A final salute, and the line of pilots comes toward us. Fuji'i-san bows, but says nothing.

"Be brave, little sisters," one of his men says. "We will crash brilliantly for you. You must persevere."

We bow and the six pilots press letters and mementos into the hands of the Nadeshiko girls they know best. Some of these letters contain wills to be mailed to their families. One of the pilots gives the last of his pocket change to his Nadeshiko. "I'll have no need for it from now on," he tells her.

Mariko and I stand back with Sachiko and Kazuko. We wish our brothers well and stand firm as the ground crew pull the chocks from beneath their aeroplane wheels. They hand-start their engines—these body-crashing planes are so unlike the ones that ferry important officers back and forth. Tokkō have neither guns nor powerful engines. That's for the escort planes, the ones that lead them out to sea and witness their glorious attacks. No, their aeroplanes are simple, most notable for the large bombs attached to their bellies. This is the sign of ultimate sacrifice.

"Scatter bravely and well!" we say to these boys like cherry blossoms, like fireflies that light the sky for only a day.

A few of the engines sputter, but they all catch, and the planes take off in a roar of sound, a cloud of petals scattering softly to the ground.

Mariko wipes a tear away with the dark sleeve of her blouse. She reaches for my hand, and we wave goodbye.

CHAPTER 19

TARO

Spring 1944

Taro watched Hakata Bay disappear from view as the train trundled toward his new home. Even Nakamura sat in reverent silence. Tachiarai Army Flying School was south of the city of Fukuoka, on the northern tip of Kyushu. It was there in the thirteenth century that Mongols attempted to invade Japan. But the gods chose to protect the home islands, blowing the invaders back out to sea with the kamikaze, or "divine wind."

Now, instead of wind, the Emperor sent aeroplanes. Taro sat a little straighter at the thought.

"Hey! Girls!" Nakamura broke the silence. Heads turned. Sure enough, there were girls standing on a hillside above the tracks as the train slowed round a bend. "Ah, too young." He scowled.

"What are they doing?" one of the boys asked.

"Drills," another replied with a shove. Taro swallowed a sudden feeling of sorrow. They were elementary schoolgirls, each with a sharpened bamboo pole. A teacher stood before them, shouting instructions Taro couldn't hear. The girls stood at attention, raised their poles, and thrust them in unison at an invisible enemy.

"My mother told me the women in our mura also train like this," he said quietly. When he had finally asked, after his graduation, she had been proud of her calluses. She was ready to defend the home islands against the gaijin invaders to the end. "The day after Pearl Harbor, my old schoolteacher said this conflict would be over in months. He claimed the Americans would beg for peace on our terms." Taro ran a hand over his short hair. "I wonder what he thinks now."

The train rumbled on, past the girls with their makeshift weapons and determined faces, moving steadily toward its destination.

A few minutes later, one of the COs ordered everyone to close their window shades. "Troop movements are top secret," he said. "It won't do to have you waving at every schoolgirl in the prefecture."

The boys sat soberly after that, the darkened windows like a wall between them and the life that came before.

"They better put me in a plane quick," Nakamura declared. "We're going to win this war."

———

Blue sky, dust, and the scent of aeroplane fuel greeted them as Taro and the other cadets assembled for their first roll call.

"Welcome to Tachiarai Army Flying School! I am your squadron leader, Lieutenant Saito! You will be divided into flights of twenty, two flights to a squadron. You will bunk together, mess together, train together. What is the duty of a soldier?"

"Loyalty!" the cadets shouted. It was the first tenet of the Imperial Rescript for Soldiers and Sailors. They would be expected to recite it, start to finish, whenever an officer demanded.

"Loyalty," the squadron leader repeated. "That's correct. Now, when your name is called, line up before your assigned barracks. You will be given two uniforms and a flight suit. You are soldiers now; you will dress as soldiers. Swords are to be worn at assembly. Do not shame yourselves."

With that, Saito turned on his heel and strode off.

"Akama Toshiro!" the flying officer in front of the first barracks called. Taro waited as boy after boy accepted his clothing and joined the formation in front of his new home. Watching the new faces lining up, Taro began to feel a bit homesick for the familiarity of Oita. Fortunately, when his name was called, he and Nakamura were once again teamed together in the same flight. Dismissed, they were allowed to settle into their bunks until it was time for the evening meal.

"What a dump!" one of the boys exclaimed. The barracks were underwhelming. Inside, the wooden walls were dusty and unpainted. What paint there was on the exterior had begun to flake in the sun.

"It's not so bad!" Nakamura declared, claiming a bed in the middle of the row. There were ten cots on each side of the narrow room. "At least there are no spiders."

Taro noted the cobwebs in the corners. "Don't get ahead of yourself, Nak," he said. "Maybe there's a broom we can borrow."

"And a bucket and a mop and a can of paint," Nakamura added. "See? Stick with me, Peach Boy! We're gonna do just fine."

At 0600, Taro woke to the call of a bugle playing reveille. He rose with the nineteen other cadets in his flight. In unison, they rolled up their sleep sacks and stored them in their cubbies before washing and dressing for the day. Even though it was called flying school, much of it took place on the ground. The army didn't have enough fuel to waste on untrained pilots. And so, despite the brown silk summer flight suits that had been handed to them on arrival, they mostly wore their drab uniforms and fell into a routine of military instruction—calisthenics, fencing, and martial arts—along with aviation mechanics and meteorology in the morning, and navigation, communications, and "flight training" in the afternoon. Then there was dinner, study time, and curfew at 2200. Once again, there was little time left to practice violin. The call of the bugle to wake, to mess, to assemble, and to sleep was the only music he heard.

"Flight training" meant the cadets built their aeroplanes before they flew them—detailed models intended to teach them how the aircraft worked. Taro was reminded of the hours spent with his father as a boy, carving lightweight wood into struts and wings. This model of aeroplane was newer, but it took the same amount of time and care.

Nakamura couldn't do it.

"Aaagh!" He threw a pile of sticks across the room like an old man reading I Ching fortunes. "I've glued my fingers together again."

"We can't fly until we know our planes inside and out," Taro chided him. "You'd better not wash out over this and leave me here alone."

Nakamura grumbled and groused as he picked up the wood again.

"Fine. Show me how you did this."

———

When the models—miniature Ki-9 trainers two hand spans long—were complete, their company graduated to simulators.

"Finally, a flight suit!" Nakamura crowed the first morning, smoothing down the silk jumpsuit. It was a hot summerlike day, and the thin fabric stuck to their sweat in places like a second skin. The fit was a bit snug across his broad shoulders, but he wore it proudly. "I saw some Ki-55s on the airfield this morning. Maybe we can at least sit inside them today."

Taro patted his friend on the shoulder. "Don't count on it," he said. The Tachikawa Ki-55 was an advanced trainer. Nakamura was asking to run before he could walk. "And don't forget your model plane."

Taro was right. The simulators weren't aeroplanes. Not even full fuselages. Nakamura groaned when the flying officer introduced them to the device. It was nothing more than a seat on a sled with a rudder and control stick attached in front.

"Nakamura," the instructor said, "you've been so eager; you get to go first."

Taro swallowed his smile as Nakamura shuffled into the seat.

"You have your aeroplane?" the instructor asked. Flying Officer Akagi was a thin man with an equally thin mustache. His uniform was always pristine. Taro had decided this was the man to emulate at Tachiarai. He stood straighter now, determined to learn from any mistakes Nakamura might make, to prove himself from the start.

"Sir!" Nakamura held his model aloft. It wasn't the prettiest version of a Ki-9, but it was sturdy and accurate—unlike the seven other models he'd thrown across the room before this one.

Akagi used a bamboo switch to point out the controls on the simulator—how the levers controlled the throttle and flaps, how to make turns.

"Cadet! You will make the proper actions with the simulator and adjust your model in accordance with those actions, as if it is in flight. You bank left, it banks left. Like so—" He grabbed Nakamura's wrist, twisting it so the little model tilted left. "Understood? Now, prepare for takeoff!"

Nakamura jumped, then mimed going through takeoff procedures, his model still in his left hand.

"Bank left!" Akagi shouted.

Nakamura pulled the joystick to the left, tilting his aeroplane model in the proper direction.

"Bank right!"

Nakamura banked right but forgot to move his model as he managed the controls.

"Wrong!"

The bamboo switch came down suddenly, slicing an arc of red across Nakamura's cheek.

Taro flinched, but Nakamura did not. "Hai!" he shouted, correcting his model. From then on, he followed Akagi's instructions more closely, but still earned two more cuts of the switch before he was done.

Nakamura returned to the line silently, blood running down his cheek. Akagi sneered at the cadets. Taro stared over the flying officer's shoulder, unwilling to show him any emotion.

"This is not grade school, children! This is the Imperial Army! What does the soldiers' Rescript tell us?"

"The soldier and sailor should consider loyalty their essential duty. Who that is born in this land can be wanting in the spirit of grateful service to it? No soldier or sailor, especially, can be considered efficient unless this spirit be strong within him—" the cadets began. Some officers allowed them to recite only the highlights, but they were learning Akagi was a harder sort. Word for word, he drilled the Emperor's wishes into their hearts day and night.

Akagi cut them off before they could continue. "That's right! If you fumble, drop your model, treat it as a toy, are you of use to the Emperor? No! Your spirit is weak! You are less than useless! Remember what his Imperial Majesty says! 'We rely upon you as Our limbs and you look up to Us as your head.' What do we do with an arm that is useless? We cut it off!"

Akagi regarded the line of boys before him. Taro could feel the sweat building on his top lip, his neck. He willed it away. Beside him, a drop of blood fell from Nakamura's cheek onto the ground. His first blood shed for the homeland. Taro gripped his model. He would not fail.

"All right, then," Akagi said. "Next!"

Cuts, slaps, and punches. Those were the rewards for nervous fumbling. By the end of the day, no cadet was unscathed.

In addition to the cut on his cheek, Nakamura had red marks up and down his left side beneath his flight suit. Taro had welts on his cheek and one hand. He had grown up doing just such maneuvers and received two lashes when he forgot himself and started making engine noises to go along with the motions. Still, Akagi had given him a begrudging nod when he finished his simulated flight.

"Do we have Akagi for all our training?" Nakamura moaned as they got ready for lights-out.

"I hear he came up from infantry," one of the other boys said. "They're rough over there. My brother has a friend who says they regularly punch cadets in the face! I guess we're pretty lucky."

Nakamura snorted, touching his wounded cheek tenderly. "Yeah, lucky I'm so pretty, or I'd regret this. Eh, Taro?" He threw a grin across the room. "I hear girls like scars."

———

Taro's class graduated to new simulators, ones that were attached to wheeled platforms. The boys would push with all their might, propelling the devices along one of the runways to simulate the feeling of flight. Flying Officer Saito took over for this training. He was a jovial type and not so hard to please as Akagi.

"Are we ever going to actually sit in a plane?" Nakamura wondered over dinner a couple of weeks later. Spring was warming toward summer, but the excitement of being at Tachiarai had begun to cool, replaced by a nervous tension. "We only have nine more months to get up to speed. My brother says when he joined up, cadets got two years."

"Wow." Tomomichi, a round-faced kid with spiky hair that no comb could control, almost choked on his rice. "Two years! They probably spent four months just building models!"

"Ugh. I hadn't thought of that," Nakamura groaned. "Fine. I can handle a couple more weeks. But I can't wait to fly."

But there was more to ground school than models and control panels. They had to learn how to handle maneuvering in the air, which was a lot different from being pushed along the ground by five sweaty boys. For this, they trained in a large Ferris-type wheel, like a metal hoop made from a ladder. The trainee stood inside in a shape like an X—feet braced against U-shaped cross bars, hands grasping a second set above his head—while his classmates rolled him along so that he twisted upside down, sideways, all the directions an aeroplane could go. It was dizzying and, worse, nauseating. More than one trainee emptied his stomach in that gizmo.

Only after Lieutenant Saito saw that each cadet could manage it without getting sick did he announce, "First flight's tomorrow. You'll each go up with me or with Flying Officer Takei. Get a good night's sleep. Write your families. Tell them what you are doing, and that it's dangerous. There are no guarantees once you're in the air. Such a letter is good exercise for your moral fortitude. Besides, if anyone screws up, I don't want to be the first to break it to your mothers."

With that vote of confidence, the boys were released for the evening.

———

"Ah!" Taro scooted back in his bunk. Nakamura's face loomed overhead. "What are you doing?"

"Are you ready?" Nakamura whispered in his indoor voice.

"What time is it? Did I miss roll call?"

"Nope. It's"—Nakamura grabbed Taro's wrist—"four a.m., according to your fine timepiece." The watch had been a surprise gift from Taro's father, delivered by army packet to Tachiarai shortly after Taro arrived.

"Why are we awake?"

"It's first flight day, son! Step one in becoming an Eagle of the Eastern skies!"

Taro's head felt like a sandbag. He yawned, making his ears pop. "Sounds like a movie."

"Yep! The one they'll make about us, just as soon as you put on some pants." Nakamura's indoor whisper was getting louder. The other trainees were beginning to stir.

"You're not going to let me go back to sleep, are you?"

"Nope. Come on, I'll buy you a cup of ocha before reveille."

———

Taro was going to be sick. The tea had been a bad idea, and tea had *never* been a bad idea. So he had to admit it was nerves, not the ocha, churning his stomach while he waited for his chance to fly.

He and the other trainees stood on the flight line at the edge of the runway, a green field stretching out behind them. Nakamura had already taken off, swaddled in the front seat of an old biplane, while a senior pilot took the helm from the back seat. So far, three of the boys had thrown up, and that was just as passengers.

"Kannon, please let me make my father proud," the boy next to him muttered, a prayer to the goddess of mercy. Taro's hands grew clammy, and a sheen of sweat sprang out on his top lip. His father was a pilot, an aeronautical engineer, no less. What would he say if his son lost his lunch on the first day of flying? Yes, he'd flown before, but that had been years ago. This would be his first flight without the safety of his mother's lap. The thought of flying that way now made him smile.

"Inoguchi, next!" the instructor called out.

"Hai!" Taro approached the idling plane, careful to avoid the propeller, and hauled himself up into the open cockpit. The Ki-17 was a biplane—with double-decker wings and room for two fliers seated one behind the other. Once Taro was seated, the instructor pilot shouted at him to attach his earpiece to the speaking tube.

"Hai!" he said into the funneled mouth of the tube by his side. He buckled into the harness, pausing to attach the emergency release to his parachute.

"Watch your feet!" the pilot said through the speaking tube. "Don't touch anything. Feet off the pedals. I'm in control here, got it?"

"Hai!"

"Parachute attached? Buckled in?"

"Hai!" Taro shouted to each question. And then the plane was rolling.

He listened to the basso rumble of the plane, the increasing tempo of the wheels along the runway, *ta-lok, ta-lak, ta-lok*. It reminded him of something. The percussion, the bass. *Boléro* by Ravel. The music swelled inside him, pulling him along on a caravan of sound until the drums dropped into silence and they were in flight. Oboe and clarinet called like songbirds. The world fell away from his feet, and he was swallowed in blue.

Taro wanted to spread his arms out to his sides, above the walls of the narrow cockpit. He wanted to open his mouth and bellow along with the engine, the wind, the rush of noise.

It wouldn't do to keep this foolish smile on his face once they landed. He could imagine his father's disapproval.

This was serious business, he told himself.

But the smile remained.

"I told you," Nakamura said that night as the newly christened pilots toasted each other with shōchū from Lieutenant Saito's private stock. "We were born to fly!"

CHAPTER 20

HANA

The house is quiet when I return this afternoon. My mother is in the other room, sewing in the fading April sun. We make the most of sunlight these days. From the doorway, I can hear the bubble of the pot on the stove. Okayu again, but the rice porridge is thin. Tonight I have something to add to it, though. I slip off my shoes in the entryway and pad across the tatami mats into the kitchen.

"Okā-san, I am home." I bow to her and pull a sweet potato from my waistband. "Look, a treat for us!"

My mother looks up from her sewing and smiles, even though her lips are pursed around the dull backs of three pins. She marks her place, pulls the pins from her lips, and says, "Ah, a satsumaimo! Did you work the farm today? It must have been a good harvest to send you home with such a big potato!"

"Hai." The lie comes easily to my lips. I bow and put the potato in the coals to warm.

We have only served at the base for three short weeks. But the repetition of our work makes the time seem longer. It's chop wood, carry water again and again, as my father would say, though his work was measure and cut, cut and sew. Sometimes it's necessary to live this way, one step at a time. But if my mother knew we girls were spending every day with tokkō pilots, she would worry. My father's enlistment was bad enough. And since the cave-in, she worries all the time.

In truth, the airfield *is* a more likely target for bombs and fighter planes. And the soldiers are rambunctious sometimes—rumors have flown about their carousing at the restaurant next door. The Kempeitai military police were even sent to investigate, but Tomihara-san runs a clean shop. It's the government that runs brothels of comfort girls, not Tomihara-san. But my mother has a patriotic heart. She would want me to continue to be a good citizen, especially for such fine young men. At least that's what I tell myself when I feel the guilt of omission.

I stoop by the fire, moving the pot off the center of the heat.

"Go change your clothes," Okā-san says. "I'll stir the pot."

I nod, grateful to get out of my monpé and into a clean yukata. I am tying the belt across my waist when a voice calls out from the street. There is a man at the door. I pause in the hallway, hidden by the sliding screen, while my mother greets the visitor.

"Ah, yes! I know these kimono. A good weave, very fine fabrics. Certainly, we will do all we can. Yes, careful stitches, no unnecessary cuts, nothing taken away. She will be able to adjust them again if needed. Certainly. Five days, no more. Many thanks to you."

I have been holding my breath, not realizing it. I breathe now. The mineral scent of damp pavement. A brief shower chased me home. Not enough to delay tomorrow's flight. But now there is freshness that has been lacking in the stale back rooms. I slide the shōji screens open onto the back garden, hoping to direct the breeze throughout the house. The days are getting longer. Above the trees, the sky is still light.

"Ah, yes, a breeze. Just what's needed," my mother says in her usual shop chatter. She talks to herself, even when I am here. And she talks to my absent father when she thinks no one is listening. Now she steps over the coat she has been sewing, her arms full of a beautiful rust-and-salmon kimono.

"Look at this, Hana. Do you know what this is?"

I follow her to the window, where we admire the rich fabric in the fading light. I rub it between my thumb and forefinger, feeling the fineness of the crepe. "Kinsha?" I ask, trying to identify the silk by its feel.

"Not quite. This is chirimen. Look how beautifully it drapes," she explains, carefully unfolding the bundle.

"Who brought it in?" I ask. No one in Chiran would wear such a gorgeous kimono. It is the most beautiful thing I have ever seen.

Okā-san clucks her tongue. "Who, indeed. A farmer, of all people! This is not his kimono! Or, at least, it wasn't originally. This belonged to Reiko's mother. You know, she was a kimono model once, before Reiko and her siblings were born."

My eyes goggle. "Tomihara-san?" I try to picture her round, motherly face dusted in rice powder, with painted lips and elaborate hair, like in the old magazine photos of the Floating World in Tokyo, where famous actors and musicians flitted in and out of nightclubs and restaurants.

"You forget, Hana-chan, every woman in this village had

a life before she had children! I myself was considered a great beauty in my home mura."

Okā-san came to Chiran as a bride seventeen years ago, only two years older than I am today. Back then, it was common for men to visit other villages to find a bride. My father met my mother less than an hour from here while he was on holiday in Ibusuki. The town is famous for hot springs and onsen spas and especially for sand-bathing, where guests are buried in the warm sands heated by the underground springs.

As Otō-san tells it, he was a modest bachelor looking to save a few pennies. Rather than go to a resort and have the attendants help him in and out of the sand, he dug himself a pit down at the beach and scooped the sand over himself. He fell asleep in the sun and woke only when the returning tide tickled his nose. Fortunately, my mother was passing by with her family. Her face was the first thing he saw above the sand and water. She thought his head was a toy left on the beach. Okā-san and her family rescued my poor father, and he spent all of the money he had saved to buy thank-you gifts for them all.

Those same beaches are covered in barbed wire and defense trenches now. All in preparation for the American invasion.

My mother still has the gift of small hair combs Otō-san gave her. Only now her hair is pulled into a sensible bun. She says she will wear them again when the war ends and Otō-san is home.

The young girl shines in my mother's face as she smiles. The face that my father fell in love with. I wish I could press that look between the pages of a book and keep it forever. Instead, I return the smile and help her fold the kimono back into a neat bundle.

"Anyway, if Tomihara-san has sold this beauty to a

farmer"—she says the last word with disdain, even though a moment ago she was praising the bounty of our local farms—"it is because of all those pilots she takes under her wings. It must be good for business, having the army choose your restaurant as the official eatery for the base. But she should serve them what she can afford, what the army can pay for, instead of trading her treasures for treats for those men!"

My face goes warm, and I bow my head, uncertain of a reply. I've not heard my mother speak like this before. It is un-Japanese of her to criticize the war effort in any way. Those "men" are dying to protect us. What would she think if she knew how young they were?

"Ah, but don't listen to me," Okā-san says softly. "I am merely sorry to see this beautiful kimono go to some dirty farmer's wife. And not even as a kimono. 'Pants,' he says! All of this gorgeous fabric to make monpé! I will have to use every last scrap to make them bigger, no doubt, to accommodate her girth."

I find myself laughing and cover my mouth to suppress it. The kimono has fabric to spare. "Okā-san, the farmer's wife is no fatter or dirtier than we are. Food is scarce everywhere. Never mind lighting a fire to heat bathwater!" Soaking in the furo once marked the end of each day. Now we save the fuel and soak thrice weekly instead.

My mother scowls and sighs. "I suppose you're right. But that satsumaimo has me in a tizzy! It's only a sweet potato, but look how it makes my mouth water! I hope it'll be ready soon, Hana. It's unbecoming to be so empty-headed. It must be hunger. I forgot to eat today."

A sourness fills my mouth. She hasn't forgotten to eat. She's been saving her rice for the evening meal. I remember the sweet green taste of the spring rice at the base, so delicate, so far from the chalky taste of tonight's gruel. I will save my bowl tomorrow and share it with Okā-san for dinner. Perhaps I can find something to trade to the kitchen staff for a few pieces of salted plum as well.

Tonight, when my mother splits the satsumaimo in half, I tell her I'm tired and wrap my portion for her to eat in the morning.

CHAPTER 21

TARO

Summer 1944

"Momotaro-san, Momotaro-san, where are you going, Momotaro-san?" Nakamura sang as he drummed the side of the bed. Taro jumped up and saluted his friend.

"I'm going to take my first solo flight!" he belted. Ever since their first day in the air, training had accelerated. It was as if their superior officers had looked at the calendar and realized how much they had to teach in less than a year. Today, Taro would prove he had what it took to be a real pilot . . . or he would wash out and be sent to work as ground crew or, worse, a flight navigator for someone else.

But he wouldn't let that happen. Like Nakamura kept saying—he was born to fly.

"Good for you," Nakamura crowed. "But I've just done it!"

Taro scowled. "How do you keep getting in front of me? Nakamura comes after Inoguchi!"

"Yes, but Kenji comes before Taro," Nakamura says.

"The Western name order!" Taro realized, rubbing his forehead in memory of the day they met. Nakamura grinned.

"Yep. The CO has our names backward. Must be clerical error. You haven't noticed by now?"

Taro deflated into laughter. "And where was I while you were soloing? I would have cheered you on."

Nakamura shrugged. "Okay, so it wasn't supposed to be my official solo, but Saito and I got to drinking last night, and I convinced him to let me have a practice run. I went this morning, and he said it was good enough to count. If they weren't so tight on the gas rations, I'd go again this afternoon. But I figured I should leave enough in the tank for latecomers like you."

Taro snagged his towel and swatted at his friend. "Keep laughing, Kenji Nakamura. I'll get my wings soon enough."

"And I'll cheer you on. When are you up?"

Taro glanced at his new watch. "Twenty minutes. Walk me to the line?"

———

＊

The old Ki-17 rattled, idling at the edge of the runway. It felt strange, sitting in the cockpit without the safety net of an instructor behind him, but he was prepared. Taro hummed along with the engine as he finished his preflight checklist. Lieutenant Saito stood to the side of the runway, waiting for a hand signal to send in two other cadets to pull the chocks from his wheels. Taro took a steadying breath and gave the sign. Behind Saito, Nakamura gave him two thumbs up and a ridiculous grin. Taro swore he could see Nakamura's ears waggling, even with the narrowed vision the aviation goggles provided. He resisted the urge to stick his tongue out. The ground crew cleared the runway, and he pressed the throttle forward.

Flying was like music. Part math, part art. There were equations to explain everything that was happening, from the bump and rattle of the wheels to the careening scream of the wind in his ears. The way the landscape began to blur. The moment when the stick needed to be pulled back—

—and how the plane leapt into the sky.

The Ki-17 rose, sunlight fracturing off the unpainted wings, dazzling him for a moment. The wind wrapped itself around the nose of the aeroplane, lofting the wings into the sky. Warm weather could hold a plane close to the earth in summer, the air too thin to lift it easily. But the cool morning air condensed the sky into a ladder that was easy to climb. Density and gradients, pressure—those were the scientific terms to explain what Taro was doing in the sky.

And then there was art.

The sky was a pure bright blue that seemed to deepen as he looked into it. And the roar of the engine mixed with the rattle of his bones until he felt like a purring lion.

He smiled—he always smiled when he flew. And, even though he could not hear himself over the engine, he began to hum. First the Mozart piece that continually plagued him. Then the songs his mother used to sing. Even Nakamura's teasing version of "Momotaro." He sang them all, the thrum in his chest playing counterpoint to the rumble of the aeroplane, and it seemed to him as if they were two friends, the Peach Boy and the Pheasant, soaring over the land of their birth.

Taro brought the plane in for a decent landing, a little wobbly at the end, but it put him safely on the ground. His legs were also a bit wobbly as he dismounted from the aeroplane and the ground crew swarmed past to ready the bird for her next flight.

He presented himself to Saito with a sharp bow and a serious face.

"Not bad, Inoguchi. Next time, try smiling. You've done well," the first lieutenant said. Taro managed to hide his shock until Nakamura grabbed him by the shoulders and pulled him away laughing.

"What's going on?" Nakamura asked, jogging alongside Taro on their way to the hangar. The summer day was hot and humid. A sheen of sweat had glossed over everything, including Taro. He wiped his forehead as they ran, and shrugged.

"Who knows?"

The commandant had called an assembly just after breakfast. Taro had been studying maps in his head over his meal, too focused on his navigation lessons to listen to gossip. They had moved on from their solo flights to aerobatics and then formation flying. Every pilot needed to know how to lead and how to be a good wingman. That meant, among other things, being a good navigator. Soon they would have to show they could do it on their own. It was no wonder he and Nakamura hadn't heard the scuttlebutt.

When they arrived in the hangar, the commandant was standing rigidly in front of a map of Japan, his face like a forecast for stormy weather. Nakamura and Taro fell in line with their flight and stood at attention. When the last of the cadets appeared, the commandant nodded and began.

"We have learned in recent days of two great tragedies!" he announced. "Imperial forces on the island of Saipan"— he slapped a finger against the map, indicating a tiny dot of an island in the Philippine Sea—"fought bravely for nearly a month, but were unable to repel the brute force of the American navy. Although their bodies were weak from hunger, their spirits were very strong. Gyokusai!" He shouted the word. "Every man, woman, and child on Saipan did what all Japanese should do in the face of unavoidable defeat! Let this be a lesson to each of you. Your life belongs to the Emperor. Your honor reflects his greatness. May you all have such strength when the moment arrives!" He paused, mopping his forehead with a handkerchief.

The July heat weighed down on Taro almost as much as the news. *Gyokusai!* They had all killed themselves rather than be captured. It should not have come as a surprise. After all, hadn't they been preparing themselves for such an event, should the war be lost? But to hear of it happening—was the war indeed coming to this brutal end?

"Secondly," the commander continued, "the Imperial Navy has suffered the loss of several ships in the Philippine Sea. It is an embarrassment. Mistakes have been made. Such costly errors are not to be tolerated. As of yesterday the prime minister, General Tojo, has been made accountable. The Tojo government has resigned."

Gasps filled the room, including Taro's own. It was one thing to bear the defeat at Saipan in silence, but this? With no government in place, Japan was an aeroplane without a rudder. It was a disgrace to the Emperor. How were they expected to fight? How were they expected to win?

The CO raised his hands for quiet. "Remember what the Imperial Rescript tell us. You are the Emperor's arm!" he declared stridently. "Not the prime minister's. Not the government's. There will be a new government, a new prime minister. But the Emperor is the Emperor forever! Do not forget that. You must train harder. Strengthen his arm. Strengthen your resolve. Remember the words of Lieutenant General Mutaguchi Renya as he faced difficult challenges in India: *If your hands are broken, fight with your feet. If your hands and feet are broken, use your teeth. If there is no breath left in your body, fight with your spirit. Lack of weapons is no excuse for defeat!*"

A great heat rose inside Taro, erupting in a wave of sound. "Banzai! Banzai! Banzai!" he yelled, and the other cadets yelled with him. Governments may come and go, even generals like Tojo might rise and fall, but Japan was forever. The Empire would live. They would make sure of it.

CHAPTER 22

HANA

"The ships are moving," one of the boys tells me as I fix a tear on the collar of his spare shirt. "But no one seems to know where." I am using white thread to match the fabric. It glides through my fingers like the strings of a koto, following the silver flash of the needle. I keep pins in my mouth, as if I will need them, like my mother last night. This way, I will not be expected to speak.

"So we have another day of waiting," the boy continues. He lies down on the grass and sighs. "It's a pretty day, isn't it?"

I nod, dragging the thread in and out around the tear. I must not be rude. I am not invisible. Although if I could be, I would disappear. Become a pair of magic hands that mend shirts and socks unseen. Floating servant hands that pour the tea and serve the rice. That make the beds and, being magic, do not feel the tears on the pillowcases of boys who believe today is the day they will die.

It is strange to me that this boy's fate depends on ships moving miles away across the gray-backed sea. Even stranger that those ships are moved by men who sit even farther away, across an entire ocean, in rooms with no windows, no light. Just smoke and radios, maps and power.

That's what I imagine, at least. Does the man in America who tells the ships to come closer to our shores know that I am here sewing a small tear shut, fixing what I can in this terrible time of war? Am I who he wants? Is it this Nadeshiko sitting in her dusty monpé pants, a shirt in her lap, who makes him hate us so?

I do not think so.

I am a gnat on the cheek of an elephant.

He cannot see me. He cannot feel me here.

But he swats anyway.

And I die.

CHAPTER 23

TARO

Fall 1944

"It's not enough." Taro shook his head. "They can't expect us to be ready with only thirty minutes of flight time each day. My father had over five hundred hours before he was considered ready. If this keeps up, we'll have less than half that by the time we deploy."

"If we're lucky," Nakamura agreed gloomily. Night flights had signaled the end of their intermediate flight training. Now all that stood between them and graduation was eighty more hours of required flight time. A woeful lack of aeroplanes made the waiting insufferable. And so they were on the basketball court, taking turns shooting hoops. It was better than sitting in the barracks, better than hanging out at the cafeteria waiting for their next meal. And far better than watching the lucky cadets on the flight line that afternoon. "They say we'll make up for it once we get assigned, though."

He lined up his shot and missed. Taro caught the rebound.

"Not with hands like that," he quipped, and dribbled past

Nakamura, lofting the ball into the air. It smacked off the rim and bounced away. They watched it go.

"What if it's over by the time we finish training?" Nakamura asked. "The war."

"The way they're rushing us through, it seems unlikely," Taro said. But it wasn't unlikely. Even here in Tachiarai, they could tell the war was going poorly. The few aeroplanes they had were barely held together by the ever-vigilant ground crews. Just last week, Tomomichi had crashed one of the Ki-9s because of a faulty engine. When a replacement failed to show up, everyone's flight time was cut even further. With all the fuel in the world, a hundred men still couldn't easily share fifteen planes.

Taro jogged to pick up the escaping ball. He took a wild shot from where he stood. It smacked the backboard and spun off toward Nakamura, who leapt to catch it.

"Good one, Inoguchi."

"Yeah, well, I'm bored of this," Taro said.

"Me too. Let's go find a drink."

Nakamura fired the ball back at Taro, who caught it in the stomach. It was slick with sweat.

"That was on purpose."

"Yep."

The mood at the PX wasn't any better. They each bought a bottle of Calpis, downing the cold milky drinks so fast it set Taro coughing.

"What's the news, Ojii-san?" Nakamura asked the old man behind the counter while Taro caught his breath.

The old man shrugged. "Same as always. We lose some ships, we send some planes. They lose some ships, they send

122

some planes. All I really know is my wife is hungry, and she's unpleasant when she's skinny. Marry a fat woman, I say. The best insulation in a cold, uncaring world."

He grinned, and Nakamura slapped him on the back. "Thanks for the advice, Ojii-san. Did you hear that, Taro? Let's go into town tomorrow and find some fat women."

"You gotta go a lot farther to find a fat one these days," the old man said. "Why not just have another Calpis instead?"

He uncapped two more bottles and pushed them toward the boys. "On me. I was young once. Never jumped around in the heat after a ball, but I know what it's like."

Taro bowed his thanks. Nakamura rubbed his head. "Momotaro, such a good kid."

"Someone's gotta be." He shrugged.

"Oh, there is some news," the old man continued. "A new plane came in—"

They grabbed the old man by the shirt, pulling him halfway across the counter. "What plane? Where?"

"Relax, relax!" the old man said. "Put me down! It's not for flying, it's for looking at."

"What's the point of that?" Nakamura wanted to know.

"Search me. But it's in Hangar Two. The commandant said so when he picked up his smokes this morning. They're going to give you a whole show about it, just you wait."

They thanked the old man and paid for the extra drinks to make up for mussing his shirt. Quick showers, combs in damp hair, and the two were back in uniform, waiting for the news.

And it was news.

Hangar Two was a high wooden structure, home to half the

planes on the base in times of peace. With the increasing risk of American air raids, the aeroplanes were now hidden in the fields beneath the trees, encircled on three sides by embankments nicknamed "octopus pots" for their U-shapes. They were designed to protect the planes from bombings. Pearl Harbor wouldn't have been half as successful if the Americans had done a better job of hiding their aircraft instead of lining them up on the runway, where one explosion could trigger a dozen more.

But this, as the old man had said, was a plane for showing, not flying. It stood in the center of the cavernous hangar, surrounded by a hundred curious faces.

"The Mansyu Ki-79 is an advanced trainer, not unlike the Nakajima Ki-27," Lieutenant Saito said in a pleased voice as he paced in front of the open cockpit of the single-seater plane. The sleek fuselage sat at an angle—its large front wheels pointing the body upward, while tiny rear wheels held the tail section close to the ground. Painted olive-green and sage camouflage, it boasted a deep brown propeller and a vibrant red circle on either side. "You'll have heard about the Seventy-Nine, maybe even seen one. But this one is special. Look under the wings, what do you see?"

Taro and his company mates surrounded the plane in a half circle. They dropped into crouches to examine its underbelly.

Tomomichi was the first to spot it.

"There's room for more than the two standard bombs," he said.

Lieutenant Saito nodded. "That's right. The standard Ki-79b holds two fifty-five-pound bombs. This one can hold over five *hundred* pounds. This is a Tokkō Tai attack plane."

Taro felt the room go still and very loud at the same time, all of the air sucked up in a sharp group inhale. He had heard of them, of course, a new secret weapon of the Imperial Army and Navy. Special pilots, hand selected to destroy the enemy with every ounce of themselves. *Kamikaze*—the word had been whispered across base. Like the divine wind of history, sent by the gods, these new pilots would sweep the Western forces away.

Taro could hear the ticking of his wristwatch. The pounding of his pulse.

And then the questions began.

Tokkō Tai? Who did the plane belong to? Had another tokkō attack commenced?

The twinge of excitement Taro had felt upon hearing about the new aeroplane returned, but this note was different, sharper. Nakamura was smiling, as were Tomomichi and even Lieutenant Saito. Everyone was. Just an hour ago, the war had seemed hopeless. And hadn't they seen the schoolchildren in town drilling with bamboo staves, like those schoolgirls they saw from the train? Every citizen was preparing for the imminent invasion.

But now this plane and all it represented promised a turning of the tide, the deliberate sacrifice of a few to save the many. It was the embodiment of *Yamato-damashii*—true Japanese spirit—at its greatest. It was bravery like this that would see Japan prevail.

The half circle of cadets drew closer to the aeroplane, as if it were an animal they could pet. Taro found himself reaching out gingerly to touch the familiar coolness of painted metal. Not so different from the aeroplanes they already flew, but imbued with a purpose beyond any he had ever known.

And then a new question rose in his own mind. Why show them this aeroplane—this tokkō plane—now?

His mother's face flashed in front of him for a moment. The two kinds of tears in her eyes, laughter and pain.

"We thought you boys should see what it really means to be a pilot of the Imperial Army," Lieutenant Saito was saying.

And like that, the image of his mother was gone, replaced by the magnificent plane before him. An honorable plane. An inspiration.

He slid his hand along its flank like the rest of the boys, admiring the grace of its fuselage. Awed by the power it could contain.

Nakamura might have started it, or maybe it was Lieutenant Saito, but soon, all of the boys were shouting—to the Emperor, to the aeroplane and her brave pilots, to Japan—their voices echoing throughout the cavernous hangar. "Banzai! Banzai! Banzai!"

May you live ten thousand years!

CHAPTER 24

HANA

"Hana! Are you coming?"

I've just returned the last of the sewing to the barracks, nudging the basket inside with my foot. The boys will claim their items when they return. The base had seemed quiet, the open barracks door looming like a hungry mouth, until Mariko popped up out of nowhere, calling my name.

"Going where? I think we are done for the day, neh?" I gladly turn away from the darkened maw.

"Done working, yes," she says, tugging at my sleeve. "Some of us are walking to the river. The comfort girls are putting on a show. Come with us!" Together, we climb down the hillside to the road.

"I can't. My mother needs my help today. I told her I would come straight home."

Mariko makes a pouting face. "You need to have fun, too, Hana. Next time, you have to come."

"I will," I promise. Although the thought of watching those women, girls really, singing and dancing just makes me homesick for when we all used to sing and dance. We would laugh and drink tea and eat bean cakes. Now all we do is work, go hungry, and worry.

Mariko clatters up the road and waves at me before cutting across the field to the river. I told her Okā-san needed me, and she does. But, for a moment, I don't move. My arms are tired, and my fingers ache. I wiggle them and roll my shoulders. No one can see me. It is utterly silent. Just me, the trees, and the air. I am the only person in the world. This is peace.

And then I hear a bird, or perhaps the wind sawing through the trees. It freezes me, frees me. I have lifted a foot toward home, and it hangs there, half an inch above the gravel. What is that sound?

I close my eyes, slowly turning, until my ears point the way. It's coming from the barracks. I open my eyes, ease my way back up the hill, and lean against the rough bark of the triangle roof.

Someone is playing an instrument.

It has been years since there was music in my life. Real music, not military marches or schoolgirl songs.

My heart moves sideways. It's gorgeous.

The melody trembles like sakura in the wind. I find I have left the safety of the roof. I am standing in the doorway, listening to the lone musician, the boy with the black case in his duffel. He stands in the center of the barracks, playing a Western violin.

I take a step inside.

There was a moment when I was dead, swaddled in darkness, a moment of utter stillness. My ears were ringing because of the bomb, a constant hum, like the first note of creation.

And then there was light.

Just a tiny dot of it, streaming in as if it were all the light in the universe.

And it grew. And grew.

Until there were fingers, hands, faces, and blue sky.

And voices screaming, "She's here! She's alive!"

Now my ears ring with that first note once more. Through the doorway, a dot of light. And fingers, hands, a face like the open sky, and music singing, *I am here. I am alive.*

I stand in the sunken barracks, and no stone hands reach out to suffocate me. The sweep of music is holding up the roof, and I realize I am unafraid.

The song ends. The musician opens his eyes. A catch of breath, and he sees me. I do not know what to say, so I bow in deep gratitude. He is startled. He nods, his eyes still on me, a doe he is afraid to frighten away. I pause, a fox unwilling to startle the hare.

And then, eyes on me, he takes a deep breath, straightens, and begins the song again.

If I stay too long, I fear I will cry. So I pull back from the doorway and climb the hill toward home. But I am listening.

And when I am too far away to hear the music, I still feel the song.

CHAPTER 25

TARO

Winter 1944

Brass buttons, double-rowed and shining like twin suns. Olive twill slacks side-striped in scarlet. The uniform jacket, trim and braided. The smart cap with its black sun visor. Taro flexed his hands inside their white gloves and gave each a sharp tug down to his wrist. His shoes were mirrors, his eyes bright. He was an officer now.

"Hmm," Nakamura said beside him. "Not too bad, Lieutenant! No one would ever know you're lacking in moral fortitude."

Taro smiled. "Or that you have the tail of a pig."

Nakamura snorted a porcine laugh and held out his hand in a Western shake. By now, Taro knew not to bow into it. He clasped the offered glove and shook it.

"This is it, boys!" Nakamura said a bit louder, so the rest of their cohort, newly bedecked in dress uniforms, turned their attention his way. Of the hundred boys they'd started with, only fifty-seven remained. The rest had moved on to ground crew or other airfield staff. "Today we graduate. Tomorrow we fly for the Emperor!"

"Banzai! Banzai! Banzai!"

Taro clapped Nakamura on the back and finished packing his duffel. They would leave directly from graduation to their first deployment on a twelve o'clock train to Akeno Air Base in Mie Prefecture, on the main island of Honshu. From there, after a few months of fighter training, who knew where the wings of his Ki-43 would take him? At least, a new Nakajima Ki-43 was his hope. They had all heard rumors that new recruits were less and less likely to get the best planes. Matériel and men—both were running low in this confounded war.

The barracks door flew open, and one of the younger cadets burst in, cheeks red from exertion. When he saw the graduates arrayed in their finery, he stumbled to a stop and bowed deeply.

"Please excuse me for the interruption! There is news! One of our graduates body-crashed today in a battle against the Americans!"

"Body-crashed?" Nakamura asked.

"Yes! He sank a battleship all by himself! Tokkō pilots are the bravest men we have, and this one was trained right here at Tachiarai!"

Nakamura laughed. "A lot of army pilots are trained here, Cadet. That's not so special."

But Taro didn't laugh. "Who was he?" he asked. Was it an accident? he wondered. Pilots unable to return to base safely had been known to fly into enemy ships on occasion. It was a terrible choice, but an understandable one if the plane's damage was great.

"Endo Kosuke! He graduated earlier this year. He volunteered for one of the new tokkō units. He left as a corporal, but they're promoting him to sergeant major now!"

The boy was excited, his cheeks still flushed, his eyes glistening. Endo's new rank had nothing to do with it—all tokkō received posthumous promotions. No, this was hero worship, Taro realized. The boy was talking about a gunshin, a war-born god.

"Tokkō," he breathed. The image of the Ki-79 so proudly displayed in the hangar rose in his mind. Had Endo been there that day? Had he been swept up by the chorus of cheers? Or was it fate that led him down the path of the kamikaze?

Taro bowed his head. "A moment of silence for our brave brother," he declared. The rowdy graduates and the beaming cadet sobered immediately. "He was very brave," Taro added.

"Hai. Hai!" the boys agreed.

Not boys, Taro told himself. Men, each of them. Old enough to serve in whatever way they could. Pilots, tokkō, sailors, soldiers, every last Japanese would do his part. In ancient days, even the women could be samurai, and so they would be again in this time of great emergencies.

The silence stretched, expectant, heavy as a swollen cloud before the storm.

"I am proud to be Japanese today," Taro said softly.

Nakamura straightened, pulling his hat onto his still-damp hair. "And I am proud to be a pilot. Come on, boys. Let's graduate and end this war."

———

Dearest Mother and Father,

We graduated today with top honors. You will be pleased to know Nakamura Kenji and I have been assigned to the same squadron as part of the 103rd. In a few minutes, we will board the train to Akeno for our advanced fighter training, and then be deployed as the army sees fit. I am sorry Mother was not able to attend today's ceremony. You would have seen I have added three inches to my height! Not too tall to fly, but it has made me better at basketball and improved my reach in fencing.

Fortunately, my violin is still a good size for me. I had worried it might get too small to handle. Mother, if you speak to Ayugai-sensei, please let him know that I continue to practice, and that I am now able to bow as he always urged me to, thanks to my growing arms!

You have heard the news, no doubt, of the losses at Leyte. But today, one of our own graduates sacrificed himself in a true show of Yamato-damashii. It gives us great pride to see the bravery of such pilots. The lost battle does not deter us! Had we but been ready to join the fight sooner, we might have turned the tide. My brother pilots and I know that we serve a greater cause, and we are eager to do our best.

If I am able, Mother, I will write again when I have my assignment. It is my wish to fly over our house the way

Father did so many years ago. I will let you know if I am able. If not, think of me and know that I am thinking of you.

Your son,
Taro

CHAPTER 26

HANA

Otō-san's koto lies covered in a silk cloth to protect the wood from dust. I hang back in the doorway to our second room, not wanting to disturb this space. Not wanting to lay eyes on the butsudan, the incense, the photo of my father treated as an ancestor. He did not know what lay ahead for him when he went to join the war, so he told my mother, "Think of me as already dead." That way, the pain would not be unexpected should the worst happen, and the joy would be a hundredfold should he return. On that day, his koto would make music once again.

I have imagined my own photo beside the butsudan since that morning in the sweet potato field. But today, for the first time, it feels as if I might come home. The thought frightens me. It's so much easier to be dead. To be silent as my father's koto.

Tears sting my eyes, and I blink them back. It's just a room. Just a photograph. Just an instrument. Not a snake beneath a cloth, but a dragon.

I cross the tatami in three swift steps and kneel beside the draped form. The fabric is purple kinsha silk, textured with a wave pattern, gray on the underbelly, soft lilac on top. I lift it from the instrument and fold it carefully. The koto glistens in the light, breathing.

She stretches before me, almost six feet in length, a gently curving arc of lacquered kiri wood. Thirteen strings, white as snow, made from twined silk, run the length of the dragon's body from her head to her tail. The strings are tightened by knobs and supported by ivory ji, or bridges. The ji have not moved since my father last tuned her. I lightly touch the tips of my fingers to the ivory, feeling what my father used to feel.

"Will you play?"

I jump, snatching my fingers away from the strings. Okā-san is standing in the doorway. Her face is in shadow, and I can't tell if she is angry, sad, or merely curious.

"I . . . I don't know . . ." I press my hands and forehead to the ground. "I'm sorry, Okā-san. I heard music today. Beautiful music . . . and it made me think of Otō-san and how we used to play."

With a soft swish of cloth, my mother enters the room and kneels beside me.

"He would be pleased you are remembering a happier time, Hana. There is no shame in that."

I look up, surprised. "But I don't wish to disturb you, or his things. I only . . . I did not think."

Okā-san smiles, but not at me. It is a sad, thoughtful look. She reaches out to the koto as I did, and touches the top of one ji.

"I sit beside this sometimes and pretend I can hear him playing." She looks at me, and again I see the girl she once was. "I wish I could play it. I suppose I would, if I could."

She says nothing more, but folds her hands in her lap and lowers her eyes. And I can feel it without words. She is asking, and not asking, giving permission, but only if I will take it.

I look at the koto, no longer a dragon, once again a snake.

Outside the wind is blowing. There will be no rain tomorrow. No music in the morning.

"Perhaps . . ." I say, but the moment is past and my mother is rising.

"The rice is almost ready. I mustn't let it burn." And like that, she is gone.

The moment trembles in her wake. The lilac cloth unfolds with a whisper and settles into place with a sigh.

I'm sorry, I want to say. I should have played for her.

But now it's too late.

CHAPTER 27

TARO

February 1945

Taro stood at the end of Akeno's second runway, playing the aeroplanes in on their landings, sending them off on sorties. Far from the Ki-43 he had hoped for, he'd been assigned an ancient Ki-79 that had been grounded by a faulty engine. And so, despite the cold, he took the time to practice, letting the notes float away into the open air. The buzz and grind of propellers, the *clunk-chock-clunk* of wheels speeding up and lifting abruptly made a strange counterpoint to the flowing violin. Taro squeezed his eyes shut, trying to leave the airfield like the aeroplanes did, climbing the sky on notes instead of wings, letting the sonata bleed across the sky.

Fighter planes were andante, then accelerando, then allegro. He matched the rising speed, the basso boom as the planes jerked into the air, the rapid vroom as they disappeared into the clouds. If he could play the flight, he wondered if it counted as air time. As if violin and aeroplane were one and the same. Master the strings, and he'd master the wings.

He had only been at it for a few minutes when Nakamura came skidding to a stop beside him.

"Taro! Taro! Put your fiddle away. The captain wants us in the ready room. Something's up!"

A trill of excitement burst in Taro's chest. He tucked the violin into its case and jogged alongside Nakamura. "A mission? Finally! It's been days!"

"Days and days, with nothing but bad news," Nakamura agreed. "But I hear they've got something great up their sleeves this time. Did you hear about the Ohka?"

"Those awful gliders? We're pilots! They don't expect us to drop from the sky in those things." The Ohka was little more than an airborne torpedo, large enough for a bomb and a single pilot. No guns, and little in the way of maneuverability, the Ohka were flown out to sea and dropped from a bomber plane. It was up to the pilot to guide the explosive into the deck of an enemy ship.

"Those 'things' are what will win this war," Nakamura said with conviction.

"But they have no weapons," Taro said.

"They are the weapon. Just like the Kaiten torpedo boats. The vessel is the bomb!"

Taro frowned, losing step with Nakamura's easy gait. "We were taught to fight with bullets and sharp maneuvers."

"Then you weren't listening." Nakamura grinned back at him. "We were taught to fight with fortitude. Where's your shining spirit?"

Taro blinked. They had reached the barracks. He ducked inside and settled his violin case into his cubbyhole. He stretched his back and cracked his fingers in the cool dimness of the bunk-room, Nakamura's jest nipping at his mind. Where was his shining spirit? The walk to the ready room was slower, weighed down by this question. It was true, their instructors at Oita and Tachiarai had encouraged them to develop their inner strength. The Emperor's speeches were always geared toward being shining citizens. But Taro's spirit had been bound long ago by catgut and rosin—earthly elements, not lofty ones.

The scent of rain washed the air, sending a cold breeze to tickle his collar and lift the ends of his hair. But it could not clear his confusion. Had he betrayed his country by choosing music first?

Shame burned his cheeks as he entered the ready room. His flightmates were already lined up. Captain Hibara appeared a moment after Taro fell in.

"Gentlemen! As you have heard, the tide has turned against us of late. We need to make a decisive move against the enemy. Toward that end, we are forming a new attack squadron, and we are looking for volunteers!"

The room lit up. A murmur of excitement, stiffening backs, broadened shoulders. Taro could feel the entire room bend forward to listen closely.

"I say volunteers, because this is not your usual duty. If you are an only child, or have a wife, I ask you to consider closely before deciding.

"This is a tokkō unit we are forming. You all understand tokkō are gunshin warriors, and as such, it is a great honor to make this sacrifice. I need ten men willing to join. Who among you is with me? For, yes, I will be going too. You needn't decide right away. We will meet again in the morning . . ."

The captain trailed off, his well-prepared speech forgotten. His eyes, trained at some middle spot between himself and the men he was asking to die, suddenly widened in surprise.

Taro had stepped forward, without even thinking. And Nakamura beside him. And Hideo, and Tomomichi. Every single pilot in the room had volunteered without hesitation. There was nothing to consider. Taro had known it the moment the question was asked. He was an army pilot, just as his father had insisted all those years ago. At twelve, he'd been prepared to give up fifteen years to military service. Now he would give all of them. Whatever it took to live up to that role.

Captain Hibara bowed his head, and when he looked up, his face was full of emotion. Pride, Taro realized. And something else. Sorrow?

As one, Taro and his unit bowed. Today they were no longer just pilots. They were tokkō. The decisive action. The means of ending this war.

———

Only later, in the barracks, did the true meaning of their commitment sink in. Hideo could be heard sniffling in the corner. Nakamura and Tomomichi were sharing a whispered conversation. Taro himself lay on his futon, staring at the ceiling, arms folded beneath his head. He was trying to remember his mother's face.

You would have two soldiers in this house, she had said to his father that day long ago. And now Taro himself had betrayed her wishes. But he did not know if it was wrong or right to do so. If Japan lost the war, she would be lost too. The thought of his mother, practicing with sharpened sticks like the schoolgirls in town, promising to take her own life, was nauseating. But the thought of her alone, a gray-haired widow sitting beside the ancestral tablets, adding the names of her husband and son—was it better? He could not say.

"Taro?"

Nakamura stood at the foot of his bunk. His face was pale and more serious than Taro had ever seen him.

"Nak?"

"The captain mentioned writing our jisei." Jisei . . . death poems. A Buddhist tradition for those facing their own demise. Taro had read the jisei of famous monks and poets in school. And now . . .

"We're pilots, not poets," he said, attempting a smile. Nakamura cleared his throat.

"Well . . . some of us want to try." He ran a hand over his hair and looked away. "Would you play us something on that fiddle of yours? It might help . . . settle the boys."

Nakamura. From that first day on the bus to Oita to this, the end of their journey, he had been there at Taro's side. And he had always hated the violin, Taro realized. But he also knew what it meant to Taro, who was not a poet, but a musician.

The kindness almost choked him. Without a word, he reached under his bed, pulled out his violin, and began to play.

Later, Nakamura laid a piece of paper on Taro's blanket. Taro had just put his violin in its case. He looked up in surprise. "A love letter from the girls back home?" Taro asked. The mood had lightened as he played. He smiled at his friend.

But Nakamura shook his head. "For my mother," he said.

Taro stood up and bowed at the waist, taking the jisei in both hands. Nakamura's calligraphy was surprisingly beautiful, bold black lines on the cream-colored page, in the tanka form, similar to haiku, with two extra lines of seven syllables each.

See the dragonfly
His wings cannot go backward
Is this bravery?
Now I am a dragonfly
I will be brave for Japan

CHAPTER 28

HANA

The sun is a pearl in a silvery sky when we arrive at base this morning. The men often depart before sunrise, but not today. Mariko and I clamber down from the back of the truck and take a moment to pinch our cheeks and straighten our blouses, dusting the backsides of our monpé. There will be families here today. We want to look our best so they will know their sons and brothers have been well cared for.

Sensei leads us in rows down to the airfield. This time, it will be the boys from our barracks flying, so we are in front. Reiko's mother, Tomihara-san, is there with two other women from the neighborhood association. The boys will have been to see her last night, slipping her their final letters home. Ones the army censors will never see. On the flight line, heads turn and we see new faces. Some families have made the trip to see their sons off. Not every pilot is able to send word of his final flight. Plans change quickly to match the movements of the war. Even then, travel is difficult, especially for civilians. They do not always reach the base in time. But today, a few have succeeded. Mothers in formal kimono, carefully packed and carried a long way, so as to look their best for their sons. Fathers—some in Western suits, most in clean work clothes. A couple hold hampers, the remnants of last meals shared with their children. It looks like a line at a train station, an extended family going on holiday.

But there have been no holiday outings since I was twelve years old.

"Oh, Hana, look!" Mariko gasps.

But it is not the parents Mariko is pointing to with her eyes. It is the lead aeroplane, and the one third in line. Kazuko and Sachiko must have arrived early. Both planes are covered in cherry blossoms. It is as if the earth has given shape to these aeroplanes, showering them in blessings. The pilots who fly these two will surely scatter magnificently across the sky.

We look at each other with big eyes and break away from the group, rushing up the hillside through the damp grass to gather our own cherry tree branches. We clamber back with a few sad twigs, heavy with dew. I shake mine a few times, but lose more blossoms than water.

"Hey!" Mariko exclaims, dodging the shower of drops I send her way.

"Sorry. Do we have time to decorate?" I wonder, but then the boys are lined up, the ceremonial saké cups are drained, the white funeral boxes and scraps of paper with the pilot's jisei are on the little table. The ground crew is ready, and it is time to wave goodbye. We take our places in the line and bow deeply as the boys from our barracks come forward.

Nakamura gives a small box of chocolates to Sachiko. "These

were sent by my mother. I don't have the stomach for them now, but perhaps you will," he tells her.

Sachiko bows and thanks him, her hair a curtain across her smiling face. She produces a hachimaki and holds it out proudly. "For you, Kenji-san." She has learned his first name. "I have painted the rising sun with my own blood!" She holds up her pricked fingers, and now I know why she winced yesterday when washing clothes. Beside me, I hear Mariko sigh. Sachiko is always so extreme, and usually we laugh about it. But today it seems as though she is the only one who has made a worthy gift for our elder brothers.

The boy who told me about the delay offers Mariko a letter to be sent to his mother. "I finished my jisei last night and would like her to have it," he tells her. "And this is for you. It's all I have." He hands her a few worn coins from the depths of his pocket.

Mariko's face is very red. "Yamada-san, all I have to offer are these flowers. They are a poor gift, but I hope they will brighten your aeroplane."

It's Yamada-san's turn to blush. He accepts the flowers. "I had thought to leave the world behind this morning, but your kindness I will take with me."

I don't expect any special tokens or thank-yous today, or any day. Unlike the other girls, I keep to myself. I don't know any first names, nor any intimate details of our pilots' lives.

And then he is there before me. The boy with the violin. I look down at my fading flowers and cannot meet his eye.

"Miss . . . I'm afraid I don't know your name," he says. His voice has a warmth I didn't expect. A realness I do not wish to hear. If he becomes real, he will die and I will know it. I bow to hide my embarrassment.

"But you . . . thank you for sewing my uniform. It is quite clean and suitable now . . ." He hesitates, and we both seem to feel the absurdity of the moment. My armpits are hot. My pants, damp and heavy from the trek through the grass. I am reminded of the fragrant burden in my arms.

"Elder brother, these are for you," I say, and thrust the branches toward him.

But his hands are already full.

"And this . . . this is for you."

The black case is suddenly the only thing on this airfield, the only thing in the world. This boy, whose name I do not know, is giving me his violin.

I gasp and look up, needing to see if it's true. If there are tears in his eyes, I can't tell. They may be my own.

"Arigatō gozaimasu." I thank him profusely. "This one is not worthy of such a gift."

My voice catches in my throat, and he tilts his chin up, blinking rapidly. I look back down at the ground, and he gently removes the flowers from my arms, replacing them with the music case.

"This one," he says softly, "is unable to take it with him. Music should live, neh?"

I bow from the waist. A single tear drops from my eye to the ground. The field is too wet to show where it fell.

"Please, may I ask your name?" I can't believe I am inviting this, but I could not stand to learn it after he is gone. I can barely breathe.

"Inoguchi Taro." Such simple syllables. No titles, no rank. Such a common name.

"Benkan Hana," I reply.

"A pleasure," he says softly. Unlike many of the other boys, he does not say it is the last pleasure he will experience, or that mine is the last face he will see. I hear the rustle of his clothing, and I know he is bowing. Then a gust of air, and he has departed.

Only when I hear the engines growl and rev do I rise from my own bow. I hold the black case to my chest like a newborn and watch the planes take off one by one, dark birds against the brightening sky.

For the first time, I am unable to wave goodbye.

CHAPTER 29

TARO

March 1945

The house seemed so small, two stories of dark wood, with an outside hallway wrapped around the ground floor like a porch. Taro closed the gate behind him and stepped into the yard. Over the wall, across the street, he could see Mrs. Tanaka's laundry hanging, rimmed with frost at this early hour. The old dog that slept against the house was gone. The more things changed, the more they stayed the same.

He'd reached the front door, lowered his duffel to the walkway, and bent to the task of undoing his boots, when he was struck by a memory. He went back out into the street. The sky was gray-blue today, not the vibrant sky from the day his father had flown overhead, but one that threatened gathering clouds and the promise of rain.

The shōji screen slid open. Taro's mother struggled into her geta and ran to him.

"You're home! You're home!"

Deep bows and, later, clasped hands. Once his duffel bag was put away, the boots were in the entryway, and they were sitting

149

over cups of steaming hot tea, she chafed his cold fingers in her own. The calluses he had noticed at graduation were still there. Somehow, they were a comfort now.

"From your last letter, I thought you'd be going straight to your air battalion."

"So did I," Taro explained. "But they gave us a little bit of leave first. Nakamura has gone home, too. Some of the boys live too far away, but those of us in Kyushu and the south are lucky."

She smiled. "You must be tired. I will prepare your futon. Perhaps you would like a bath?"

"I would very much, but it's too much trouble," Taro said. "Please don't treat me as a guest."

"But you are! A welcome guest!" his mother insisted, pouring more tea.

"I would rather be your son."

She put the teapot down then, and looked at him. "Taro," she said, the way she'd always said his name. Like it was good news, a joke, a reason to smile. Only her face did not match the sound. He was no longer her little boy, Taro realized. He loosened his collar. Why was he still in uniform? A yukata would be better. He should change right away. But it would be disrespectful to excuse himself now.

"Any news of Father?"

His mother's gentle smile wavered. "Only that he is well. I am afraid he is in the south now, in the Philippines, but he does not say. Only that he is thinking of us. And proud of you! I'm sure he has yet to get the news of your graduation. My letters take so long to find him. But he knew it was imminent and awaited it with much anticipation."

Taro bowed his head slightly. "I am glad to hear it." And he was. At graduation, he had thought of his father and how proud he would be. But any celebration was tainted by the future now. Taro took a sip of tea to hide the unexpected bitterness in his throat. *You would have two soldiers in this house.* Soon there would only be one. How would his mother forgive his father— forgive *him*—for accepting a tokkō assignment?

"Taro? You have something on your mind, I see. Not a young lady, is it?"

Taro blushed. "No! I haven't even seen a girl up close since Shōnen Hikōhei, and even that was in passing."

"Ah. Well." His mother looked embarrassed now. "One hears rumors about women and pilots."

"Do they?" Taro feigned shock, but he knew. Nakamura had made sure of it. "They can't get enough of us!" he'd crowed to Taro after a day's leave from Akeno. "Just wear your uniform, you'll see."

Taro had worn his uniform home, but he'd been too distracted to notice anyone noticing him.

"And Ayugai-sensei?" He changed the subject.

"Did you not get my letter? Sad news. Ayugai-san was in Tokyo performing for some important people when the city was firebombed. He survived," she added quickly, "but I'm afraid he was gravely injured. His wife wrote to tell me he has lost the use of his hand!"

"No!" Taro felt the bottom drop out of his stomach. "I must go see him!"

"But he is not here. He is still in hospital in Tokyo. When she is able, his wife will have him moved to Sapporo, where her family is from, and hopefully out of harm's way. Tokyo is a dangerous place to be these days."

Taro had heard of the firebombings. Allied planes would drop incendiaries at night onto the old wooden buildings of the Imperial city, targeting civilians and military alike. It was a cowardly act meant to force the Emperor to surrender. But Japanese were made of tougher stuff. Women, children, and the elderly might suffer, but they would do so gladly, for they were Japanese and that meant something.

But poor Ayugai-sensei. "If I write him a letter, will you see that it's delivered?"

"Of course," his mother said. "He will be glad to hear from you."

"And how is old Mrs. Tanaka across the street?"

"Oh, she is getting along fine. You know Mr. Tanaka was a navy man? So he's away on business for the navy, but because of his age, he is not in the fighting. I bring her food when I can. It's hard for her to get to the market anymore, and the lines are so long I hate to think of her standing in them. If I bring her ration book and a note, they let me shop for her. Our tonari-gumi is very good at that, I think. Others are not so lenient."

Taro looked down at his tea and the small plate of roasted soybeans his mother had placed beside it. "Food rationing. I almost forgot. I brought you some things from the base."

He rose and padded into the next room, where his duffel bag lay against the wall. "They take very good care of us on base and see that we are well fed. At first, Nakamura and I stuffed ourselves every night."

He returned carrying a bundled paper package. "But it's

unseemly for an officer to be a glutton, especially pilots who must be able to fit into our planes!"

His mother smiled, and it lightened his heart. She had grown thin, careworn. Her hair was losing its color and its shine. "I hope you will find something in here useful."

She carefully untied the package, setting aside first the string—which she looped around her hands and tied in the middle to keep from tangling—and then smoothing out the paper so it would not tear. With each item removed, she gave a small cry of surprise or pleasure.

"We have not seen chestnuts in months! Oh, but this is too much! Oh, Mrs. Tanaka will be pleased!"

And with each exclamation, Taro's smile grew sadder and sadder. A handful of condiments and treats could not bring enough joy for what would come next.

At long last, he gave in to the hot bath and the warm yukata before a dinner made extravagant by wartime standards because of his gifts. He went to sleep that night on his old futon in his own room. He had yet to tell his mother he would be body-crashing within the month.

It was a restless night.

In the morning, he dressed in a fresh yukata and went to the window. From his usual spot, he could now see most of the street. The house seemed very small. He gathered his violin, went downstairs, slipped into a pair of his father's geta, and stepped into the backyard.

The sky was as gray as the day before, but that could not be helped. He lifted the violin to his chin and played.

Mozart, that perfect piece, the one that had eluded him,

glided easily from the strings. The song that once gave him wings did the opposite now. As he played, the house, the yard, the moss-covered stones, the lichen-laced roof tiles—all of it became real, as if he were playing the world into existence.

A boy. In a yard. At home. His mother inside, waiting. This would all be true forever.

As the last strains of melody melted into the sky, a sense of peace filled him. He had done it. He had played from the place he could not reach before.

Lieutenant Saito had often told his students that the ancient way of the samurai, the true code of Bushido, meant the way of death. All warriors must live as though dead so they could face battle without fear. Bushido, in that sense, was a way of peacefulness.

Taro bowed to the north, toward Tokyo and the Emperor and Akeno, where his old lieutenant was likely saying the same thing to his new recruits. It had a different meaning as a tokkō pilot. A truer meaning.

A weight dropped from his chest. He turned toward the house and stopped.

His mother stood in the doorway watching him. Her hand covered her mouth. There were tears in her eyes.

"Taro-chan . . ." She bowed to him. "Ayugai-san would be pleased."

He spent the day with her around the house, visiting a few friends and Mrs. Tanaka. He wore his uniform for everyone to see. The rest of his duffel lay packed and waiting. The violin he placed in his old room as a memento for his family. He wrote to Ayugai-sensei, telling him what he could not tell his parents. He would body-crash in honor of his teacher, he said. The

Americans would suffer for the crime of stealing his music. He told him of the moment in the garden and asked his old teacher to beg his parents' forgiveness on his behalf. Not telling them was cowardly, but he could not bear to see his mother's pain.

But his mother watched him every moment, and the tears never left her eyes.

She smiled when she took the sealed envelope from him. She addressed it herself, and tucked it into her coat to mail on the way back from the train.

"Wait! You mustn't forget your violin!" she said, carrying it down from his room.

"Oh . . . I think it will be safer here," he tried to say, but she insisted.

"Taro-chan, music is your life. You mustn't leave it behind."

His throat tightened. He took the violin.

And then she walked him to the station just as she had his father so many years ago. Only, this far into the war, there was no crowd, no parade of tonari-gumi members. No schoolchildren with flags. Just a young man and his mother, and a lifetime of unspoken words between them.

"If . . . if you should meet a young woman, Taro, I would like to meet her," his mother said as they stood on the steps of the station. "It would be good to have company. To know someone else out there cares for you. There is so little happiness in this world, it would be good to find what you can."

He held his mother's calloused hands, lending her his warmth.

"I'll see what I can do," he joked, and she smiled and let him go.

CHAPTER 30

TARO

March 1945

"Did you tell her?" Nakamura's voice was loud in the smaller bunkroom. With only eight beds, instead of dozens, their new housing reflected their status as Tokkō Tai. Nakamura was hanging his head upside down off the foot of his bed so that his face was very red. He was playing with something bright that Taro could not make out. Taro sat on his own bed, staring at his violin, pretending to polish it with a soft cloth. Tokkō training began in an hour.

"I couldn't bring myself to," Taro admitted. The shame he felt was palpable. "It's strange. I felt such a sense of peace; I thought of Lieutenant Saito's Bushido."

"Ah! You're samurai now?" Nakamura laughed.

"I'm serious, Kenji. It felt as if nothing mattered more than what we are doing. Even telling my mother was not important."

Nakamura rolled over to look at him. "Was?"

Taro sighed. "Was. It seems important now. Did I take the coward's way out?"

Nakamura shrugged. "Who's to say?"

"I suppose you told your family?"

Nakamura gave him a lopsided smile. "Best and worst thing I've ever done. My grandmother slapped me, my grandfather got drunk with me, my sister's girlfriends all asked to marry me, but I had to say no because my mother made me this."

He held up the toy he'd been fiddling with. It was a bride doll. A petite pale-faced woman sewn of cloth and hand painted with rosy cheeks and smiling lips. She wore a miniature wedding kimono of elaborate silk dotted with cranes.

"Meet the wife!" Nakamura said, sitting up. "Her name is Nobuko—at least, I think that's what my mother said. She's going to serve me in the afterlife."

Taro felt a pang in his stomach. "It's . . . I mean, she's beautiful."

"Eh, she's okay. Not fat enough to guarantee happiness, like that old guy said. But she'll do. The kimono's nice—cut from my mom's wedding outfit. Little sis wasn't too happy about that, but I told her by the time she got married, Western dress would be all the rage. That caused a ruckus. If we win the war, Western clothes will probably be banned for a thousand years, or so she told me in many, many more words. Sis is the only one not impressed by me. I'll have to take out a big battleship just to make her blink."

"So that's what you missed out on. A slap, a hangover, an angry sister, and you could be married to a doll, too."

Taro imagined his own mother carefully cutting up her wedding kimono, painstakingly painting a little face. He gripped the neck of his violin and tried to summon his fortitude again. She would understand. He was doing this for her. He was doing this for Japan.

"Oh, and the women," Nakamura added. "Just watch the love letters I'll be getting from here on out. Girls love pilots, but they go crazy for tokkō."

Taro surprised himself with a laugh. "Nakamura, your 'secular' fortitude is impressive."

Nakamura smirked. "Laugh all you want. By next mail call, you'll see."

———

Tokkō training was very different from fighter training. Instead of learning swift maneuvers and how to dogfight, the new CO instructed Taro and his flight in the fine art of trust.

"You will have no guns, so you won't be able to engage the enemy. You must trust your escort planes to take care of them for you. In this way, you are no different from a bomber plane. You have one job. Do it well. The others will do theirs, and they will report your success when they return."

From there, it was charts and graphs and spotter cards. How to recognize an enemy ship from a distance. The best places to target—preferably near the ammunition storage or fuel tanks. Either would provide a sufficient blast to cause maximum damage and disable a ship.

"There is nothing more pointless than sacrificing yourself without hurting the enemy," the CO said. He was a ruddy-faced man. Rumor had it he drank too much. Taro didn't doubt it. The man had trained over four hundred tokkō.

"The deck of this aircraft carrier is armored. Crash on deck, and if you are lucky, you cause a fire and take out a few sailors.

Hit the fuel stores, though—" He tapped the chart on the wall highlighting the spots where highly volatile aviation fuel was held for the thirty-six fighter planes and fifty-four bombers on board. "And you become gunshin warriors, lifted to Yasukuni in the arms of beautiful kami."

They discussed wind speed, when and how to drop out of the sky, to skim the waves, to hold steady.

What they did not discuss was spiritual fortitude. Perhaps the CO was not capable of it. Or perhaps it no longer mattered. They were committed. They would follow through.

And that was it. One day of training, and then they had little to do but wait for an assignment. Taro imagined rooms full of generals in impressive uniforms, somewhere in Tokyo, moving chess pieces along a great board the size of the Eastern World. When they were ready, they would push their knights into position. And Japan would be preserved.

———

Nakamura hadn't been kidding about the love letters. They came in, three a day, then five, then a dozen. Word had spread around his hometown. Entire schools of girls, and even grown women, were writing him by the time the boys got their orders to ship out. Some of the girls even sent extra letters to be given to his friends. Taro read one from a twenty-two-year-old schoolteacher in Kagoshima. When Nakamura saw him blush, he took the letter back "for careful review."

He also gave the postmaster clear forwarding instructions: Chiran Imperial Army Air Base, Kagoshima Prefecture.

Nakamura had a fan base now. He wasn't going to miss reading a single line.

Taro wrote a letter home to tell his mother where he would be, but he did not mail it. The censors would not allow him to say what mattered most, and even if they would, he still could not bring himself to tell her the truth. His actions would have to speak for him.

CHAPTER 31

HANA

"Hana! You are so lucky!" Sachiko says after we return to the barracks. I have cradled the violin all the way back across the airfield, careful to watch my step on the broken ground. Even with her precious box of chocolates, she can't leave me be. "Open it! I want to see!"

"No," I say, but it's a whisper. Mariko takes over for me.

"Come on," I hear her say brightly. "These beds will not change themselves."

"So stingy!" Sachiko says loudly to one of the other girls. "I would share my chocolates with her, but we can't even have a look at her little love gift."

Mariko hisses sharply, and Sachiko falls quiet. For a time, there is only the sound of soft sheets tugged from futon and damp pillowcases dropped to the floor, and then the starchier sound of new sheets being tossed, tucked, and folded into place.

All this time, I stand with the violin in my arms.

At last, Kaori-sensei comes to me. "Here, Hana-san. I will put it in the commander's office for safekeeping. You may have it back when you go home." She gives me a sympathetic smile and a nod of approval. Only then do I realize I am inside the barracks. Even without the music of Inoguchi Taro's violin.

Releasing the black case, now warm from my own body, is like giving away a limb. The blood flows back into my cramped arms. I did not intend to hold it so tight. I shake my fingers until they loosen and flex my elbows. My next breath is filled with the rich scent of dirt and the musk of last night's sleep. A rough green blanket hits me without warning.

"Good," Mariko says, smiling. "Take that end and help me. I told the other girls we'd handle the rest."

That explains the silence, the expansive space beneath the peaked roof. The girls have gone to the river to coo over their gifts and share their swooning stories. There are no clothes to mend or meals to serve. We will go home early today by design. It's allotment day for our mura—when the trucks carrying rations arrive. Government-sanctioned foods and staples will be sorted and doled out by Mrs. Higashi and the ladies of the neighborhood association. As the town tailor, my mother will receive her few bolts of cloth, and a line of people waving their clothing ration tickets will form on our street, each hoping to claim a few yards of cloth for a new shirt or a pair of lightweight monpé for the coming summer.

With only the two of us in the barracks now, my claustrophobia has faded, rising only when I think about it. I focus on the rough scratch of wool and the smooth coolness of the wooden sleeping platforms as our hands glide down the blankets and under the futon.

"Did you know him?" Mariko asks me on the third bed.

"No more than the others," I confess. "But . . . yesterday, I heard him playing. I listened, and he knew I was there."

"I didn't know we had a real musician among us. Though, I suppose Nakamura-san was making fun of him the other day."

"Was he?" We finish the last bed and stretch our backs. This is always the worst part, the awful silence between units. If we give ourselves time to think, then we know our young friends are dying, like moths in a flame. So we don't think. We move. Except for now, the frozen moment between one task and the next. Like a breath caught in the throat. An awareness of being alive. The sound of a young man playing the violin.

"Come on," I say, mimicking Mariko. "These sheets won't wash themselves."

"Let them wait," Sensei says from the doorway. "The truck is here. These will keep until tomorrow."

After the laundry has been stored away, I take up the black case again. It rests on my knees softly as the truck takes us back into town.

"Oh! Did you hear?" Sachiko pipes up. I can smell the chocolate on her breath. "Miyakawa-san came back last night! Reiko should tell the story, really. Won't you, Reiko? No? Well, Miyakawa-san was the one who loved to visit Tomiya Shokudo and was always asking Reiko and her mother and sisters to sing for him. He body-crashed yesterday with the morning flight! The night before, he promised Tomihara-san he would return as a hotaru and said, 'I will come back at sundown. Please sing "Dōki no Sakura" one last time.' And just like that, last night a giant firefly flew into the garden and entered the dining room, and Tomihara-san took the girls by the hand and they sang to the firefly. Well, what do you think it did? It hovered in the rafters until they were done, then circled overhead and flew back out into the night! Isn't that sad? Isn't it beautiful? I'm sure Reiko could tell it better, but she's grumpy today, so at least now you know."

Reiko remains silent, her hands clasped, her eyes distant.

Mariko and I stare at each other across the truck, unblinking, daring each other not to scream at Sachiko for being a gossip. "She can't help herself," Mariko says. Sachiko frowns.

"It's her way," I say back. I sound so much like Kaori-sensei that we both giggle. Sachiko looks at us with flashing eyes.

"You have no hearts and no respect! I think it's a wonderful thing!"

We cover our mouths until the giggling subsides. She's right. But she's also wrong. It was not her story to tell.

Some of the girls start singing "Dōki no Sakura" then, but I do not join them.

I can only hear the name Inoguchi Taro, and the sound of the silent violin.

CHAPTER 32

HANA

The cloth truck is early. My mother is too distracted to notice the violin case at my side. I slip past the deliverymen and the bolts of rough indigo cloth they carry. In the entryway, I slip off my shoes and place the violin in the next room, beside my father's koto. The neighbors will have seen the delivery truck. Soon, they will be lining up with their orders.

I pull a cotton smock on over my clothes and grab the order book from my mother's worktable.

"Oh good, you're here," Okā-san says. Her hands are full of fabric as she judges what few bolts are available today. Spying the order book in my hands, she rattles off the names and yardages of the fabric we receive. I write them into the inventory and portion out the ration tickets she passes to the driver.

"Are you open?" a woman calls from the street.

"One moment, please!" Okā-san calls back. She takes the log from my hands and frowns. I show the men where to place the allotted bolts in the front room, leaning them against the walls like tired trees, cut ends facing out so we can display the drape for customers.

"Arigatō gozaimasu," my mother says, thanking the men when we step back into the yard. As the truck rumbles away, she takes my elbow. "A total of twenty pairs of pants, or thirty-five shirts. That's all we can manage in adult sizes. Don't let anyone bully you into more. For special requests, send them to me."

The rest of the day passes in a flurry of bargaining and bullying as the old women of the mura test the new fabrics between judgmental fingers, insisting my mother make muslin into silk and one yard into one hundred. Shirts are relatively cheap at eight ration points, but coats cost as much as fifty. Even if we had more than a few bolts of fabric, there is only so much each family can buy. With only eighty points per person a year, there is no haggling, only jostling for the sturdiest cloth.

At last, the orders are finalized: eight shirts, a dozen pairs of pants, and a few smaller items, all in Civil Defense khaki or deep indigo—the safest colors in times of war. The fabric has run out. Turning away the unlucky customers at the end of the line, we close our doors and catch our breaths before dinner.

The morning farewell comes back to me like a fog, too dense to navigate.

"Hana, what's wrong?" Okā-san asks as we lay out a meal of rice, pickled greens, and tea. The rice is sticking to the pot. The tea is pale, the leaves overstewed. I make a note to gather more. This is tea country. It's the one thing we should not lack. Even the air base was once a tea field. There are still wild things to be found on the edges.

A snatch of music flashes in my mind, strings playing something green and wild.

"Nothing, Okā-san. I'm just tired."

"Girl," Okā-san says. She has not called me *girl* in many years. "You are not fooling me. I see you leave here in the morning in your school blouse and work pants. That is not farm work you are doing. I trust Sensei to watch out for you, but your face grows longer every day. What is it that you will not share?"

I keep my eyes down, but the heat rises in my cheeks. My vision blurs. "Okā-san, I met a boy, and now he's dead." I look up at last, unable to hide the truth any longer. "Our class works at the air base as maids for the pilots."

"The tokkō?" My mother's face grows still. "Those men who come riding through here by the truckload and carouse the night at Tomiya Shokudo?"

I am suddenly ashamed at how it must seem. I fall to my knees and bow. "Hai, the same. Only, they are not men, Okā-san. They are boys. Seventeen, nineteen—too young. Tomihara-san treats them as her sons."

My mother stares at me over the bowls of rice, the crusted pot forgotten in her hands.

"Don't be angry with me, Okā-san! Sensei told us not to worry our parents. I did not want you to be upset."

The hardness leaves my mother's eyes and jaw. She lowers the pot and finishes arranging our dinner. "I am not angry, Hana-chan. I'm . . . My daughter is Nadeshiko in more than name. Like the flower, graceful and resilient. You do honor to your father and your country with this service. I am . . ." She does not say what she feels, but suddenly the tears burst from me. I'm choking on this honor, this service. And I am happy to be of use.

A work-hardened hand rests softly on my head. Okā-san strokes my hair, murmuring gently, until I am through. "Hana, Hana, Hana, Hana," she says, drawing out the end of my name until it is a song. "We mustn't grow attached, Hana. Attachment leads to suffering. You must let it all go." She knows I am listening, and I know she is right.

Though I have no stomach for it, she makes me eat when I am done crying. And then, together, we go into the other room to marvel at the violin.

"It's just an instrument," she tells me, although her fingers seem to delight in the curves, the proud horse head, the broad back of wood, its finish rippled beneath the surface like waves of sunshine. I nod, caressing the strings as I place it back into its coffin. Only an instrument . . .

"Hai," I tell her. She is right.

And yet that night, I say *Inoguchi Taro* in my prayers.

CHAPTER 33

TARO

April 1945

"Nakamura!"

Taro was blinded by clouds, by smoke. His aeroplane was limping. He'd fallen well behind the others. The oil pressure gauge had dropped, a black trail burned behind him as the oil ignited from the heat of his engine.

He could not make it to the target. He would not body-crash today.

Taro signaled, hoping the escort planes would see him, but they had already flown out of sight. He couldn't blame them. His smoke trail was a beacon to the enemy. But at least they could defend themselves from fighter attack. He had no weapons beyond the plane itself, and that was all but useless against an American Mustang.

Taro swallowed his regret and let his training take over. He made as tight a turn as he could, shifting direction. Descending below cloud level, he headed toward the approaching shoreline. From the corners of his eyes, he could see he was not alone. Two other aeroplanes had failed in some way. One trailed smoke. The other, he couldn't tell, but he prayed it was Nakamura. Then he prayed that it wasn't. He wouldn't wish the shame of failure on his friend, no matter how much he wanted to see him again. But who else could understand what it was to accept death, only to be rejected by it?

Chiran appeared below. Taro wrestled the joystick, lowering his aeroplane into a landing. The ground crew was already running toward him, fire extinguishers at the ready. Arms helped him out of the cockpit and hurried him away. The second plane was not so lucky. The pilot had managed to jettison his bomb along the way, but the landing gear caught a rut on the runway and snapped. The plane skidded into the ground in a shower of sparks. The pilot—Hiroshi, Taro thought—was dragged away unconscious. His plane would not fly again.

"Taro!" a voice called to him. The third pilot. The wind whipped past Taro's ears, carrying the sound away. He turned slowly, knowing.

Tomomichi, his wide boyish face wet with tears, approached. "My engine choked. I thought I was going to fall into the sea," he said. "I was a coward. I turned back. We should be out there with them."

With Nakamura. Taro closed his eyes. Nakamura.

"They body-crashed without us," Tomomichi said.

"You saw them?" Taro opened his eyes. "Was it glorious? Nakamura deserves glory. He's the best of us," he said.

Tomomichi glanced at the ground uncertainly. "I . . . I'm sure he did. The escort crews will tell us, though. My engine . . . I was not able to fly so far. But I'm sure he did well, and the Americans will know his name."

Taro took a deep breath. Together, they went to debrief and discuss their equipment failures with the engineers. Commandant Asama was waiting inside the hangar. He looked them up and down, as if making a decision.

"Cowards!" he barked. "That other fellow loses a perfectly good bomb, and you two! They blame the aeroplane. I blame the men!" He stepped forward and slapped Tomomichi across the face. A moment later, Taro's head rang with the second slap. "I should have you arrested. But you're more use to us as pilots." He turned his scowl on the engineers. "Get them in the air again, immediately!"

Asama turned on his heel and stormed off. Taro refused to rub his cheek. The pain was no less than he deserved.

"Don't worry," one of engineers said once the commandant was gone. "It's better to return for repairs than fall into the sea. We'll get to work right away. Your friends will be waiting for you on the other side."

The other side. What a terrible barrier between a pilot and his mates.

Taro knew of only one way to voice the turmoil he felt. He turned toward his barracks, but hesitated. His futon most likely belonged to a new pilot by now.

"Let's see the staff sergeant about quarters," he said quietly. Tomomichi followed him outside.

———

"We haven't filled that one yet. But, if you'd prefer, we can put you up in a different barracks," the staff sergeant said, reading his thoughts. "It's bad for morale to rattle around in the space you shared with your brothers, isn't it? No one likes an empty house."

Taro shook his head grimly. "It's where we belong. I'd prefer it."

Tomomichi turned pale, but he agreed. "We will be closer to our unit this way."

They followed the sergeant to their old barracks, where the man respectfully left them alone. Tomomichi fell onto his old futon, weeping angrily into his pillow.

Taro looked for his violin, but of course, it wasn't there. A gift from the dead, it belonged to the living now. To a girl with a name that meant "flower."

Taro walked slowly through the darkened barracks, not living, not dead. Perhaps they should have accepted the offer of a new barracks. Here, he and Tomomichi were little more than shadows on the borderlands of the spirit world. And there was only one place left to go.

———

By nightfall, no other pilots had returned. The other five were presumed to have body-crashed, although there was no word from headquarters if their strikes had been successful.

"I didn't know it would be this way," Tomomichi said. He had stopped his angry weeping and now sat on the foot of his bed, fists clenched, hair damp with sweat. "Shouldn't we at least know if our brothers were successful? Don't they deserve to be recognized?"

Taro sat on his own bunk, swinging his feet against the wooden platform like padded sticks against a dull drum. Keeping time to the beat of his own heart. "Yes, they do," he said quietly. He looked up at his unit mate. "But this is the way of the tokkō. We go to our deaths knowing all we will ever know. That's why it's better to be dead."

There was a scuffle at the entrance. A young pilot, younger-looking than any Taro had ever seen, bowed in the doorway. "Excuse the interruption. We hear you had great misfortune today with your planes. My unit is new here. We arrived late this afternoon, a day early. Perhaps . . . perhaps you would wish to join us for dinner in town?"

He bowed again, hands on his thighs. Taro could see the sweat of his palms staining the fabric darker green. Do we make them nervous now? he wondered. Were he and Tomomichi bad luck? Or was it that they had survived death, that they were spirits now? Either way, it was no time to carouse at Tomiya Shokudo. Nor would he cast a dark shadow on these new men.

"Arigatō," he said, knowing with a brief glance that Tomomichi agreed. "We are not worthy of such kindness. Our thoughts are with our brothers. We will meditate on following them."

"Of course," the boy said with a clipped bow. He left at a run. Eager to get away, if only for a moment, to the promise of life.

It was only then that Taro realized how funereal his world had become. The dirt beneath his feet was below ground level. The entire barracks was a crypt, a roof over a grave. A stone hand reached out to choke him. His eyes burned.

"What do we do now?" Tomomichi asked.

Taro collected himself. Cleared his throat.

"We can be glad we're healthy, unlike poor Hiroshi," he said. They'd each spent an hour by the side of their injured comrade. He might never heal well enough to finish his mission. "We will fly again tomorrow, or the next day. As soon as our planes are able."

"What if they aren't?" Tomomichi sounded desperately whiny. Like a child.

"They will be!" Taro shouted. His voice cracked. "They will be, or we will find new planes for ourselves. We cannot tolerate failure for long."

"Hai," Tomomichi whispered. "Hai."

Taro lay back on his futon, imagining his funeral pyre. He stared up at the wooden beams of the ceiling, picturing the sky beyond and the last piece he'd played on his violin. He played it now in his mind. It helped to calm him. He took flight on the music, soaring into the sky, past stars and moon and planets whirling in orbit around the sun. He was the night wind. He was everything. He was nothing.

His fingers twitched. His arm ached.

He was earthbound.

And alone.

CHAPTER 34

HANA

The air is damp and cool this morning as Mariko and I clamber onto the truck that will carry us down to the airfield. The rest of the Nadeshiko are already on board—all of us exhausted from the extra demands of allotment day.

"Sensei, were our brothers successful yesterday in destroying the enemy?" Sachiko asks as we settle in. She still smells of yesterday's chocolates. I suspect she dabbed it on like perfume. Nakamura was her new favorite. Now that he is gone, she will profess to pine for him. Like a geisha in a love story, she longs for what she cannot have. Hisako is different. Perhaps because she is a little older, or because she knows true loss. The boy she was to marry died at sea. Her grief is not a performance like Sachiko's. She sits quietly up against the back of the truck cabin, her thoughts her own. On clear evenings, I have seen her at the temple on the hill where we gathered yesterday's cherry blossoms. She combs her hair and dots it with flowers, looking off toward the sea that is miles from view.

Okā-san is right. Detachment is the way to happiness. Suffering is a choice.

"I have no news," Sensei tells Sachiko. "But they were good boys, well trained. I am sure they scattered brilliantly. Shall we sing a song to honor them?"

And so it is that we are singing "Umi Yukaba" at the top of our lungs—myself included. I will detach by joining the rest.

But when we arrive at the base, we see that our barracks are not empty.

Sergeant Kawahara is waiting. He helps Sensei climb down from the truck bed and speaks to her urgently while the rest of us hop down unaided.

"Girls, attention, please," Sensei says. The sergeant watches us nervously. "Sergeant Kawahara tells me that some of our brothers were unfortunate yesterday and were forced to return to base. I only need two girls to tend to the returned pilots. The rest of you will lend a hand to your classmates with the new arrivals."

Sachiko steps forward, as do the rest of us. So she steps forward again. She's brimming with desire. I can see it. Sachiko eats tragedy the way others eat salt. But I am not the only one who knows this. Kaori-sensei holds up a hand to stop her. "Ah. Wait. This is a sensitive mission. Our brave pilots are very upset and longing to join their brothers. This is a silent duty I ask of you. Hana, Mariko, you know to hold your tongues. You will take care of our unfortunate brothers until they are sent out again."

Mariko and I bow. Sachiko makes a face, and though it's unkind of me, I'm glad she's been passed over. But as we approach the quiet barracks, I hesitate.

"Hana, what is it?" Mariko asks.

"Only, it's so sad for these two to remain," I say. But that is not why I hesitate.

The song we've been singing, "Umi Yukaba," is about the honor of dying for the Emperor. A tokkō who comes back is dishonored. Some see it as cowardice. There is shame in outliving your comrades. And yet I prayed for this last night. I am afraid to see if that prayer has been answered.

"Come inside," Mariko says. "They will be hungry. At least we can make the beds."

The barracks, when we enter, is blessedly empty. But two beds are roughly made, one at the far end of the room, and another closer to the middle. I recognize it and catch my breath.

"I must go home," I tell Mariko suddenly.

She turns to me, arms full of sheets from the other bed. "Are you ill?"

"No . . . I . . . please, Mariko. I'll return as soon as I can."

"Iie, you will not leave me here, Hana! Help me make the beds at least, while they are not here. And be back before we have to bring them lunch."

"Hai, arigatō." I bow to her and rush to strip the bed.

CHAPTER 35

TARO

Taro and Tomomichi returned from an unwanted breakfast and an encouraging conversation with the ground crew engineers—their planes required new parts, but they had them on hand. They would be flight-ready by nightfall.

And there it was on the white futon, waiting.

Tomomichi didn't notice. "I'm going to the shrine to make an offering for tomorrow. Fair weather, and we will follow our brothers into the afterlife."

"Hai," Taro said, almost a whisper. He failed to see the troubled frown on Tomomichi's face as he turned to leave. Taro only had eyes for his violin.

The case was as he had left it, deep and textured, not quite pristine, with his name carefully written on a label pasted on the side. He opened the box and smelled . . . something different. What? The scent of laundry, perhaps. Jasmine blossoms. The case had been opened, the violin touched. He ran his fingers lightly along the strings, the curving horse head.

Hana.

He needed to thank her.

Closing the case, he grabbed the handle, jumped up from his bed, and hurried out the door. This time of day, the girls were hanging up laundry or helping in the kitchen. He headed to the laundry lines. There they were. Nadeshiko, fresh and bright, so many more faces than he ever expected to see again. But not Hana. He wasn't even sure he'd remember what she looked like. He had erased her. Why remember the face of one lone girl, when his father, his mother, his friends were ever present in his mind? For a moment he was glad. His moral fortitude was in place at last.

And then he found her, in the yard outside the kitchen, hanging up towels to dry.

"Hana-san?"

Her dark eyes widened. She dropped the towel she was pinning to the line and fell into the deepest of bows.

"Inoguchi-san, are you well?" she asked, though from the blush on her cheeks, she was as aware of the irony as he was.

"I am well, Hana-san. Thank you for lending me your violin," he said. The girl hesitated, then nodded.

"Of course. It is best when in the hands of a master."

Taro flushed hotly. "Far from a master. A poor student at best. I'm afraid I neglected my training in favor of taking to the sky."

Hana picked up the dropped towel and spent a certain amount of time dusting it off, but it was too damply dirty to pass off as clean. She folded it carefully and placed it on the ground.

"Hana-san." Taro hesitated. But it was only right, he told himself. After all, the violin belonged to this girl now.

"May I play for you?"

Her face, when she looked up, shone like the sun, and he wondered that he ever doubted he would know her again. He knew, the way a ship knew its port, a pilot the shape of his parents' home below.

"I cannot ask it," she said, a catch in her voice. "But I would wish for it with all my heart."

The catch seemed to travel. He cleared his own throat. "Well, then." He found a stool behind the kitchen door and perched on it. Resting the case on his knees, he pulled the violin into the light of day.

"Please," Hana said. She crouched before him, laying out another towel on the ground, this one dry and clean. She lowered her eyes as he rested the violin case on the cloth, away from the dusty earth.

"Arigatō," he whispered, not meaning to be so quiet. She nodded softly and rose to continue her work.

Taro watched her, her lean arms, her black hair knotted at the nape of her neck, her dark eyes, the sun-browned curve of her cheek. Her baggy work pants and the dark blue sailor's blouse with the white collar that looked so girlish and untouched by war. He placed his chin on the chin rest, raised his bow arm, and began to play.

CHAPTER 36

HANA

I hang the towels slowly, afraid that when the work ends, so will the song. Every so often, I steal a glimpse of Inoguchi Taro from behind the damp flaps of linen and cotton sacking. He is tall, his elbows and knees almost awkwardly far from his lean body. His cap, at first down low over his forehead, slides back and forth as he plays, craning his neck to his shoulder. It's as if the violin is speaking to him and he must listen closely to hear its voice.

This is what it is to play beautifully—this conversation between player and instrument, with music as the translation.

But even military laundry does not last forever. Nor do songs play without end. As the last strains of music fade, I find myself intently watching Taro. I barely see the kitchen staff by the doorway, listening. Only Taro, as he opens his eyes to meet mine.

Attachment leads to suffering, Okā-san said.

But perhaps that is the price of joy.

CHAPTER 37

HANA

"Do you suppose it will rain tomorrow?" I squint up at the sky. There are clouds to the east over the ocean. But are there enough?

Mariko shakes her head. "Sensei says we are up early tomorrow, so I don't think so. The clouds are moving away," she notes. And I must agree with her. We keep walking. We've opted to walk home rather than ride in the truck. Even spending all day on our feet, sometimes it feels better to move on our own. Besides, we know what the enemy sounds like. It's an easy thing to hide among the trees on foot. Trucks have a harder time of it.

We follow the river, within sight of the gray torii gate of Toyotama-hime Shrine. The tall, curving archway marks the entrance to a sacred space and acts as a perch for the messenger birds of the gods. Behind the great gateway, the shrine stands as it has for two hundred years, with its bright vermillion buildings and its clever collection of mechanical water dolls, delicate automatons powered by a water wheel. The shrine is dedicated to Toyotama, also known as the Dragon Princess, the daughter of the Sea King, descended from the sun goddess Amaterasu herself. Legends say Toyotama fell in love with a human and hid her true form. But when she gave birth to their son, her dragon shape was revealed. Her husband cast her out, but their child became the father of Jimmu, who became the first emperor of Japan. This shrine is as close as we in Chiran ever get to the Imperial might of the Chrysanthemum Throne. This, and the orders to go to war.

We used to attend festivals here as children and beg our parents for coins to purchase fortunes in hopes of great blessings. Bad fortunes were tied to the trees by the shrine steps, like little paper flags, so the bad luck could be washed away. But now, to my Nadeshiko eyes, the bold red buildings and tattered fortunes are targets for enemy bombers. The row of cherry trees leading to the shrine are merely decoration for Tokkō Tai. We keep to the far side of the river as we pass.

"What if we stop by the temple on the way home?" I ask.

"Not the shrine?" Mariko asks. We have two faiths in Japan. Shrines are for Shinto, and temples for Buddhism. Shinto tells us there is a spirit in every living thing. Buddhism teaches us that life is suffering and death is not the end. The spirit journeys and is reborn. It's no wonder that weddings are Shinto occasions and funerals are Buddhist ones. But both faiths are for peace. I find I need some today.

"No." It's too bright, too exposed, too close to the air base. But I don't say that. "The one by the school. Up the hill, where we used to play." It was not uncommon, when we were babies, for our busy parents to leave us in the care of whichever mothers were sitting in the temple yard, letting their little ones play.

We used to bring stale cakes to feed the birds. There is a nursery school there now, for the youngest children.

"Up the hill! Hana, my legs feel like clay today. You'd have to carry me!"

I say nothing, and she is silent for a while. Then, "Do you suppose the old monk is still there? The one with the bald spot he said was made by an angry bird?"

We both laugh. "We were terrified of birds for the rest of the year," I recall.

"I still duck when sparrows swoop by," Mariko says. Her cheeks are pink and merry. "You win. Let us go pay our respects," she decides, and we branch off to the higher road that will take us to the temple yard. "Then you can carry me home!"

It's the same and not the same as it used to be. No one is in school these days. There are no children playing on the flagstones, no visitors carrying pots to be blessed. But the temple and outbuildings are still somber and beautiful with their swooping roofs and carved eaves. The garden is still green, and the birds are still there, scratching and pecking in the yard. I wish we had some crumbs to give them. But now there are not enough crumbs to share.

We are sad to hear the old monk has moved on and give our best to the current monk, whose shaved head is sprinkled with white stubble. He has a warm face, and I am ashamed we have not visited before now. As we leave, Mariko points to the garden.

"Do you have any cherry trees? Perhaps we may take some boughs for tomorrow's flight," she says to the monk, explaining we are in service at the base. But the older man shakes his head.

"It will rain tomorrow. People are praying for it. Farmers. What else would they pray for?"

"Of course," Mariko says.

I try not to let my heart trip my feet as we bow and say our farewells. Last night I wished for a miracle. Today, I wish for another. The clouds to the east are farther away than ever, and yet the words of the monk echo the words in my own heart. *Let it rain, let it rain, let it rain.*

Beside me, Mariko proves herself the wiser of us two. "Funny to think of what the monk said, isn't it? Farmers need rain, yes. But why would they not also pray for peace?"

CHAPTER 38

HANA

How many farmers' prayers does it take for a day like today? How many foolish, attached girls?

It's raining. The new monk at the temple was right.

I am smiling at breakfast. My mother notices. "Ah, you must have something fun planned for today, neh?"

"No, just laundry and bed making," I say. My tongue is a liar, but my lips betray me.

"Well, as long as you obey your teacher and stay safe, I am glad," Okā-san says.

I will bring her a cup, no, two cups of green rice today if I am able. I will be able. The whole world is shining. Who needs the sun?

———

"Hana, be careful," Mariko tells me as we climb into the back of the truck. "You think I don't notice, but how could I not? You like that boy, Taro. It's not wise. It's dangerous!"

"Dangerous how?" I ask her. My well-meaning friend. Mariko has never felt the way I do today.

"Don't give your heart to a dying man," she says sadly. "You remember what happened to Lieutenant Fuji'i-san."

The memory of the man, of his wife walking with their daughters into the river, is enough to silence me. Taro is like Fuji'i-san. He has been left behind. Surely he has moved on too far to think of me.

And what would that mean, anyway? A day of smiling foolishly, of begging him to play his violin? I have chores to do, beds to make, food to serve. Socks to darn. There will be new pilots. Even the rain cannot stop new units from arriving and the war from grinding on.

The rest of the ride to the camp is a somber one, with Sachiko complaining that her socks are wet, and the others failing to rouse enough girls to sing a song.

I hop down onto the wet earth with the others, the black mud splashing our socks, our geta grinding on the gravel as the soil washes away. There is no point in washing sheets that will not dry. There is only sewing and serving and pretending to be joyful. My heart is rarely in it. And now, not at all.

"Hana-san?"

He's there in the doorway of his barracks, watching the rain. Or perhaps he is watching for me?

"Inoguchi-san, are you well?" I bow and stand there, foolish as an ox in the rain.

When he smiles, a dimple appears on his right cheek. I want to touch that dimple. "I am now. And you?"

I take a step forward, shaky on the rocky ground. It's the

rain, the gravel, I tell myself, that makes me unsteady as a lamb. I should be blushing, but I feel an answering smile.

"I am now, too."

The others are watching us. His unit mate Tomomichi, my Nadeshiko friends. Sensei has gone on to the command center, which is fortunate. I feel as though we are onstage, he and I, two players in a Kabuki sewamono. I am frozen in this tableau.

"Well, there is work for you today, I am sure," he says at last. "Perhaps when you are done, I might play for you again?"

"I would like that very much," I say.

He nods and seems to notice for the first time that we are being observed. "I would enjoy playing for all of you, if you care to listen. I'm still learning, but I will do my best."

The other girls nod or murmur assurances. They have heard from the kitchen staff, no doubt. Inoguchi Taro is a maestro.

We break our positions and scurry to our chores. It is only as Mariko and I finish making Tomomichi's bed that I realize we are soaked to the bone, all of us, from standing like fools in the rain.

———

It's a lonely meal we serve our two tokkō at lunchtime. Taro and his unit mate will not join the other unit. Instead, Mariko and I serve the two of them alone in their dim barracks. We stand awkwardly by the doorway as they sip their soup and eat their portions of rice and a stew of fish and sweet potatoes. Mariko closes her eyes, resting against the door frame. I gaze outside, trying not to look back to see if he feels what I feel. An energy presses inside me, against my skin, my chest, demanding I act or explode.

I cannot act. I take a deep breath and focus on the gray curtain of rain, the deep verdant green of the black-trunked pines. It smells like winter, even though it's spring.

At last, the scraping of chopsticks ends, and we pad down the length of the barracks to gather their trays. Tomomichi wipes his mouth on the back of his hand and nods a thank-you to Mariko. When I dare to look, Taro is opening his violin case.

For a moment, there are only the two of us.

I can smell the faint scent of rosin from the strings, the dry smell of paper, and a warmer scent—the burnished wood. And there is Taro's strangely familiar smell, of leather and sweet grass, of something warm and deep like honey and the salty sea.

Perhaps it's my imagination. Or the images the music conjures as he begins to play. I am a ningyo, a mermaid floating deep beneath the waves.

Laughter breaks the spell. The sound of a dozen geta clattering on the gravel outside. Sachiko is here, and Kazuko, Reiko. Even sad Hisako drifts down into the barracks to hear Taro play. His eyes flick toward me, as if in apology, and I know. He understands me. And I him. I nod to say it's all right. There will be another time.

And then I remember that may not be true.

His posture shifts, and he is taller, broadening himself to play for a crowd. The kitchen staff follows, and I am no longer a mermaid, but a fish tossed on dry land, gasping and lonely for where I belong.

The music changes. Taro plays folk tunes that have the girls clapping and the kitchen workers singing along.

The room is suddenly too full.

I rise and push my way through the laughter to reach the door, where I can breathe.

The rain is still coming down, heavier than ever. I look back into the barracks from my perch on the steps, over the heads of the others.

This is what I see when I look at Taro: a young man, standing tall, a shining instrument of wood held confidently in his arm, like a dance partner, his chin resting on her shoulder. I see bright faces looking up at him as he does what no one else has been able to do—make them forget. The girls are no longer Nadeshiko Tai, but schoolgirls, happy to clap and sing. The kitchen workers are no longer scullery maids and pot scrubbers, but men and women who have families, stories, songs of their own.

I see tired people turned into human beings. I see a gray rainy day turned into sunshine.

It surprises me, as if there is color in the world I have been blind to until now.

I used to look at a tokkō and see the state of his uniform, the trim of his hair. I saw how they came prepared or unprepared to face their deaths. When they arrived, all I saw were fireflies. Watching Taro, I now see the fire.

And I see something else. My father at his koto. My mother dancing beside him, turning like a blossom to the sun. I see myself as I was then, so young and plump and joyful, mimicking my mother's dance. Taro is playing "Haru no Umi"—my father's favorite song.

The tears come unexpectedly. I let them come. No one is watching.

Almost no one.

Above the bobbing heads, Taro's eyes find mine. There is a small questioning smile on his face, as if to ask, "Is everything okay?"

Those eyes guide me back into the barracks and across the floor.

I climb up onto the sleeping platform when the music ends and tell him, "My father used to play that song."

He starts it up again, and I remember my mother's movements. The two of us at a cherry blossom viewing party many years ago. Otō-san sitting beneath the flowering trees. Our neighbors swaying to the music as Okā-san and I, in our best kimono, mimic the swell of the ocean, the spread of the sky. My own gestures were far more clumsy—then and now—with the balance of a seven-year-old girl. But as Taro plays, I spin and dip a moment, my knee no longer stiff. Everyone claps. It is spring again, 1937, months before the start of war. Everything is full of promise. I will be a great musician one day, like my father, a graceful dancer, like my mother. I am a bud that has yet to blossom. Everything is full of life.

And then I come back to myself. In a barracks on a tokkō base, beneath a peaked roof instead of blooming trees. I am a girl of fifteen, not seven. A Nadeshiko Tai. In the front row, Mariko is gaping at me in such astonishment I grow shy and climb back down to earth, where I belong.

We walk home from the base feeling light as the kamifusen we once played with as children—colorful paper balls that swelled with each bounce in an open palm. I feel full to bursting, even in my drab monpé. With every step of my geta toward home, I hear *Taro, Taro*. Every syllable a bounce. Mariko laughs at me, but she is bouncing, too. It's been so long since we've been happy. She sings snatches of the folk songs Taro played, and I join in. We wander home along the river, weaving, drunk on laughter, as if we've swallowed all the shōchū, the sweet potato liquor the women of the mura make for festival days.

"What has gotten into us?" Mariko asks me as we round the corner toward home. So kind is Mariko, to pretend she does not know.

"Nothing," I say, even as a blush warms my cheeks.

Mariko's laughter falls away with a sigh. Hisako is ahead of us, watching the carp in the stream. Hisako, who loved a boy and, in losing him, lost herself.

"Oh, Hana, there is a light in your eye," Mariko says seriously.

"Yours, too," I reply, an accusation, a question. We are simply happy, nothing more. But she gives me a look and my laughter fades.

"Good night, Hana," she says.

"Good night, Mariko. Get some rest."

When I reach home, I keep my head lowered so my mother will not see whatever it was that brought such sorrow to Mariko's face. I have a favor to ask of her.

Okā-san is hunched over Tomihara-san's kimono, the one brought by the farmer for alterations. She is carefully ripping apart each seam. When she is done, she will cut the pattern and dye the cloth Civil Defense khaki, so his family can continue to work in the fields. The military has been very demanding of farmers since the start of the war. I know this from my own time harvesting sweet potatoes. And yet, the cloth is so very beautiful . . . Is that not like everything else in Japan these days? The prettiest things, worn thin, splashed in mud.

I say as much to my mother, kneeling before her on the floor, my hands pressed to my thighs to keep me from gripping my clothes, from twisting them as if I could wring an answer from the cloth. "Okā-san, you must miss making beautiful things," I say.

"Don't be silly, Hana. This is war. We make necessary things. Beauty is a pastime for peace."

I work to keep my brow from crinkling. Only a day or two ago, I would have agreed with her. Even yesterday, I would have been convinced.

But she has not heard the violin. She has not seen Taro play.

"Perhaps it is so," I tell her. "But at the air base, this rain is a cease-fire. There are two pilots—both fine young men—who were unable to crash with their brothers. They are ashamed, Okā-san, and lonely. Couldn't we make a moment of beauty for them?"

Okā-san looks up from her seam ripping to scan my face. "What are you going on about, Hana? We have work to do. Come, change out of those clothes and help me."

"Tomorrow is Sunday," I tell her. "If it is raining, might we invite them for dinner? It would be a kindness. Your dinner parties were always so wonderful. I should like to show them."

"Dinner party! You mean like those carousers over at Tomiya

Shokudo? Hardly, Hana! It's one thing to serve them at the base, but quite another to invite such men into our home. We are two women alone. What would the town say?"

She is right, and I am ashamed. They will think the worst of us. We are not an inn, a public place. This is a private home. And while I see boys, the world sees military men.

I bow in front of my mother, my forehead to the tatami mat. "I am sorry," I whisper. But something in me, perhaps the light Mariko feared, shines forth, moving me to speak yet again. "But perhaps . . . they would say it is a kindness. A duty, like the home visits the cadets once made when the air base was just a base, before the war."

She stays silent for so long, I do not know what to do. I stare at the floor, waiting. The woven rows of the tatami mat blur in my vision. Cadet home visits were restricted to families without daughters my age for a reason. Is that what she's thinking now?

"Okā-san?" I ask, hoping for a yes.

"Hana," she says. "We have so little to share, I should be ashamed. We cannot feed them well."

"Oh, but Okā-san!" I sit up, leaning toward her. "You are such a wonderful cook. We should be ashamed not to try. I will cook, too. We'll be clever with what we have," I promise.

Something shifts in her face, a cat raising its head to the sun. Once upon a time, my mother loved parties. She was known throughout the mura as the best cook, the most elegant hostess outside of an inn. But that was before the rationing. Before clothing was restricted by points and kimono exchanged hands like money. Before Otō-san went away and my charming hostess mother became a tailor who made pants for the fields.

She sighs, and I know I have won.

"How many of these pilots must we feed? Perhaps we can ask Mrs. Higashi and the women of the tonari-gumi to—"

"Only two!" I say quickly. I'm unwilling to share our guests with anyone else. "Two boy pilots—Corporal Inoguchi and Corporal . . . I don't recall his name, only that he had engine trouble. They both did. They had to turn back and are too ashamed to join the others at the inn. But in this rain, all they can do is . . . Okā-san . . ."

My mother is looking at me. Or perhaps she is looking through me, for she murmurs to herself, "So willing to die."

She clears her throat and folds away the kimono cloth, making sure to mark her place with the needle.

"Very well. Invite them for an afternoon meal." She rises and smooths her yukata. There is a brightness in her face that must mirror my own. It has been too long since we worked for pleasure rather than duty. "There is so much to do. We have millet for dumplings, and I'm sure there are some red beans in the pantry. I was saving them as a treat."

For a moment, I am so grateful I am shaking. "Thank you, Okā-san. Oh! This place is a wreck!" I scoop up the fabric lying on the floor and bundle it into a chest. "I'll sweep the mats and find some flowers for the table and—"

"Hana." My mother's voice stops me just as surely as her hand on my arm calms me down. "It can wait until tomorrow. Let us have our own supper now and set the beans to soaking. Then worry over tomorrow when it arrives."

Over our own scant dinner, we plan the meal. My mother goes to the evening distribution of rations at Mrs. Higashi's house and returns with a lotus root and a small portion of rice. I sit in the kitchen rinsing beans, sifting them through my fingers to search for any stones. I am smiling, even though the work is simple, repetitive. Taro is coming here.

I make a small pile from the stones I find in the beans. We put the dried red beans and soybeans in two bowls of cool water to soften and go to bed.

To bed, but not to sleep. I lie awake on my futon, staring into the blue darkness, a tangle in my stomach like a rope, pulling me toward the air base, the pine-covered hillside, the triangle barracks sunk into the earth . . . Is he staring into the night, too?

It is a mistake to want this. So many boy pilots have passed through Chiran.

But none like Taro.

Sorrow stretches around me, a cocoon that has smothered me for too long. The strands of silk are tearing open.

There is a crinkle beneath his left eye when he smiles. A dimple on his right cheek.

There is a look, like a lighthouse on a distant shore, when he plays, his violin tucked tenderly in his arms.

And when that searchlight finds me, it carries me to shore.

I sigh and throw off my covers. I cannot sleep. I would pace the floor mats, but it would disturb Okā-san. Instead, I close my eyes and pretend I am hearing "Haru no Umi." I see the koto in my mind's eye and recall the notes. I fall asleep listening to the rain, playing the koto in my dreams.

CHAPTER 39

HANA

I wake to a joyfully thunderous sky. Taro is coming today. I rise early, heat the water for our washing bowls, and dress quickly so I may get to work. Sunday is our day at home. We are schoolgirls, after all. If there had been a flight today, Tomihara-san would be the one to wave goodbye in our stead. But the downpour outside means no one will fly.

After a quick breakfast, Okā-san sets the red beans to simmer on our old stove while I grind the soybeans to make tofu. The suribachi mortar sits on the table, a heavy ceramic bowl with a rough pattern like swirling grass on the inside. I scoop a cupful of soybeans and soaking water into the suribachi and pound them with the wooden surikogi, using the pestle to smooth the beans into a thick, foaming paste. Each bowlful of paste is poured into a large pot, until all of it is ready to cook.

Okā-san helps me put the pot on the fire. We take turns stirring the bean paste and adding cups of water to keep it from foaming over. After half an hour, the mixture has turned grainy, like lumps of meal in soy milk. This is okara, the pulp of the cooked beans.

I ladle the milk onto a fine muslin cloth tied across the top of a large bowl. Pressing the ladle down, I squeeze the freshly made soy milk through the cloth.

We take a break from our labors while the milk continues to drain, sharing a cup of the first batch in the doorway. It tastes of summer grass.

Outside, the rain splashes down in large fat drops, loud enough to blur the sounds of people inside the restaurant next door. It's almost as if the war has gone silent. A cricket chirrups in the garden. A cat rushes past on some fur-soaked errand. Okā-san claps her hands on her thighs, and we rise to finish our tasks.

Okā-san takes the cloth, now full of soybean pulp, and scrapes it into the suribachi. She will fry some of the okara with diced vegetables and a bit of soy sauce, doing what she can to make it savory. Okara is high in protein, but low in flavor otherwise. The rest will go to thicken the soup.

I find I am humming as we work. Okā-san glances at me, and I fall silent, embarrassed by this bubbling inside me. But then she begins humming, too.

I remember this, from when I was young. Before America entered the war. Otō-san would play the koto, or he would sing as he worked, cutting kimono and Western suits from fine cloth. And Okā-san would cook wonder after wonder, and we were always full and never went to bed hungry.

We are luckier than most. In the cities, they have no river of fish, no fields of their own to grow tea and sweet potatoes. And yet I had forgotten what it is like to have so much food in one place at one time.

Perhaps I am being greedy. Okā-san and I could live off these rations for a week.

But not everyone has a week to live, I remind myself, and return to my task.

I carefully measure a few grains of calcium salts into the milk to curdle it into tofu. Before this new war, we made tofu with nigari, and it was rich and grassy and sweet. Okā-san doesn't care for the new way of making it, but nigari is high in magnesium—a vital component for the aeroplanes Taro and his friends fly. I wonder if he knows this. Perhaps I will tell him at lunch today. Our worlds are more entwined than I would have guessed.

The soy milk clumps and foams. Once it's curdled, I scoop the curds into our tofu press—a simple box of blond wood, now stained with use and age, with a lining of fine cloth and holes along the sides for drainage. I weight the lid down with a brick. White milk squeezes out onto the plate below. While the tofu drains, Okā-san combs the cabinets for seasonings for the okara.

On the back of the stove, the millet has simmered long enough. The grain is soft and ready to mash. I wash out the suribachi and bend my arms to the task. Once upon a time, this would have been tiresome. But laundry duty has changed me. My arms are wiry, the flesh hardened and thinned by work and hunger. And yet, today I feel soft and light.

Once the millet cools enough, I pinch off bite-size pieces and roll them between my palms into balls. Okā-san has borrowed sugar from Tomihara-san. She will cook the red beans into a sweet anko paste to mix into a broth for the millet. I imagine Taro taking his first bite and picture a smile on his face. Will he feel my fingerprints on his lips? I blush.

"Get dressed, Hana; stop daydreaming," my mother says. "Go and fetch our guests!" She startles me out of my reverie.

My hair is damp with steam and hanging in my face, my fingers red with work, my cheeks flushed. Where is the delicate flower I imagined, gracefully inviting Taro to dine? Hopefully hiding beneath the mess of rumpled clothes and sleep deprivation I see in the mirror. I brush my hair brutally, splash cool water on my face, and pull on a clean school uniform. It hangs off of me, no longer the daily wear of a plump child.

"No," Okā-san says to me, wagging a finger when she sees how I look. "The chest by the window. Take my lilac kimono. This is a special affair."

A kimono. How long since I've worn one that was not a simple cotton yukata, something for the home? My mother helps me don the nagajuban underrobe with its long collar and sleeves, the soft sash that ties it at my waist. I fold the kimono collar in half, and she helps me slip it on. It's a luxury to pull the textured silk over my arms. She returns to cooking as I straighten my sleeves and tie the second sash after wrapping the kimono left over right and behind. My fingers fumble at the obi, but at last it is done. I wrap my hair into a bun at the back of my head.

"That is correct," Okā-san says upon inspection, but there is a smile in her eyes that more than approves. At this moment, if love were visible, the room would be full of pink light.

I bow at the waist. "Arigatō, Okā-san."

"Aie, go! Don't trip, and don't ruin my kimono!" She waves me away with a wooden spoon. I pull on my longest coat, take our largest umbrella, slip on my geta, and hurry out into the afternoon rain.

CHAPTER 40

TARO

Another day of rain. Taro sat in the barracks of a recently arrived unit, playing hands of menko and other childish games with the new boys. He didn't feel like playing. He shuffled a spare deck of cards in his hands over and over again, enjoying the feel of the cardboard lightly scraping against his palms like the wings of a moth, like eyelashes on cheeks. He had no business with the other pilots today. They were frustrated, but he was happy.

"I hear the Americans have come as far as Okinawa!" a young pilot named Ano was saying. "Okinawa! That's practically next door!"

"It *is* next door," Tomomichi groaned. "If we wait much longer, we won't need aeroplanes at all. We'll be stuck fighting hand to hand on the ground."

Taro smiled at something Hana had said yesterday after he played Miyagi-sama's masterpiece. *My father used to play that song. And I would dance, just so.* She had spun once on her geta, somehow keeping her balance on the tips of her shoes. He had played it again later, just to see if she would dance some more. But she was shy and did not.

"How long will we be cooped up here?" another boy complained. "I don't want to sit around. Let's go into town and see what there is to see."

"Not much," Tomomichi declared. Despite his frustrations, there was a certain cachet to being a senior pilot with this new group. "Still, you can try Tomiya Shokudo. She makes good egg custard. Anything you want."

The boys fell silent for a moment. "Do you think she knows how to make okonomiyaki?" Ano asked. "I haven't had it since I joined the academy. Oh, one last taste before I body-crash, and I promise I will take out a battleship all by myself!"

There was laughter then, and ribbing, and before Taro knew it, the boys were on their feet, grabbing hats against the rain and shuffling out the door. Even Tomomichi, who looked back at Taro and shrugged sheepishly. "I know I should stay," he said. "Forgive me. I do not go to celebrate. Only . . . it is raining. What can I do? You should join us."

Taro shook his head. "I'll stay and practice," he said.

"Right, 'practice.'" Tomomichi smirked. Then his face shifted. "Oh, no! Today's Sunday. No Nadeshiko to swoon over you. I guess you *will* just practice, after all."

"Like you said." Taro shrugged. "It's raining. What can I do?"

Tomomichi laced up his boots in the doorway. "Remember the academy, Home Sundays when we would go visit the local families and eat real home-cooked food?"

"I do," Taro said wistfully. "The closest thing to home since we left it."

"Yeah . . . Well, look, those guys might leave me behind."

"Give Tomihara-san my best," Taro said. He followed Tomomichi out the door, returning to their empty barracks.

The rain drummed heavily on the roof. Taro pulled off his boots and paced the length of the beds, once, twice, swinging his arms. He rubbed a hand over his face, scrubbing away rain and the persistent smile.

It was better this way, Tomomichi gone off with the others. Taro couldn't explain it, but he was a pot about to boil over. Every time he opened his mouth, the same word kept trying to leap out. He would say it or explode.

And if he said it, what kind of soldier was he? The sting of Commandant Asama's slap was fresh. He already knew there were rumors, bolstered by dirty looks, about the true reason his final mission had failed: cowardice. They thought he lacked moral fortitude. Even the engineers who had seen the problem with the fuel line had begun to regard him grimly under Asama's angry presence. Each time, it was as if he was back in flying school, another punch to the gut and smack to the head.

Taro reached into his cubbyhole for his violin. He hoisted it to his chin, set the bow, and played, fast and wild. Angry, a stallion foaming at the mouth, nostrils flaring, rampaging against the storm. He filled the barracks and the woods outside with military marches and anthems, his violin screaming. Beethoven followed Mozart, keening into the sky.

They doubted him. His moral fortitude. His devotion to his duty.

And, worse, he doubted himself. Each time that damn smile betrayed him, each time he swallowed the sound of her name.

The bow scraped across the strings and one snapped.

Taro shivered and lowered his arms. He wiped the sweat from his face and gently set his violin on the futon. Had he damaged it? Foolish. From the moment he'd limped his plane back into Chiran, he had been a fool. He should have gone with Tomomichi. Saké would do less damage than this senseless anger.

He drew a replacement string from the case. His palms were hot, his fingers burning as he restrung the violin. Strings were hard to come by; he should be more careful.

But what need did tokkō have of new strings? Perhaps it was just his love of the violin that was compromising his fortitude after all.

He set his instrument to his chin once more, vowing to play something gentle this time.

He had only drawn the first note when he heard the sound of an umbrella closing in the doorway.

Dressed in a long coat against the weather, Hana stood just outside the entrance, framed by leaves and raindrops.

"Forgive the intrusion," she said. "But it's Sunday, and it's raining. My mother would be honored to have you—and Tomomichi-san—to our house for lunch."

His bow hand twitched, sending a shiver of music up the strings. He blushed and lowered the violin. Had she heard him playing? The screeching snap of the string, the mark of an amateur?

"Good afternoon," he said belatedly. She dropped her eyes, not quite a bow. Taro tried to stand taller, as befitting an officer of the Imperial Army Air Force. "I'm afraid you've just missed Tomomichi."

"Ah," she said, wavering as if to leave. "Then . . ." She turned back to him. "Will you, Inoguchi-sama . . . ? Please say yes."

A breeze blew into the barracks, carrying the scent of wet pine.

"Yes."

Hana watched him carefully pack the instrument into its case. "I've been clumsy today, but I just put a new string on. Perhaps your mother would enjoy it," he rambled. His hands were shaking. His pulse jolted in his ears.

He patted his pockets as if he had forgotten something, then shook his head. "I am sorry, I have nothing to protect it from the rain." It would not do to get the case wet and risk damaging the violin inside.

"Don't worry about that. Let it stay. We will have to entertain you instead." She smiled. His heart tripped over itself.

"But I'm afraid I don't have any gifts for your mother. I . . . Perhaps I should stay, too.

"Oh, wait!" He ran to his footlocker and pulled out a length of blue silk, woven in a delicate pattern. "This was my graduation sash at Shōnen Hikōhei. I no longer need it, but it is very fine material. Perhaps your mother—"

"It is too much!" Hana exclaimed.

"It's just enough."

He held the umbrella over their heads as they made their way down the road into town. "That is the temple where Mariko and I played as children," Hana said. Was she as nervous as he was?

"And that is where I first learned to skip a rock." She pointed at the stream that ran through the town. "And here I got sick on green peaches one day because they looked so pretty and I didn't think a pretty thing could make me sick. My mother warned me, but I was a stubborn child."

Pretty things can make you sick, Taro told himself, glancing at the girl by his side. The day was cool, but he felt feverish.

"I can hardly believe it," he said. "You're so quiet at the base."

Hana blushed and leaned closer to him, as if the warmth of his body was a magnet to hers. "Quiet children are often stubborn. Were you quiet, too?"

"No. I'm afraid I was as loud as Nakamura, until I began playing the violin. Now it often speaks for me."

She smiled. "What a lovely voice." Taro blushed to the tips of his ears.

A gentle fog rolled in over the hilltops to the west, scattering more soft rain.

"May I ask you a question?"

"Yes."

"When it comes time to serve meals, you rarely enter the barracks. I have seen you inside only recently, and your face goes pale when you do. Nakamura says it's because you are a flower that craves the sun—"

Hana laughed. "Such a poet! Who knew?"

"But there is more to it than that, isn't there?"

Hana's footsteps faltered and grew still. She hesitated for a long time, her face in shadow. What cave had he made her enter just now?

"Before my classmates and I came to the base," she said, "we worked with the farmers outside of town. There was an air raid—the first ever in Chiran. We took cover in trench shelters we'd dug alongside the road. Mine collapsed. It was close to an hour before they found me and dug me out."

Suddenly, her gaze pulled away from the memory and flashed up at Taro's face. She blushed and dropped her eyes to hide her embarrassment.

"I'm sorry. That wasn't a nice story. Forgive me."

But Taro was pinned to the spot. "You thought you were dead."

She grimaced. "Hai."

A polite person would not ask any more questions. A polite person would nod and move on. He knew this, yet still he asked.

"What was it like?"

She looked up in surprise. "I'm sorry?"

"The moment when you thought you were dead?"

She glanced away, as if searching for an answer, a politeness.

"Please. Tell the truth."

She searched his face with eyes as deep as wells. He could not be sure in the rain, but it seemed there were tears there.

"How can I tell you? You are tokkō, and I am a fool."

"Hana . . ."

She turned away, leaving the shelter of the umbrella. Rain spattered onto her shoulders and hair.

"I know what I should say. That I thought of my parents, that I thought about their sorrow. Or my duty. That I worried over my friends."

Her cheeks were bright red now, but she continued quickly, as if running through thorns. "But I will tell you the truth, *because* you are tokkō and because you ask it of me."

She stepped closer, out of the rain, and looked him in the eye. It was unnerving, this girl who had so often bowed or hidden from view.

"I was glad. I had no burdens. I was done."

Like a sudden downpour, her deferential shyness returned. She looked away, her voice dropping. "Since then, life feels as if it is two steps away."

Taro took a deep breath, absorbing her words, her stillness.

"'No burdens.'" He tasted her words in his mouth and exhaled. "Life becomes very simple when you know you will die. It didn't seem appropriate to say so before now. That is what it means to be tokkō, too."

She was watching him from beneath the umbrella, searching his face again.

"Do you? Have burdens?"

Taro began to walk, and she kept pace. "I have a mother who will be sorrowful. And a father who will be proud. I will never master the violin, but that is a small enough loss."

"My father used to say one does not master an instrument, only befriends it."

Taro smiled. "Well, then! At least I can say we have been friends."

"Good friends," Hana replied, and Taro smiled wider.

"How long have you been playing?"

"Since I was five."

"And yet you are a pilot."

"My father said, 'The Emperor needs pilots, not musicians.'" He mimicked his father's stern tone.

"How very fatherly," she said.

Taro laughed.

"But I enjoy flying. Have you ever been in an aeroplane?"

"Only to decorate it with flowers." She grew quiet then, as if sorry she had said it. The specter of cherry blossoms on Ki-79 wings filled the silence.

"My father is a pilot," he said abruptly. "And an engineer. He used to take us up in his plane before the war. It's quite beautiful. All of Japan spreads out before you like a quilt, under the dome of a blue sky."

"You make it sound peaceful. The planes at the base are so loud, I never thought of it that way."

"It can be."

They fell silent for a while as they walked, and buildings rose up around them. They were nearing the center of town. Hana seemed to realize it and veered to the right, toward the rushing sound of the river.

"It will take a bit longer, but there is a very pretty walk along the riverbank. Will you take it with me?"

Warmth spread through Taro's chest. "Yes."

They cut across the wet field until they found the well-trodden path. The river rushed by below them, white cataracts and swirling pools dotted with fallen leaves. The air was clear and light, chilled by the mist rising from the water. They stopped, standing close together beneath the small umbrella. River noise surrounded them like a blanket. He could feel the heat of his shoulder against her coat, smell the damp warmth of her hair. Raindrops gleamed on her head like jewels. He closed his eyes and drank in her voice.

"Taro-san?" She said his given name for the first time. He

held his breath. "When did you first know you wanted to fly?"

A shiver ran through him. He thought back.

And shared everything.

The wings of the crane, white as snow . . .
The burning blue sky.

CHAPTER 41

HANA

A butterfly of sunshine twitches in my chest, bursts into a swarm.

I am on a high wire, teetering between this moment and the next.

Before he went to war, Otō-san told me that we live on in the memories of our loved ones. It is why we burn incense and leave gifts of food at the temples of our ancestors. It is why we sing songs from our ancient days. It is why, he said, he wanted me to remember him—the way his mustache tickled my cheek, the way his callused fingers guided mine over the koto, the way he laughed. And he would remember me the same way—my laugh, my hands, my mustache. That made me giggle, and he smiled. I will never forget that moment. Even if this war should do its worst, Otō-san will live in my memory and I will live in his until memory is no more.

And now there is Taro.

Tell me everything, I want to say. I will hold on to each word, each reminiscence. But it is too forward, too intimate. Perhaps I am just a silly little girl to him. What does a tokkō, even a young one, care if I promise to remember him—who he is, who he was, who he wanted to be?

I cannot ask for so much.

And yet, it is exactly what he gives me.

CHAPTER 42

TARO

"Konnichiwa, Hana! Good afternoon!" a girl called from the doorway of Tomiya Shokudo as Hana and Taro stepped into the street, but Hana did not respond. She was listening to him. Taro could hear Tomomichi and the others carousing inside. The present dropped like a theater curtain. The walk was over.

"I'm afraid I've bored you," Taro said. They had paused at the edge of a small stream that ran alongside the road through the center of town. A few carp swam beneath the surface, heedless of the rain. The swollen sky had darkened further, and he realized just how long he'd been rambling. He shook his head. "Forgive me."

"No," she said. "Your story is a gift . . . Thank you."

Her lashes were thick and dark against her skin. Like black butterflies.

A peal of thunder rolled across the sky.

"This is my house," she said suddenly. He looked up at the one-story building, leaning slightly to the right.

"So close to Tomiya Shokudo!" he realized aloud. They were neighbors. "Does the noise drive you crazy?"

"We've grown used to it." She opened the gate and led him to the front porch. "Please." Hana slipped off her geta and folded the umbrella as Taro struggled out of his boots. The door opened with a waft of savory scents.

"Okā-san, please meet Corporal Inoguchi Taro. Inoguchi-san, this is my mother, Benkan Hisa."

An elegant woman bowed before him, delicately dressed in a salmon-colored kimono adorned with white cranes in flight. Hana seemed to stand a little straighter as her mother rose from her bow.

"You are most welcome in our home," Hana's mother said. Worry creased her face—a face so like Hana's it was as if Taro was glimpsing the future. The same dark eyes, the same curved cheek. "I am sorry, was your friend unable to come?"

Taro bowed low. "I'm afraid so," he replied. "He will be sorry to have missed such hospitality." He rose and followed the women inside.

How strange to be in a real home again. To walk the tatami mats, to see a mother and daughter moving in symmetry. To see Hana, coat removed, no longer the schoolgirl in her monpé and blouse. She wore a daytime kimono of the palest purple, flowing with the same grace with which his own mother used to move. It made her look older, a gosling turned into a swan.

They bade him sit and poured green tea. He let the rich scent of the leaves envelop him, a perfume made sweeter by the setting.

The miso soup was delicious. "I made the tofu this morning,"

Hana explained. "Okā-san made everything else." She blushed.

The low table was covered in small dishes—steamed lotus root, sautéed okara with vegetables, red bean rice, and even millet dumplings with the sweetest red bean sauce for dessert—it was a celebratory feast. Taro ate each dish with a smile.

"It's delicious, Benkan-san," he assured her mother, who waved him away and seemed pleased.

"It has been two years since we've heard a man's voice in this house," her mother said, shaking her head. "I had forgotten how much they can eat!"

"Forgive me. The food on base is . . . Well, this tastes like home. My mother's unohana is much like yours," he said, pointing to the okara with vegetables. "And the millet dumplings! I've not had anko in ages."

Hana was beaming. But from her mother, there was more waving of the hands. "Hana, you brought home a polite one. When she told me she had friends on the base, I was afraid it would be like those hooligans over at the inn. Singing and shouting. No respect for the neighborhood. No respect for their own positions."

"That is not so!" Taro said hotly. He caught himself and was ashamed. "It's just that . . . It's very difficult. They are young. And war is a difficult thing."

The way her mother looked at him, he lowered his eyes, embarrassed.

"Forgive me, Inoguchi-sama," Hana's mother said. "I know it. It is I who am being too sensitive. Too unforgiving. I cannot treat these special-attack pilots as boys. You are heroes. I will remember that."

After that, Benkan-san rose to clear the dishes. "Hana, put on water for more tea," she said.

For a moment, Taro was alone. He closed his eyes, listening to the two women in the kitchen, more homesick than he had ever been.

Hana returned first. "It will be a moment," she apologized. "Perhaps . . ." She gestured for him to follow, and led the way into another room, where a koto lay in wait beneath a rich purple silk.

Hana stood back in the doorway as he approached it. "May I?" he asked. She nodded ever so slightly, and he lifted the silk away.

It was breathtaking. The wood a deep reddish tone that had layers of depth beyond those in his violin. The ivory bridges that lifted the strings were yellow with age. The air in the room seemed to sigh, or perhaps it was the koto—or Hana—breathing.

"Do you play?"

"I used to. It's my father's. We would play 'Haru no Umi' and 'Sakura Sakura.' They were our favorites, but now it lies still. Your violin kept it company."

He turned to look up at her. "This is a good place for instruments."

She shook her head. "It's just a room."

The faint hint of incense tainted the air. The presence of the altar, the photo of Hana's father in his uniform. The rain. This moment. A stillness that could not last. She would live, and he would die.

"Will you play for me?" he asked.

216

She stepped farther into the room, then hesitated, one foot still on the threshold. "I—"

"Hana!" her mother called. "I need you."

Hana turned. Taro would remember her this way, head turned, lips parted. "Coming," she said, and it was a whisper. She turned back, apologetic. Her dark eyes tugged at him. It was too much.

A soldier must be loyal to his duty.

"I should go," he said, and looked away. He drew the silk carefully over the koto and rose to his feet.

"Arigatō gozaimashita, Benkan-san," he called out to her mother. But the doorway was narrow. Hana had not moved.

He slipped past her, an excruciating closeness that they could not allow. He could feel her breath, damp on his throat, her skin, warm and smelling of rain. Where was his shining spirit, his moral fortitude?

"Taro," she said softly, so softly, drawing out his name. And then she was gone, into the kitchen, fetching the last of the bowls.

"Thank you for coming." Hana's mother was suddenly there, blocking the path to her daughter, a bundled furoshiki cloth in her hands. "It is only a little red bean rice, some dumplings and anko, but I hope you will enjoy it. We will remember you kindly," she added, turning him toward the door with her words.

Taro struggled into his boots, hopping awkwardly outside the door. The rain was still coming down, and he had no umbrella of his own. He slipped from under the awning, lost his balance, and soaked his sock in the gutter.

"Apologies. I almost forgot." He got his boot on at last and straightened himself up to something more respectable. "It is only a small token and inadequate compared to your hospitality." He reached into his jacket and drew out the folded graduation sash.

Benkan-san's eyes widened, then narrowed in professional appraisal of the cloth. Taro was surprised at the pleasure he took in seeing the older woman's face shift from mother to professional tailor.

"Ah! Such a fine piece of work. Too fine. It is too much when we have offered so little," she said, folding the blue fabric carefully and placing it on a low table inside the doorway. "Hana! Bring the ocha, please!"

A moment later, Hana padded out from the kitchen with a small earthen jar.

"And for you, Taro, and your friends, should they ever tire of beer and saké. Tea from the bushes behind our house. It is best drunk fresh, when the leaves are still tender and green. A tea for today, and today only."

She smiled, and if she had not, Taro would have sworn she was saying something more. She gave him directions for steeping and stood in the doorway to see him off down the road.

"Sayounara, Benkan-san," Taro managed, with a bow. His last sight was of the woman in her doorway like a sentry, and the pale shadow of her daughter beyond, the hallway a dark night, her face a distant moon.

CHAPTER 43

HANA

Okā-san is angry with me. She does not say so, but she is quiet this evening, bustling to and fro, gathering her things for the tonari-gumi ladies' meeting. Okā-san has given her offering—the tea—to Taro. Now she has banished me to the backyard to pick some more. Not an easy task in the rain.

I have abandoned my umbrella to keep it from tangling in the branches. The first few plants have been picked over. I have to go farther into the yard to find more of the best leaves. They stand out bright and soft against the gray, aging shrub. I pinch them off carefully. The rain carries their biting scent as I break them from their boughs.

The bowl in my hand is half as full as it should be, my harvest rising on a slow puddle of rain. I tilt out the water and keeping picking, but it is getting dark. Behind me, a single light shines in the window where my mother gathers her notes. She will need to shutter the windows soon. She keeps the records for fund-raising and will be reminding each household what they owe tonight. I will not shame her. I move along the hillside, picking and searching as I go. With every step, I think, *Taro, Taro, Taro.*

How does it happen this way? One moment, I am a frozen pond, and now I burn. Inviting Taro was my idea. But I had planned on inviting Tomomichi, too. It was the only way Okā-san would have allowed it. If she had known he'd be coming alone, she'd have worried. But she could not deny offering what solace she could to two boy pilots who were willing to die so bravely for us. It is not my fault Tomomichi was not there, although I had hoped he would not be. Taro. He was all I wanted. But I should have known, as soon as she saw us in the doorway, as soon as I introduced him to her, that it was dangerous. Too dangerous, like Mariko said.

Okā-san could read it in my face. Perhaps she could read it in his. I could not, not at first. I sat beside him, pouring tea and trying so very hard not to tremble. Trying to behave as a Nadeshiko, as a little sister would. And yet . . . one can sit across the room and still feel so close. How is it that our sentences tripped over one another, but were in essence the same?

"Hana!"

My mother is in the back doorway, peering into the gloom.

"Coming, Okā-san!" I gather my last pinch of tea leaves and make my way to the house.

"There you are! It's getting late. That's all?" she asks, peering into my bowl. She flaps a hand. "Oh well, it will do. I'll bring some tofu, too. Put those in a bag for me, yes? My sack is by the door."

"But, Okā-san, I am coming with you, am I not? To serve?"

Okā-san's mouth forms a line. "You have had enough revelry

for one day." Her face softens as she looks at me. "And you are soaked through! Where is the umbrella?"

"In the yard. I forgot it in my hurry."

"Yes, well, at least it is made for rain. Go fetch it and then dry yourself by the fire. It won't do to catch a cold. Mrs. Kawagoto's girl will manage on her own."

"Yes, Okā-san."

And so I find myself alone after sundown, wrapped in a warm yukata, combing my hair and listening through a slightly open window to the boy pilots at Tomiya Shokudo.

I wonder if Taro is with them. My mother kept me busy so I could not see which way he went. I like to think of him strolling back toward the air base, thinking of me. But it's too sad to imagine him lying alone in his bunk, staring at the ceiling, knowing what tomorrow may bring. No, it is better if he merely crossed the street to Tomiya's and is surrounded by the warmth of his friends.

A tentacle of jealousy curls around me. He will be there, laughing and smiling with Reiko and who knows who else. He will eat new food, drink new tea, and it will wash away the flavors my mother and I worked so hard to prepare. The tofu I made with my own hands. He will forget about me. How could he?

And this is when I understand my mother's warning. With attachment comes suffering. With joy, sorrow. With peace, war.

CHAPTER 44

TARO

Clack! Clack! Clack!

Taro stood in the rain, unsure of his next step, then he heard the familiar sound from his past. He followed it now just as readily as he had when he was a boy, through the garden gate and into the cool dimness of the Tomiya Shokudo. The shōji screens were pulled partially back to let in the evening air, the overhanging roof protecting those inside from the rainfall. The mouthwatering scent of roasting fish and the sound of laughter lured him inside.

Clack! Clack!

It seemed almost ridiculous, the loud snap of the old man's clappers in the dining room. The clappers had summoned no one but Taro—the rest of the audience was already in the room, having just finished the afternoon meal. Tomihara-san and her daughters had removed all of the low lacquered tables. Still, the old man snapped his clappers in a way that said they could not convince him to do otherwise. And it seemed to have an effect. The soldiers grew quiet, and in the back of the room, the old men of the village seemed to settle in with a collective inhale of anticipation.

"You came!"

Tomomichi's round face lit up, and he made room for Taro on the tatami beside him.

"Sweets! Sweets!" the kamishibai man cried. This one was even older than the kamishibai man from Taro's childhood. He was missing teeth and looked like a well-used piece of leather. Like a belt, Taro thought, creased by tightening.

A few of the boys dug into their pockets to purchase what candy the old uncle had. After a moment, Taro bought a handful as well. He would give some to Hana and the other girls at camp, if the little boys in the front row didn't eat them all first. They giggled and bowed, thanking him in deep, hoarse voices. One kept looking back at him, even as the first presentation began. He held up a small model Ki-27. Taro had to swallow hard. He used to be a skinned-kneed boy in shorts with a model, too.

"Kintaro!" Uncle Kamishibai cried, announcing the beginning of the children's story. Kintaro, the Golden Boy, was very much like Momotaro, except Kintaro was meant to be real. The son of a samurai, he did brave deeds that made his parents proud.

Only this time, the kamishibai's window did not show a brave boy in samurai dress. Tomomichi shoved an elbow into his ribs. "Oho! He's dressed like us, Taro!" It was true. Kintaro was dressed as a boy pilot. Around his head was a white band painted with a blood-red rising sun. Beside him, also in army khakis, were his mates—rabbits and dogs, all dressed like soldiers. And instead of the traditional boat, they were flying to the demon island in an aeroplane.

The boys in the front row cheered as Kintaro and his companions parachuted out of the sky. The old man sang a battle song, and the children sang with him, red cheeked and smiling. The little boy with the model plane flew it over his head making zooming noises. As the story ended with the defeat of the terrible white demons, everyone clapped, and the older children in the room rounded up their siblings to lead them off to bed.

"And now, the news from Tokyo," the old uncle said. This time, when he opened his candy drawer, he dug a bit deeper and offered a few dusty cigarettes for sale. Several of the townsfolk bought them. Taro had an entire pack in his bunk. He'd been planning on giving them to Nakamura as a mission gift, but had forgotten when the time came. Now he wished he'd brought them, with their better-quality tobacco, to share with the guests at the inn. Or perhaps he should burn them as an offering at the temple. Nakamura could enjoy them in the afterlife.

The colorful pictures of Kintaro and his rabbit buddies were replaced by an image of the Sea of Japan. Seven battleships sailed south—Japanese ships, defending the home islands.

The news was grim. There were no songs, no funny voices. At the end the old man replaced the last card with an image of the flag, and everyone in the room, Taro included, stood up and sang the national anthem. Taro felt his jaw tighten, his resolve set like cement around his heart. The world was getting closer. Time was coming to an end. He must be ready.

Like Kintaro. Like Momotaro. Like Nakamura.

Someone slid the garden door open wider, letting the

overheated air and stale scent of cigarettes rush out of the room. Taro looked out into the fading light. Reiko was there, and her sisters, and three other Nadeshiko besides, crouched on the edge of the veranda to make room for the soldiers.

It was then he realized how close he was to Hana. The Tomiya Shokudo garden shared a wall with her own.

"Taro, did you bring your fiddle?" Tomomichi asked.

"What? No . . . it's raining."

"Yoshimura here has the keys to the truck. Go fetch it. As long as it's raining, we're going to stay here and drink."

"Is that wise?" Taro asked, but Tomomichi was already lifting another glass of shōchū to his lips. Taro scanned the faces of the boys in the room. And the garden wall outside.

"Yoshimura, wait for me," he called, and followed the driver into the evening rain.

CHAPTER 45

HANA

I am drying my hair by the fire when I hear it over the drumming of the rain. The first strains of "Haru no Umi." On a violin. The sweet notes rise up from next door. Taro is playing for his friends. But why this song, as familiar to me as my own hand? The song of my childhood.

And then I know. He's playing for me.

Mother is across town at the tonari-gumi meeting.

The house is dark, and I am alone. With my father's koto.

I go to the parlor, let slip the silken drape, and open the window despite the rain. The koto is almost as large as I am, so I am careful, very careful when I carry her closer to the window. I shield her from the weather with my body. Slipping the picks onto my fingers, I kneel before her and adjust the ji, softly tuning away months of neglect. Taro's song pours through the window, rich and deep. I listen for the next bar of music, and begin to play.

Chiran listens. The town, the empty street, the raindrops, the clouded moon. The pine trees on their hill, the tea shrubs, picked and raw, the wind sawing through their branches. The sodden earth, the moldering bed of leaves, the temple with its new old monk and smell of ancient incense. The river, the mountains, the ocean, the island of Kyushu. Japan listens, and even my father must hear it, my mother in her meeting, over her notebooks, her numbers, her damp ocha leaves. Everyone must hear us playing, Taro and me.

The world is silent but for the two of us. Violin and koto. We play until the last strains of music fade.

The world waits in silence.

"Hana?" I hear his voice through the slats of the wooden fence.

"Wait," I say. I grab a blanket and umbrella and run outside. "I'm here."

I lean up against the weathered wood, slick with rain and moss, and wonder if that's his heart I hear beating, or my own.

"Hana."

So much in a simple name.

"Taro."

There is nothing else to say.

CHAPTER 46

TARO

Taro leaned against the soaked wooden wall and felt the slight pressure of her body against the other side.

He closed his eyes against the pain of perfect belonging.

CHAPTER 47

HANA

And, just like that, the rain stops.

My heart breaks, even as it blooms.

CHAPTER 48

HANA

Some moments should have no after. The whole of creation should stop and let them linger. Time should not embarrass itself by moving forward, bringing only pale imitations of a perfect night.

Perhaps Okā-san understands this. And that is why, when I step onto the back walkway and slide open the screen to the second room, she says nothing. Merely sits in the dark, her shawl still draped across her shoulders, wrapped in the scent of the rainy night. She says nothing. Only watches as I hesitate, remove my shoes on the walkway, slide the shōji shut, and fall to my knees, prostrate.

I don't know if I'm crying or laughing. Perhaps I make no sound at all.

If she asks me to explain myself, I won't. I couldn't. If she raises her voice in reprimand, or even moves to light a lamp, I will break apart, I'll shatter.

Perhaps she knows this, my mother.

For she says nothing.

And, after a moment, I rise, shamefaced, and rush off to bed.

There is a knot in the pit of my stomach. And a light inside my chest that shines.

I can hear her moving in the other room, putting things away. Opening and closing drawers, sighing as she tidies the house.

This is the quiet music that lulls me to sleep, eventually. A sleep I hope I never wake from, so the dream will not end.

Because some moments can never have an after, no matter how much we want what might have been.

CHAPTER 49

TARO

Taro walked along the river until it could no longer lead him back to base. He retraced the path he had traveled with Hana, pausing at each tree or rock she had pointed out to him. Where she had eaten too many unripe peaches. The temple where they used to play as children. Her junior high school leaned against the slope on the road above.

Taro hesitated. Carving away from the road, he climbed the hill to the temple, his violin case clutched in one palm. If the monk was awake, perhaps they would speak. Taro would light some incense and ask him to deliver a letter to his mother. Or to Tomihara-san—many of the boys gave her their true last letters. Ones the army censors would never blacken or redact. So their families received two notes—one, a jisei showing an acceptable face, the other a farewell from a son about to die.

Taro had not written anything. On his first mission, he had been too unsure of what to say. But now he knew what his jisei would be. He only had to write it down.

The temple entrance stood on an angle up the steep hill.

Taro stepped beneath the carved wooden gate. To his right lay a garden. To his left, the heavy weight of the temple, shaped into curls and flourishes like the Buddhist depictions of the heavens. No lights were on. He would not wake the priest tonight.

He bowed to the temple and entered the garden.

Over the little bridge above the koi pond, beneath the bower of bamboo fronds. Leaves dropped lazily from the trees overhead. He did not know what kind they were. He found himself wishing he knew. Hana would know.

The benches were too wet to sit on. Instead, Taro placed a hand on the stone lantern gracing the corner of the little bridge. Stone was permanent, eternal. He wished a piece of him would pass into the stone, would look down the hill toward Hana, watching over her as she lived ten, twenty, a hundred years without him.

"That's what I wish," he told the stone, and the stone listened. "Please. Give to her what will be taken from me. Let her live a hundred years."

I do not fear death
It grows late and I tire
But look—a flower!

CHAPTER 50

HANA

I wake up.

The futon is smooth and hard beneath me. The coverlet lies heavy on my body. Throwing back the sheet brings a shock of cold air. It's morning, like a hundred other mornings, and my body knows what to do, even if my spirit is wandering.

I wash my face, brush my hair. Dress. I light the kitchen fire and make tea, leaving a cup for Okā-san, who is in the next room doing who knows what.

There are two eggs today, from the farmer who brought in Tomihara-san's kimono. The new pants are almost finished. The eggs are the beginning of a payment plan.

I scramble one lightly and cook it with a bit of onion I find in the root vegetable basket by the back door. A cup of cold rice turns it into breakfast. My body eats. My mouth sips tea. My mother joins me.

We say nothing. She does not ask after my health. My voice will not rise to ask after hers.

I wash the bowls, finish my tea, and take a shawl from the

rack by the front door. Mariko is already coming down the road. It's too early for the truck. And I am in no mood for Sachiko's prattle. So I bow to my mother and ask Mariko to walk with me to the base for yet another day of waving goodbye.

But it's not just another day, is it?

Fortunately, my body does not know this. It walks down the road, away from the samurai houses and the rushing river, up the sloping hill, and onto the air base. The darkness helps make this possible. Perhaps I am sleepwalking. When the dream ends, I will wake up.

Kaori-sensei is waiting at the gate when we arrive. We bow, and I let Mariko speak for us. She has been speaking this whole way, I think. My ears have been listening, but my soul is not present to hear her.

When the other girls arrive, we all take the slow walk to the runway. The sky is paling now, as if it's received bad news.

The aeroplanes are already on the tarmac, dim shapes on the black runway. And the pilots are already present, standing before a small table where Commandant Bulldog barks a speech about war and fortitude and Japan.

I would kill him, if I were able. I would shake him until his head fell off, and I would shout into his neck to stop this war.

But that's my spirit talking. My body bows, a smile already shaping on my lips. It knows its duty, even when my soul does not.

We have no cherry blossoms today. Between the rain and the early departure, nature and time have conspired against it.

Instead, we Nadeshiko will be the flowers, pink-pinched cheeks and bright faces lining the branch-black runway.

There are no parents here this morning, no mournful wives. Only Tomihara-san, and two of the women from the mura. Dawn departures are hard, but she has never failed.

A clatter of geta announces a newcomer, someone who does not know the mournful pace of the tokkō farewell. A family member, after all, I suppose.

"Hana!" Mariko whispers urgently, tugging at my sleeve.

I turn.

Okā-san is coming down the path. She wears her best kimono and holds a bundle in her hands.

She sees me. We see each other, but I don't know what to say. Instead, I watch her take her place with the other tonari-gumi members, and I return to my duty. I watch the boys drink a toast to Japan from tiny ceramic cups. I smile.

The boys thank Tomihara-san first, bowing deeply before her and the tonari-gumi women. My mother is no longer with them. Mariko shuffles aside, and my mother comes to stand beside me. I feel ill. After so many goodbyes, all more or less the same, I don't know what's happening. The rhythm has been broken, like a snapped koto string. Jangling, ruining the song.

Still, I smile. I am Nadeshiko. I am Japan. I am in control.

And then Taro is there, standing before me in his flight suit, violin in his hands, deep brown eyes on mine. And my soul comes slamming back into my chest like a fist. I gasp. My smile fails.

Okā-san is the first to speak.

"Corporal Inoguchi-san, it has been an honor. Please accept this poor offering as thanks."

She unravels the bundle and holds it out to him across both hands.

It's a hachimaki, the helmet-scarf once worn by samurai. A white headband, like the one Sachiko so boastfully gave to Nakamura with the Rising Sun dyed red with her own blood. Only this sun is an appliqué of richly woven silk, carefully stitched to the center of the linen cloth with rays of red light streaming to the edges.

She must have worked all night.

I bow to my mother as he accepts her gift. He removes his flight cap, and she helps him tie it on.

"If you have a message for your mother, I will see that she receives it," she says.

He feels around in his pocket and gives her a small envelope—his letter, his jisei, and perhaps a lock of his hair.

It's all I can do not to tear it from her grip and throw it away. I want to burn it, to destroy it, to destroy the very reason it exists.

But there is no use denying what comes next.

He steps up to me.

"Hana-chan," he says, the term of endearment clear. My body flushes hot, then cold, then hot again. His voice is warm and rough as sunlit trees. "You gave my violin a good home once. I hope you will do so again."

I can't look at him. I can't do this. I can't say goodbye.

"No, Taro-chan. Please. Keep it with you." I look up through tears I can't hide. "Listen for my koto. Play to me from the other side."

And there it is, that face I couldn't see beyond the fence last night. Beneath the red-and-white hachimaki, his brow furrows. His jaw clenches, holding back emotion. But his eyes hold nothing back. I will never forget his eyes.

He swallows hard, a lifetime of things that he will never say. That I will never say.

He drops into a bow. I do the same, my hair brushing the top of his flight cap. I clasp my hands to my stomach to keep from reaching for him. To keep my heart from falling out.

And then we rise.

"Sayounara," he whispers. And I conjure a smile.

He mounts the steps to heaven.

And the girls wave.

Goodbye.

CHAPTER 51

HANA

There are no miracles. No fat fireflies bumbling into the barracks. No ghostly violin.

When I go home that night, I play my father's koto until my fingers are sore. I play as if each note is a knot in the thin barbed wire that is holding me together.

My mother listens in another room, so I cannot see her weeping.

CHAPTER 52

HANA

The first day is the hardest. Waking to a world of doubt, unsure if the ride to base will be cruel or kind. Did our brothers successfully body-crash yesterday? Will he be standing there in the shadowed hall of the barracks, head hung in shame? Or perhaps he will feel no shame because he'll be here with me.

I was alive for fifteen years and dead only a few weeks before Taro brought me back. It is hard to shut off the tendrils of light I've begun to feel. To will myself back into death. But I try. The truck bounces up and down the track, moaning its way to the truth.

We strip the beds (his bed); we wash the sheets (his sheets). We light incense on a flat stone behind the barracks, and even Sachiko is silent. Of all the days to have no news. I would flatten her face with my fist if I could. But it's not her fault. The sea was cloudy, the escort pilots complained. A thick marine mist rolled up out of nowhere. They have nothing to report.

———

Days later, we learn two American ships were damaged. Neither was destroyed. Is it better to be a glancing blow than a missed one altogether? The new batch of pilots behave as if it is a great victory, carousing at Tomiya Shokudo, hoisting cups of shōchū and chanting their toasts to the new unnamed gunshin. Eight planes departed. Which ones struck true?

———

"Wondering will drive you mad," my mother says one day. It's another Sunday, and we are hanging newly washed officer uniforms out to dry in the sun. The higher-ranking staff like to have their government-issued clothing tailored to flatter. Washing is the first and last step in ensuring the best fit.

"I know, Okā-san. But I don't know how to stop."

Okā-san carefully drapes khaki trousers over the drying rack, then comes to me. Her hands are warm and damp when she takes hold of mine.

"Hana, it is both simple and hard. We continue. One foot, then the other. Just as we have since your father went away."

I have not thanked my mother for attending Taro's farewell. Sufficient words have not been invented for what I feel. Instead, I try to be a better daughter than I have been these past months. I try to be helpful, to listen. To attend in my own way.

I listen now and proffer a bow.

"'Fall seven times, get up eight,'" I quote the old saying.

She pats my hand, her palms firm and sure. "Exactly so."

CHAPTER 53

HANA

We are climbing the hill to the barracks when a roar like thunder shatters the birdsong and fills the cloudless sky.

American bombers fly overhead, darkening the air, and I am back in that sweet potato field. Only there is no old woman to grab my hand and rush me toward a fatal trench. Instead, Kazuko and Mariko shove and push us all into the trees. I find myself pressed against a stand of bamboo as thick and sturdy as the staves we use for self-defense.

A concussion of air. Black earth explodes. Again and again, bombs drop, like the pounding notes of a military march. A chorus rises of screams and prayers.

I close my eyes and listen for the violin that will lead me to him.

"Hana? Hana, it's over now," Mariko whispers.

I open my eyes.

Dust in the air. The thrum of engines moving east. I am still alive.

Kaori-sensei claps her hands, and we assemble as best we can in the bamboo forest. "Girls, girls! Sound off. I need to know everyone is here!" She calls out our names, and we respond. She asks if we are injured. Mariko has a splinter—she used her sewing scissors to carve a prayer into the bamboo—but otherwise we are fine and accounted for.

"Ah, well, that is good," Kaori-sensei says, relief in her voice. "Now we must assess the damage."

"How did they know where to find us?" Sachiko cries out, her voice pitched high with panic. "We were beneath the trees!"

"I do not know," Kaori-sensei says gravely.

But the reason is evident when we climb the hill.

The damp spring winds are blowing more warmly, and the branches that cover the barracks roofs have gone dry. Sensei does not reprimand us. Our duty has gone unnoticed by everyone. It is only luck that we have survived and the barracks are unharmed.

We set about gathering fresh boughs to rectify our mistake and then do the work of dusting each other off.

But something has changed.

Perhaps the army no longer has the stomach for it. Or the Chiran ladies' association has seen one too many smiling farewells. Or my mother has had a word with the right officer.

We are pulled from tokkō duty the next day. Reiko comes by to spread the word. Tomorrow we will wear our monpé and middy blouses again, but we are to report to the school that is now a hospital. The Nadeshiko Tai will become nurses.

CHAPTER 54

TARO

Taro flew.

Sunlight on windscreen. Engine rattle. Green fields. The final circle over the peak of Kaimondake. The farewell waggle of the escort planes' wings as the battleships came into view. The taste in his mouth like gravel as his mind switched from seeing to calculating, sighting the sweet spot on his target as the rest of his unit did the same. The small faces of American sailors turning to look up in fear. The clench in his stomach, a fist that held his fortitude in place. The bump of his violin case, jarred loose from where it was wedged beside him.

The sudden scream of interception.

Mustang wings and bullets.

Taro reached for his trigger, but found none. This was not a fighter plane. It was a bomb.

The gas line ruptured. Hydraulics failed. He fell out of the sky, topsy-turvy, unable to see the fleet, to even crash onto one of its decks, anything to make his death a strike against the invasion. He was going to die in the sea—

A sudden fog, the marine layer dense, blinding. Then gray water, a strip of golden white sand. A tiny islet, a narrow beach, barely more than that.

New instincts took over. A struggle to control the aeroplane, lift the nose, lower the flaps.

Sparks on sand.

Ruptured spray of pungent fuel.

Taro slammed into the earth in a clap of thunder and lightning.

His war was over.

CHAPTER 55

TARO

"Sir! Sir! We've got you!"

Sea spray. Aeroplane fuel. Smoke.

He was alive.

CHAPTER 56

TARO

"Sir! Sir!"

Taro tried to sit up, his lips forming the word *yes*. The scorch of disinfectant. The ache of bones. The scent of death.

"Whoa, whoa. Lie back down. This is serious business!" A light pressure on his chest, and the world exploded, falling into blackness.

───

"Inoguchi Taro, Corporal, Imperial Air Force," Taro confirmed through parched lips. He was sitting up now, propped against the wall of a weather-beaten hospital tent. The canvas was rotting. The air, deeply humid.

"Good. You understand there's paperwork to file before we can let you go. Normally I'd let it slide, but, well, we have to be sure. Where you were spotted is so close to the American fleet, you might be a spy."

The doctor was a jovial little man with a soft, square face

and horn-rimmed glasses. He should be fat, Taro thought. There was a comfortableness to him that an extra thirty pounds would solidify. But the war had made him thin.

Just as the war had made Taro a joke.

"Thrown back by the sea," the doctor muttered over his clipboard. "I wouldn't believe it if your accent wasn't perfect and those fishermen hadn't vouched for you. They say you lit up the beach like a signal fire. Somehow, they got you out before the flames reached you. Wibaru and his family have had a fish camp on that spit of land for generations. Lucky for you we get fish from them. Lucky for you they were even out today. The gaijin are so close, even our fishermen aren't safe.

"Imagine our surprise when the catch of the day was tokkō!"

The man liked to talk. Taro didn't mind. It gave him something to focus on, instead of the drifting sensation. He was a leaf twisting in the wind. A boat without an anchor.

"That thousand-stitch belt really did its job," the doctor continued, and handed Taro his senninbari. A thousand red Xs hand stitched by a thousand women. His mother standing at the temple, at the train station with fabric and thread, to keep him safe. It was cut up the middle now, sliced clean by surgical scissors. The white cloth now bloodstained and blackened with smoke. Taro ran his hands over the little red bumps.

"A concussion. A few broken ribs," the doctor explained. "We had to cut the belt off you to bind them." He turned for a moment, scooping something off a rolling metal stand.

"I'm sorry to say your hachimaki didn't make it."

The white strip of cloth with its embroidered red sun was a blackened husk, nearly unrecognizable. Taro reached for it, but the doctor tossed it aside. Taro's hand dropped into his lap. It was for the best. He should hold on to nothing. Not the head-band, nor the memories it carried.

"Pretty lucky, all in all," the doctor surmised. "If you weren't tokkō."

Taro's eyes suddenly stung. His violin had likely burned with the plane. But the belt had survived, and he along with it. He should never have worn it.

"What about the rest of the unit?" he asked, his throat froggy.

A look flashed across the doctor's face. The man's mouth tightened. He glanced at Taro, then back down at the chart.

Judgment. Taro was a coward in his eyes. Or a spy.

"Really, I couldn't say," the doctor replied.

First Nakamura, and now Tomomichi. Everyone.

"I should be dead," Taro whispered.

"What's that? Yes, you should be!" The doctor handed him a glass of water. The efficient brightness was back. "It's the damnedest thing. Well, sit tight, and I'll see if I can get any answers. If you check out, we'll get you on a transport to the nearest base. I know you're eager to get a new plane."

"And if I don't 'check out'?" Taro asked. The water had helped. His voice was stronger. But his hand shook as he placed it on the tray beside his cot.

The doctor shrugged. "Well, I'd say prison camp, but more likely we'd just shoot you here. It's a crazy thing, to come through a crash like that unscathed, only to be shot as a spy. Or a traitor. Let's hope I can get that confirmation."

He strode away, the bald spot at the back of his head staring at Taro like a disapproving eye.

CHAPTER 57

TARO

"What's that you're humming?" The old fisherman rowed hard, putting his back into it.

After a month in hospital, Taro was heading back to duty at last. Or so he hoped. With the enemy controlling the waters around the southern islands, they were forced to take a round-about route. Kyushu was weeks and miles away. Taro sat uselessly in the bottom of the boat, sand flies nipping at his ankles, the itch of white sand and flaking paint where the gun-wale pressed into his back. He shrugged and fell silent. There was nothing to sing about, no violin to play, and yet there was music ringing constantly in his head.

The old man frowned, squinting against the glare.

"I've rowed many young men to their death," he growled in his heavy Okinawan accent. "But you're the first who has been unable to catch it."

He laughed like a barking fox. "When my son found you, I said, 'Throw him back!' Too much trouble for this old man. But we were afraid they'd find your wreckage on our little beach and wonder why we did nothing. So here you are, sad as can be. Ha! I say life is a gift. If the gods want you to keep it, they must have a reason."

Taro had thought that himself, for a moment. But that was lunacy, desperation. Hope. It was not Bushido. "I am tokkō," he said firmly. "My life is already gone."

The old man smirked, shifting his grip on his left oar. "That why you're so heavy? I'm rowing a dead man? What does that make me? Jizo-sama, I guess," he said. Jizo was the ferryman for the dead.

"Or maybe I'm that old bitch Sodzu-Baba. I might make you give me that pretty hat of yours as payment," he leered. Sodzu-Baba was said to live on the banks of the river between life and the afterlife, demanding payment from the dead in coin or in clothing. Taro had no coins to give. He would see that the next base offered the old man something. Though what value was the life of a twice-failed tokkō?

Taro turned his face toward the water, watching the distance to shore steadily close. For a terrible moment, he wondered, *What if I am dead?* What if this was indeed Hell, and the old man was Jizo himself, ferrying Taro across Sanzu-no-Kawa, the River of Three Crossings, the river of the dead? What if he was doomed to chase his death in the afterlife, to always think he had failed. Perhaps that was his punishment for not body-crashing when he should have. For thinking, even for those few days, that another life might have been his. That Hana might have been his.

"Keep rowing, old man," Taro found himself growling back. He would gladly chase his death across the Sanzu River and the seven seas in payment for those eight short days. And when he had finally paid his debt, he would fade away to nothingness, and that empty state would be bliss.

———

"Corporal Inoguchi Taro reporting for duty, sir!" Taro snapped to attention. The humidity inside the base headquarters was overwhelming. The walls bamboo instead of plaster, the roof thatched instead of shingled. Even the uniform he wore was borrowed and had seen better days, but at least he felt like a soldier again.

Until the commanding officer looked up from his desk, his eyes distracted, his skin sallow.

"No planes," the CO said.

"Sir?"

"You want a plane. We don't have any. And if we did, there'd be no fuel. The best I can do is get you on a transport boat to the mainland. See what they can do for you." He consulted a schedule on his desk. "It's going to be a while. We've got bigger worries than getting you back home."

Thrown back by the sea. The doctor had been right. The fisherman had been right. This was Hell after all.

Taro bowed to the CO and stepped into the heat of the day.

Old Wibaru had dropped him near a spotting station on an island whose name he could not remember, where a small group of soldiers manned an outlook on the single mountaintop, armed with a portable radio antenna and sharp binoculars. He'd caught a ride with their dispatch messenger on a motorboat to a two-peaked island, where the supply sergeant scared up a tropical uniform for him—khaki shorts that went to the knee, brown shoes a half size too big, and a tunic that billowed about the waist when he tightened the belt.

"We're plumb out of aviation insignia," the man had said wryly. "But I can draw an aeroplane on your sleeve if you'd like."

The man had meant it as a joke, but shame had burned Taro's face. Perhaps he should have killed himself when the old fisherman had left him in the shallows of the island. He could have walked into the ocean and let his body be devoured by the sea.

But Command was expecting him. He was still of use to the Empire.

Or so he'd hoped. Now he wasn't so sure.

CHAPTER 58

HANA

"There she is! The flower of Chiran!" Second Gunnery Sergeant Taiko croons as I enter the room.

June is fast approaching, bringing heat and the welcome comfort of routine to our work at the hospital. What was once an upper-grade classroom is now a dormitory for soldiers recovering from surgery. Taiko-san had shrapnel removed from his right leg and lost two of his fingers. He will be maimed for life, he says, but for now he is surrounded by pretty young women and likes to pretend he is in a hero's afterlife.

"What nectar do you bring today, fair Hana?"

I no longer blush when he says such things. Taiko-san is not the first soldier to hide his pain with bluster. I switch my tray to my hip and reach for one of the small cups it holds.

"I have your pain pills here, and if I may set this on the edge of your bed, you can have the sweet nectar of water to wash it down."

Taiko-san sighs dramatically. Without his fingers he has been unable to shave. His tanned face is scruffy. We Nadeshiko have offered to help, but I agree with his assessment of our skills with a straight razor: "You haven't even seen your fathers shave in years!" he cried when Mariko and I saw he could not manage on his own. "Why would I trust these good looks to such unskilled hands?"

There is a barber in town, an elderly man who is popular with the officers. Kaori-sensei says she will talk to him and convince him to visit soon.

Taiko grimaces as he swallows his pills. "Ah, sweet bliss! Thank you, Little Flower," he says with a sigh. A change comes over his face, dulling the edges as the soporific sets in. "No wonder the Germans surrendered," he murmurs. "They didn't have blossoms like you!"

I bow my head, unable to imagine the fate of schoolgirls in Germany since the terrible announcement came two weeks ago. Their Führer is dead. Their army destroyed. American and British tanks roll through their streets and villages. First Italy and now Germany have fallen. Yet Japan fights on.

I look at Taiko-san's missing fingers, the hand clutched to his chest like a fist. He is half asleep, but still joking. His spirit is stronger than the medicine he takes.

"Next time . . ." he says, waving his good hand in the air, "bring some peaches . . . Heavenly food is best for heroes."

Beside Taiko-san, a new patient watches us with mild eyes. His chart says his name is Captain Sato Toshiro. He has a broken leg. The sheet has slipped from his cot, showing his cast.

"Fall seven times, get up eight," I tell him, rearranging the coverlet.

He takes my hand. I recoil, but he is gentle, neither pulling me toward him nor gripping too tightly. It forces me to look him in the eyes.

The sunlight from the window brightens his irises into deep brown pools. His lips move, shaping a silent word.

Arigatō.

For some reason, this catches at my heart. I nod a swift bow and pull away.

When I finish dispensing medication, Mariko is in the hallway waiting for me. She clutches a note in her hand.

"Oh, Hana! There you are! Come with me." She takes my hand and leads me to a storage closet. Checking the hallway for unwanted eyes, she pulls me inside. The smell of disinfectant is overwhelming, and the room is close, but I know it's only for a moment. The first of these secret councils sent me into a panic. Such a small space. I expected the walls to fall in on me. But my heart failed to race. My pulse failed to quicken. Instead, I suffered the stench of bleach and musty mops. My claustrophobia must have left me for good the day we were bombed at the base. With no place safe, why fear anything at all?

"Look!" She unfolds the note and spreads it out between shaking hands.

Another love poem from the young captain in Room Six. He and Mariko have been making eyes at each other ever since he woke from his fever. "A case of malaria," the doctors had said. Thanks to quinine and Mariko's insistence that he looked "just like the actor Fujita Susumu," he was recovering well. Well enough to start courting, as it turns out.

"Daisuke-san has asked me to wait for him!" Mariko all but shrieks. "Hana, my heart is pounding! I feel faint."

I smile at my friend. "Mariko, you sound like Sachiko. What's happened to my sensible friend?"

"Oh, Hana, she's in love! And he's not a farmer! If I marry a captain in the army, who knows what life will bring?"

Her voice paints pretty pictures of long cars and fancy dinners. Warm, sunlit eyes and a whispered word. I shake the image away. I can see the underbelly of that dream.

"Mariko, look around. This hospital is full. Even the tokkō flights leaving the base have dwindled."

"What are you saying?" She frowns, hearing my words but not listening.

"Please don't make any promises. At least not until the war is over."

She folds up her love poem and puts it into the pocket of her apron. "Is it so wrong to be in love, Hana? I should think you of all people would know it's what makes this war bearable." She bites her lip, but it does not stop the sudden flow of her tears.

I bow my head in shame. "I want you to be happy, Mariko. For as long as you live. Not just for a week, or a day."

"Well . . ." She wipes her face on her sleeve and snuffles a little. "I suppose that's reasonable." She straightens her apron, and my Mariko is back. "But try to be happy, Hana. Don't be afraid of a little hope."

She opens the closet door a crack, looking both ways, and we slip back into the stream of life.

That night, as I kneel before my father's koto, fingers plucking the length of the dragon body, I play a song for Mariko and her captain. And one for blustery Sergeant Taiko. This is my routine now; the way other girls brush their hair one hundred strokes, I play nightly, and my mother listens as she finishes her evening's work. I play happy songs, folk tunes, love songs—anything but military marches. And though I tell myself, *This one is for Mariko,* or *This one is for Taiko-san,* I find myself hoping someone else is listening, even from the other side of life.

CHAPTER 59

HANA

There will be a special broadcast at noon today, Imperial Headquarters announces on the radio. "The Jeweled Sound of His Imperial Highness" himself. Neither I nor anyone I know has ever heard the Emperor speak. It can only mean one of two things—peace, or gyokusai.

The days have grown hot and humid as summer dampens the air. Now anticipation chills us to the bone. Noon comes and we are all on pins and needles, Nadeshiko, patients, and doctors alike. We crowd around a radio one of the doctors has rolled into the break room. The divine voice of our Emperor fills the room. We are breathless.

The transmission crackles and pops, the formal Japanese archaic and hard to follow. He speaks of "extraordinary measures" and a "new and most cruel bomb." When he is finished, we wait for the radio announcer to clarify.

It is August 15, 1945. After fifteen long years, the war—first in China, then against the West—is over. And we have lost.

Some of the doctors shout in anger. The nurses clap hands

over their mouths or weep. We Nadeshiko look at one another in confusion. As word leaks into the wards, the soldiers translate the message a dozen different ways.

"Extraordinary measures means it's come to gyokusai," Taiko-san tells me. "The Americans will invade. We must fight to the death. Even you, Little Flower. I hear you practicing in the yard with your schoolmates. This is good. I can no longer hold a stave, but you will kill two soldiers for me, yes?"

"For you, I will kill three," I say with a smile. My Nadeshiko skills no longer falter, but I am afraid. It seems so long ago that Mariko worried about marrying a farmer and I wondered if we would live to turn sixteen. My birthday is two weeks away. Can we survive what comes next?

CHAPTER 60

TARO

"It's over!"

Word spread fast across the little outpost. Three men had come running down from the radio truck with the news. The commanding officers had disappeared into the Quonset hut office, shoulders hunched, faces grim. Taro joined a cluster of men outside the barracks.

"The Emperor himself just announced it!" one of the radio-men said, impressed. "The war is over!" he declared again. "The transmission was rough, and the Emperor has a high way of talking, but it's done. We're through!"

"No," said a second radioman. "He said it was time for 'drastic measures.'"

He was young, Taro thought, a boy, really.

They were probably the same age.

"Drastic measures. That means gyokusai, doesn't it?" the boy asked. He was sweating, but it wasn't just from the run.

Taro's mouth went dry. These men would line the beach with whatever weapons remained—guns half empty of bullets, military-issued swords patterned with rust by the humidity, staves of wood and bamboo. All across the home islands, men, women, and children would hoist their pitchforks and kitchen knives, their homemade spears, hardening themselves to be the last rock upon which the Americans would dash their army.

His mother, with her callused hands.

His father, in a limping silver plane.

Hana.

Hana.

Hana.

He had failed.

He had failed to save them all.

CHAPTER 61

HANA

Fathers have returned from war, blown in with the curling leaves of autumn. But not all of them. Many died. And the ones who have come home are not the same. Mariko's father lost the use of an arm and an ear. Sachiko's father is whole on the outside, but his anger is bigger than his skin. Her mother bears the brunt of its presence. Sachiko has lost her silliness since his return.

There was no gyokusai, no valiant last stand on the beach. Only this—a tired military stumbling home again and a sinking feeling that never seems to end. The West is in the East now. Our fathers, who should have been hailed as heroes, are instead defeated men.

And my otō-san. He came home on a warm day in September with loose teeth and a head balding from malnourishment, the result of having only a week's worth of rations for a months-long campaign. Infantry is not kind to soldiers. His unit was told to grow their own food on the battlefield, my mother tells me later in a whisper. My otō-san is not a warrior, nor is he a farmer. He is a tailor from a small town. Yet he survived.

For a day and a night, he wept in my mother's arms. I could hear her comforting him through the shōji screens to their room. He spoke of starvation, abandonment, and darker things I was careful not to hear. In the morning, he was a skinny older man, but still my otō-san.

Now he wears his smile like a bandage, a sling for what is broken and may not mend. I smile too, let my Nadeshiko grin be a splint to help him walk tall again. It's my turn to dig in the earth, to pull him back into the light. I play the koto for him until he can play it again himself. Now there are two musicians in the house. I play every night. Sometimes he joins me.

Each day, there is news of arrests on the radio, of soldiers and officers "purged" as criminals. The Emperor has been allowed to keep his Chrysanthemum Throne, but he has surrendered his divinity. As if one can simply agree to no longer be a descendant of Heaven. This is the new world we find ourselves in. The Emperor is merely a man. His generals and admirals are on trial for crimes against peace, against humanity, for crimes of war.

I do not understand the accusations the Americans and their allies are levying in these trials.

Imperially sanctioned rape, murder, and torture in foreign places.

Otō-san was in a foreign place.

Where is the shining war of the boy pilots, bright buttons, and fresh faces full of *Yamato-damashii*? When I looked at a tokkō, I saw Japan. I *was* Japan. Now I look around and I'm not sure what I see.

In whispers, I ask Okā-san what it means.

Okā-san turns off the radio with a resounding click. She touches my cheek, something she has not done since I was a child, and she tells me, "The war is over, Hana. We will not speak of this again."

CHAPTER 62

TARO

A thin sheaf of papers, some money for a train. That was the way the war ended for Corporal Inoguchi Taro. The Japanese at the base in Kyushu looked haunted, weary. They processed his discharge under the watchful eyes of foreign men.

The home islands were overrun with loud, stinking Westerners. They were everywhere. Oni on the islands—his islands. His home.

As soon as he was able, Taro donned civilian clothes. He was not a soldier. He didn't deserve to be a soldier.

It was a strange feeling, then, to disembark at the station where he had seen his father off to war as a little boy. Where his mother had said goodbye for the last time, months ago. He had chased his death all the way back to Kyushu, and now he had followed it home.

A cold wind blew across the platform, carrying the scent of winter. From the next car, a group of men in white hospital robes wheeled and hobbled their way off the train. Taro averted his eyes. How could he face men who had sacrificed their bodily health, when he, who was tokkō, had returned home unscathed?

It had meant something, once upon a time, to be a musician. And then a cadet, then a pilot. It had meant everything to be Tokkō Tai. But what was he now?

Someone who could not look a wounded veteran in the eye. Someone who hid in his civilian clothes and hurried home, ashamed to look back.

The city and some of its people had been scarred by fire, by bombs, but his neighborhood and house were still standing. Taro was grateful for that. He crossed the little garden and climbed onto the porch.

His father answered the door, hair white, face lined with unfamiliar woes. He wore the same yukata Taro had borrowed on his last visit. It hung loose on his father's hungry frame.

"A child returns," his father said.

Taro tried to read his father's face before he bowed.

"A child returns," he agreed.

When he looked up again, the expression in his father's eyes had solidified. The mouth pulled up in a sneer.

"I thought my son was a man."

Taro's jaw clenched. He stood stock-still. His military spine stiff and straight. He saluted his father, his superior officer.

His father walked away.

The house, so solid and familiar, neither welcomed nor reprimanded him. He could not expect the same from everyone else.

And then his mother was there, in the doorway, just as she had been months ago. But this time, she didn't bother with shoes or propriety. She ran from the house and threw her arms around him as she hadn't done since he was a little boy.

"At least you are home," she said into his shoulder. "At least you are home."

CHAPTER 63

TARO

The first night had been the worst. Taro's father had refused to join them for dinner. After a sleepless night on his childhood futon, Taro rose the next morning determined to find somewhere else to stay. The house was too small to shoulder the shame he had brought on his family. He said as much to his mother over rice and natto.

"The shame is not all your own," she had replied, much to his confusion.

He was gathering his bags when his father blocked the doorway.

"It would inconvenience your mother," he announced.

And so Taro had stayed.

From there, it was little different from his early days in flight school riding the simulator. Only this time, his father held the model, and Taro followed along, mimicking his motions. His father opened a small engineering firm, applying his aviation skills to rebuilding the country. Taro worked beneath him, drafting plans and running errands until an office boy was found.

They never spoke of the war, nor of the future beyond the company's concerns.

Not long after he had returned home, Taro slid open the shōji door to his room to discover a black case lying on the little table there.

"Do you like it?" his mother had asked, padding up behind him on eager cat feet.

Like a wave of color in a black-and-gray world, he felt the wash of river water, the downspout of rain, a girl in a kimono beneath an umbrella sharing her story. *I had no burdens.*

"Yes," he said. "But . . ."

How could he explain to his mother that the violin belonged to another Taro, one who had died on the beach in a burning aeroplane? That he did not deserve to feel joy—that he was dead?

"There are some children in the neighborhood whose parents would be interested in lessons, I think," his mother continued, pleased. "I thought perhaps . . . ?"

Taro bowed a thank-you. "Father keeps me very busy."

He did not like to see her face fall. "Of course," she replied. "Of course."

He sat alone in his room for some time after that, the violin case unopened. Beside it sat the letters his mother had tried to show him—one sent by the commanding officer at Chiran, another from Tomihara-san, and the last from Hana's mother. Each had sent their condolences, as promised. Before the time the army learned otherwise, the others believed he had died a hero. How could he face them in his disgrace?

He would not repay their faith in him with the truth. Nor

would he risk losing his father's forgiveness by picking up the violin. The Emperor had even less use for musicians now.

It was one thing to choose death, quite another to choose life. Taro would not make a choice.

1946

CHAPTER 64

HANA

Cling! Cling!

The bell at the front of my parents' shop jingles as the American enters.

"Hey there, Hana-san, is your dad around?" Lieutenant Thomas Grossman is a giant of a man, almost two meters tall and half as broad. He has become a regular at Tomiya Shokudo and at our tailor shop. When the Americans finally came to Chiran, they took over the air base for their own headquarters. Our bamboo staves went unbloodied. Instead, we gained customers. Nothing in Japan fits a man the size of Lieutenant Grossman, so my family has plenty of work. In fact, enough for us to move our business out of the house and into a small shop on the main street a half block away.

I smile my Nadeshiko smile, and the lieutenant grins back. I will never grow used to how often the Americans show their teeth. Not all Americans are as friendly as Lieutenant Grossman. But Mariko assures me his grin is not meant as a threat. Her fiancé, Daisuke, knows this. He studied English in college before the war and now works as a translator and attaché for the American forces at the base.

We could use a translator here in the shop. Lieutenant Grossman's Japanese is as bad as my English, but he can only be here for one thing. I hold up a hand to ask him to wait. I have been out doing deliveries, so I take a moment to remove my shoes and jacket before slipping behind the curtain that divides the small shop between the counter and the back work area. Here, customers can try on clothes for alteration, and my parents can sit close together—their knees almost touching, although there is more than enough room for them to spread out—as my mother hand stitches and my father runs our newly acquired sewing machine.

"The big foreigner is here," I announce.

Otō-san smiles up at me, but Okā-san scowls.

"Hana! We treat all customers with respect," she says.

"It is respectful!" Otō-san says. "Grossman-sama is proud of his size. He boasts of it nonstop, Tomihara-san says."

My otō-san is the opposite of Lieutenant Grossman. The war whittled him away until he was nearly skin and bone. Okā-san poured all of her worry into fattening him up again. Now Otō-san has a potbelly, but his arms and legs have stayed skinny.

"He can lift three sacks of rice in one arm," Otō-san says, making a small muscle with his thin biceps. "He says they all are this size back home in Nebraska." Otō-san struggles with the foreign word, the ill-placed *b* and *r* side by side. Only Western tongues would make such an ugly pairing. Japanese is a much more accommodating language.

Okā-san clucks her tongue, but she is smiling. Otō-san had always been able to do that, make her smile. Another thing that was rationed during the war.

While Otō-san goes to tend to the American, my mother adjusts the combs in her hair and gives me a sly look.

"The post came while you were away."

I rush to her, eyes scanning the workroom. "Did it come? Where is it?"

Okā-san pauses to carefully fold the jacket she is altering. She reaches into the drawer beneath her worktable and produces a cream-colored envelope.

I'm too nervous to open it. "Read it for me?"

Okā-san shakes her head. "Where is my Nadeshiko with her nerves of steel?" she jokes. But she takes the envelope and slices it open with a small paper knife.

The paper crackles as she unfolds and smooths it flat. She clears her throat.

"Dear Benkan-sama, we are gratified to inform you of your acceptance to—"

I snatch the paper from Okā-san's hands, then hand it back to her, ashamed. "I am so sorry—"

"No, take it." She reaches it out to me. "It's good to see you so lively for once."

I take the paper and devour it with my eyes. I have been accepted. I am going to Tokyo to study koto music under the great maestro Miyagi Michio.

———

Mariko is not so happy to hear the news. "You'll be one of only a handful of girls there!" she exclaims. It's true, the music school is accepting women for the first time. War has changed much in Japan. I choose to think we women have proven capable. But rumor has it there are no longer enough men left to enroll.

I cluck my tongue.

"Mariko, we have worked in an army hospital. We've cared for tokkō—don't you think I can handle myself at a music school?"

She twists her mouth into a frown. "But it's in Tokyo, Hana. Such a big city. And so very far away . . ."

And that is the trouble with it. Chiran is a tiny town on the southern tip of our country. Tokyo is on Honshu, more than a thousand kilometers away. For the first time in our lives, we will no longer be a short walk apart.

"Think of it this way. Once you're married, you'll have no time for your old spinster friend. You'll have too many fat children to chase around."

"Iie! Don't say that! You're not a spinster—we're barely seventeen! And no matter what Daisuke says, we won't have more than two babies, three at the most. And I'm waiting until I'm nineteen."

"But you're getting married in two months. How will that work?"

Mariko stamps her foot in frustration. "Oh, don't bother me with questions! I'll miss you, Hana. You will be here for the wedding, won't you?"

I take my oldest friend by the hand and give her a gentle squeeze. "Of course I will. Who else will explain to Daisuke that he won't get his wedding night for two more years?"

"What are my girls laughing about so heartily?"

Mariko and I gasp, and laugh even harder. Daisuke stands in the doorway of Mariko's house, still in his work clothes. No longer a uniform—he now wears a Western suit.

"Toshi-san, do you hear them cackling like geese? Have you ever seen such pretty girls sound so brash?"

Laughter in the doorway makes me fall silent, although Mariko still has the giggles. Sato Toshiro, the handsome captain from the hospital, has decided to stay in Chiran. Daisuke says it's because of the opportunities at the base with the Americans. Mariko says it's for me.

He follows Daisuke into the room, and I drop my eyes. Mariko says you can't be a spinster at seventeen, but I am stubborn. We quiet ones often are. He has yet to ask, at any rate, because every look I give him says no. Today is no different.

"Oh, sad news!" Mariko says, reminding me of Sachiko and her constant gossip. "Our little flower is a big-time musician now. She's moving to Tokyo!"

Daisuke crows and congratulates me with a handshake and a big grin. His time around the Americans is rubbing off on him. Toshiro-san is much more reserved in his congratulations. "I will never have your ear for music," he says, "but you must have worked very hard." Those dark eyes are so sincere. "Chiran will be much smaller without you."

I can feel Mariko swooning on my behalf, but my balance is better than that.

"Arigatō gozaimasu," I reply. "I'd best get back to help my parents close the shop."

I rise, and Mariko jumps up after me. I can feel her eyes on me as I bow my farewells. Toshiro is still in the doorway when I pass, and I remember another doorway, another brush of cloth, one year and a lifetime ago.

Any doubt leaves my mind.

I may be the one for Toshiro, but he is not the one for me.

———

That night, my parents and I celebrate my good fortune. We also shed a few tears. And when they have dried, my father and I uncover our kotos. More and more often, I am the only one who plays. But this is a special night. We build a duet that fills the house and rises into the evening sky. On the far side of the wall, the American soldiers carousing at Tomiya Shokudo fall silent, listening to the music on the wind.

I will remember this night when I ride train after train, climbing the length of Japan. I will look out the window at landscapes I have only ever imagined, recalling how I once felt these islands were my body, these mountains my bones.

When we skirt the destruction of Nagasaki and Hiroshima, I will shrink back from the sight. We in Chiran have only recently heard the details of the Americans' "new and most cruel" bombings. But even the rumors we've heard will not compare to the reality of what I will see.

This duet in the night will bring me comfort. I hold on to it for whatever may come.

1947

CHAPTER 65

HANA

Sensei says it will be a somber ceremony, but the other students call it a celebration. Yasukuni Shrine—the monument to our war dead that I had hoped to visit one day—is having a festival, the Mitama Matsuri. July will be a month for honoring those who died in service to the war. Like during Obon, the Buddhist festival for the dead, the shrine will be lit with thousands of lanterns. There will be music and processions and remembrances. We students of Tokyo Music School have been invited to play. Miyagi-sensei shares the news in class today. A cold hand grasps my stomach at the thought.

I should have visited before now. I should have gone every day to pay my respects. But I could not. It felt too much like saying goodbye. And Tokyo is a place where it is easy to forget the past. So much of the city was destroyed in the war; modern buildings are rising all over the place. This is a new Japan, unlike Chiran, with its samurai houses, the same families behind the same stone walls for generations. Tokyo is full of new life. Gaijin bloom like wildflowers here, and seven languages are spoken on every corner, a patchwork of color and newness every day. Even our classroom is new, the paint still fresh on the walls.

I feel new, like the city. Each day we play our instruments, I feel more cemented to my self. And yet the thought of playing at Yasukuni surprises me, scares me a little. For all of my newness, I have not been willing to say a final goodbye.

"Hana-san, are you well?" Sensei asks. Although he is blind, he pays attention. The other students have not stopped gabbling their excitement. But my voice has not joined in.

"Hai, Sensei. Thank you."

I am well enough, I tell myself. But that night, as I play in my dormitory room, I weep and don't try to stanch the tears.

CHAPTER 66

TARO

"Are you finished?"

"Almost." Taro gave the plans a final once-over. He nodded and grabbed the edges, rolling the blueprints into a tube. "Please tell my father I am done."

The office boy nodded—he couldn't have been more than twelve or thirteen, but he was a diligent worker. He ran the plans down the hallway to Taro's father's office. The drawings would be turned into actions, then steel. New buildings were springing up all over the city. New vehicles. New civilian aeroplanes. Several of them were his father's design. A few details were his own. It was satisfying. At first, even the smallest of pleasures carried a tinge of guilt. But he was learning to take the bitter with the sweet.

Taro rolled down his shirtsleeves and checked the clock on the wall. He had half an hour to make it to the station. He grabbed his coat and bag and ran.

The platform was crowded. Families traveling, and businessmen. It was as if the country were a limb that had fallen asleep, and now it tingled with the flow of people, coming back to life.

He found a seat by the window, folded his coat in his lap, and watched the city roll by. The rattle of the train suited him. The strange flat clouds in the sky, like brushstrokes of white on blue. He fell asleep with his head against the window. It was the deepest sleep he'd had in years.

CHAPTER 67

HANA

Even in a city as large as Tokyo, Yasukuni Shrine is bigger than I could have ever imagined. We students cluster around Sensei, entering the grounds early to set up for the day's festivities. Oblong white lanterns are hung in great stacks along the causeway that cuts across the grounds, forming a tunnel of white walls and open sky. Thirty thousand lanterns, Mayoko tells me. She is from Kyoto, and a marvel on the shamisen.

We pass by the great bronze statue of Ōmura Masujirō, the founding father of the Imperial Army, and two great stone lanterns that tower above us like trees. The causeway continues under the Daini Torii, the second gate—the first, the Great Gate, having been taken down during the war. The Daini Torii is made of weather-blackened bronze, two great pillars held apart by a wide beam, crossed at the top by an even greater beam. The skin on the back of my neck shivers as we pass beneath its shadow, but not from cold. This is a sacred place.

July in Tokyo carries a heat and humidity like I've never known. By the time we reach the wide protection of the Shinmon

Gate, I am sweating. My days of hauling wet sheets and marching up hills are behind me. I've become a soft city girl now.

Sensei has us set up in the shade of the Shinmon, where its
thick cypress pillars hold up a slanted roof. The doors of the
gate are open, each marked with massive golden chrysanthemum medallions. Beyond this portal lies another gateway and
then the Hall of Worship. Other musicians and performers continue on deeper into the grounds. There are teahouses and even
a Noh theater here. They will all be full today when the gates
open to the public, and tonight when the lanterns are lit.

Once we are settled, Sensei excuses himself to light incense for
the dead. The others wander off in twos and threes to explore
the grounds, until only Mayoko and I are left.

"Who did you lose?" she asks me. Mayoko is a year older
than I am. Old enough to know that it's not a matter of if we
have lost loved ones, but of how many. She had a sister, a schoolteacher engaged to an Okinawan man, who died in the gyokusai
there. It pained me to learn of it. The Lily Corps girls were the
same age as the eldest of the Nadeshiko and a few years beyond.
But while we served in the halls of our old school building, they
tended soldiers in tunnels and trenches in the midst of battle. Of
the two hundred forty girls and their teachers, only a handful
survived the invasion and the aftermath. Such different paths for
each of us, it's hard to fathom.

Mayoko is looking at me, but I do not know what to say.
"We served tokkō during the war," I say at last. "I should pay
my respects to them."

She nods and does not follow me, opting to stay with the
instruments.

But I do not know where to go. They say there is a great book of names here, of all the dead. If I were to ask a priest to find one name for me, what would it serve? Would I feel better? Different?

I think not.

I purify myself at the Ōtemizusha font, ladling tepid water from the basin over my left, then my right hand. I pour water into my mouth, then purify the ladle, too. And then I approach the prayer hall to make my offering.

I drop a coin in the box and step forward, bowing twice. I clap my hands once, twice to show appreciation and respect. A final bow, and I am backing away. It is a strange feeling. As though I am here and yet not here. I feel closer to him playing the koto than I do in this holy place. I cannot bring myself to say goodbye.

I am grateful when the festival opens, and Sensei tells us to prepare ourselves. When he is ready, we bow to our instruments, we bow to the crowd. Sensei claps his hands twice for our attention, and we begin.

CHAPTER 68

TARO

He should have come sooner. He could have. But that didn't matter; now he was here.

The massive torii gate rose before him like a doorway. He walked the aisle of unlit lanterns, pushed and pulled by the growing crowd. So many Japanese in one place. He felt an unbidden surge of pride. And then he was through the wooden doors of the Shinmon Gate and following the flow of people to the steps of the Hall of Prayer.

Here, Taro stopped. He would pray and leave offerings—a coin for each of the pilots in his two squadrons. But first he would make the offering that mattered most.

Finding an edge of the steps where people could move around him with ease, Taro sat down on the warm stone. He pulled a pack of cigarettes from his pocket, purchased along with a booklet of matches at the station.

"Kenji-chan, you know I don't smoke. These are for you."

He lit the first cigarette, coughing as he drew smoke into his lungs to keep it burning. He waved the stick in the air like incense. He lit the next cigarette, and the next, until the entire pack was burning, lined up like aeroplanes on a runway, on the bottom step of the temple.

"Hey, you can't do that," someone said. An attendant was staring at him accusatorily.

Taro bowed without rising.

"Apologies. They are for the dead. But I would be happy to offer one to you."

The man recoiled and backed away. Taro bowed again, and the man returned it automatically before fading into the crowd.

Nakamura laughed.

Or at least Taro thought so.

He went to the water pavilion and chose a ladle. With each scoop of water, he felt lighter, cleaner. With the final drops poured into his mouth, the taste of bitterness washed away. He was grateful. Grateful.

He bowed, clapped. With the tossing of each coin, Taro said farewell to his friends.

The whole of Yasukuni spread out before him, like the entirety of Japan, of the world, no longer at war. Each and every citizen of every country uncertain of what would come next.

He could feel hopeful, he decided. Or sorrowful. Worry still creased his father's brow, even when he slept. The old world was on trial—the men they had followed, the lives those men had spent for the illusion of future prosperity. Korea, China, the Philippines, Japan. None of them would ever be the same. The only thing that was certain was change.

That was what living meant, after all.

He made his way through the crowd, past the prayerful and

the performers—here a stage play, there a lone musician, there an entire band.

The three gates rose before him. He would pass through each, returning to the world.

A sound brushed his ears. A tune familiar. The song sliding into its frame like the pictures of the kamishibai man. A place, a time, a face, all as they had been two years ago.

Taro turned. The crowd parted momentarily, opening a tunnel of light.

At the end of it, a young woman sat on a cloth on the ground surrounded by a small group of musicians.

Her hands flowed across a beautiful koto.

"Haru no Umi" on koto and shamisen.

He stepped toward her as the music ended. The drumming continued, a tattoo in his blood, a pounding his heart could not contain. Lashes like black butterflies. Eyes wide as rivers, deeper than wells. A memory of dancing, of cherry blossoms in the rain.

CHAPTER 69

HANA

The strings of my koto fade into silence. The crowd murmurs, applauds. I have come to Yasukuni to honor those who were lost, to pay my respects to the dead. And now it is over.

A pang of emptiness washes through me. What was I expecting? No glowing fireflies. No ghostly violin. I slide the picks from my fingers. The performance is over. The day at an end.

The crowd parts and moves on. Around me, my classmates prepare to do the same.

I reach for my koto case, but something stops me. As if my name has been spoken out loud. I look up.

And there are miracles.

For there is Taro.

Taro. Taro. Taro.

I raise my hand, trembling. And wave.

Hello.

AUTHOR'S NOTE

Research is one of my favorite rabbit holes. I don't remember what I was chasing that day—some tidbit on World War II aviation, no doubt—when I found myself staring at a photograph online: A row of Japanese schoolgirls in dark middy blouses and shining bobbed haircuts stand smiling and waving at the edge of a runway. Their arms are full of cherry blossoms. Their eyes are on a departing fighter plane. It was black and white, the resolution poor, but the image struck me. I read the article that accompanied the photo. And that is how I first learned about the Nadeshiko Unit girls of Chiran Junior High School in Japan. It's also how I learned about the Chiran Peace Museum, dedicated to the memory of the 439 tokkō pilots who flew out on their last missions from Chiran's Army Air Force Base. Kyushu is the southernmost island in the Japanese home island chain. Chiran was one of the closest bases to the action—a mere two-and-a-half-hour flight to Okinawa. I was hooked. I wanted to know more. Fortunately, M. G. Sheftall's in-depth book, *Blossoms in the Wind: Human Legacies of the Kamikaze* was waiting to fill me in. (See page 306 for more books on the subject.)

The first official tokubetsu kōgeki, or "special attack" unit, was formed in the fall of 1944. Japanese forces were flagging. A new plan of attack was needed if the Empire was going to win the war. In previous months, some pilots had crashed into enemy ships of their own accord—perhaps due to damaged airplanes. But now the style of attack would be sanctioned and planned. As with any war, the final numbers are uncertain, but according to some estimates, there had been nearly two thousand tokkō sorties, scoring less than five hundred hits on Allied ships, and sinking forty-five. As a result, over seven thousand British, American, and Australian sailors died.

According to *The Mind of the Kamikaze* by Takeshi Kawatoko, a fact book published by the Peace Museum for Kamikaze Pilots in Chiran, 1,036 men died as tokkō pilots. Other sources put the total number of tokkō upward of 3,800. (It's possible the Peace Museum's numbers are restricted to army pilots. There were also navy pilots and Kaiten torpedo attack units.) By the museum's count, of the thousand-plus pilots, 269 were university students and 335 were boy pilots, like Taro and Nakamura.

Chief in remembering the fallen pilots was Tome Tomihara. Known as "the mother of the tokkō," Tome did all she could to make the young pilots comfortable during their time in Chiran. After the war, she raised money to build both a shrine and the museum in Chiran. Her restaurant expanded to an inn in order to accommodate the families of those who served and died. During the Allied occupation, Tomihara-san cared for the incoming American soldiers with as much kindness as she had the Japanese before them. She is known throughout Japan as an exemplar of kindness—the Mother Teresa of her country.

Chiran Girls' School closed in March 1944 when the students joined the war effort. The Nadeshiko Unit (the flower is part of the school crest) sent its sixteen-to-eighteen-year-olds to Nagasaki to work in a torpedo factory, while the lower three grades worked in the potato fields or dug air raid shelters. On March 18, 1945, American planes called Hellcats attacked the area. Some villagers were killed. The next day, the girls were reassigned to the tokkō at Chiran Army Air Force Base.

Many of the girls' experiences in this book are inspired by the school diary kept by Maeda Shōko. The original diary is kept under glass at the Chiran Peace Museum. An English translation can be found in Samuel Hideo Yamashita's *Letters from an Autumn of Emergencies: Selections from the Wartime Diaries of Ordinary Japanese.* It was common for people to keep personal diaries in World War II Japan, and compulsory for students. Teachers would review the diaries weekly to make sure the students' spirits were high. From this book and others, I was able to read firsthand accounts from students, adults, and tokkō pilots. Unfortunately, many of the young people's diaries have yet to be translated from Japanese. I was lucky to find Dr. Yamashita's translation.

The inclusion of "comfort women"—mostly non-Japanese women forced into prostitution for the Japanese military—is based on general history, rather than specific evidence of their presence in Chiran. Despite considerable research, it's only in Maeda's school diary entries from April 1945 that I found a mention of "comfort-troop dancers." It's unclear if these dancers are "comfort women" or perhaps part of a USO-like entertainment group, but I chose to take the opportunity to acknowledge the legacy of these unfortunate women.

It was the philosopher George Santayana who said, "Those who cannot remember the past are condemned to repeat it." Japan's treatment of the events of World War II continues to evolve. Peace museums exist across the nation acknowledging the events of and lives lost during the war. On my research trip to Chiran, I was joined by several schoolkids on class trips. It was both sad and heartening to see them comprehend the human cost of the Pacific War. The scene was repeated later that week on a visit to the Peace Memorial Museum in Hiroshima. There, my guide expressed surprise at seeing so many school groups present. When I said it seemed to be a rather obvious destination, she replied, "They used to just go to Disneyland."

Times are changing. May we change with them, and for the better.

GLOSSARY

AMATERASU ŌMIKAMI • the sun goddess, the Shinto deity from whom the Japanese Imperial family is said to descend

ANKO • red bean paste

ARIGATŌ GOZAIMASHITA • polite form of "thank you" often used by store clerks

ARIGATŌ GOZAIMASU • polite form of "thank you very much"

BANZAI • an exhortation to live ten thousand years

BUSHIDO • the samurai code of honor

BUTSUDAN • a Buddhist altar used for paying respects to deceased family members

-CHAN • (suffix) shows affection

CHIRAN • a town in the south of Kyushu

CHIRIMEN • a type of silk

DAINI TORII • "Second Gate"; the second gate at Yasukuni Shrine

"DŌKI NO SAKURA" • "Cherry Blossoms of the Same Period," a popular war song

DOMO ARIGATŌ • "thank you very much"

FURO • a Japanese soaking bathtub

FUROSHIKI • a cloth used for wrapping and carrying items and gifts

GAIJIN • outsider, non-Japanese

GEISHA • a traditional Japanese hostess and entertainer

GETA • traditional wooden platform shoes

GUNKOKU-SHŌNEN • "military youth"; students in a military academy

GUNSHIN • a war god

GYOKUSAI • "shattering of the jewel," an honorable suicide in the face of defeat

HACHIMAKI • a samurai headband

HAHA-UE • mother (very formal, polite, old fashioned)

HAHAGATAKE • a mountain in Chiran

HAI • yes

HAIKU • a form of poetry originated in Japan consisting of three lines with five, seven, and five syllables respectively, or some version thereof. Images of nature are common, as well as a revelation.

HANA • flower

"HARU NO UMI" • "The Sea in Spring," a piece for koto and shakuhachi composed by Miyagi Michio in 1929. It was inspired by the image of the sea from his childhood, before he lost his sight.

HONSHU • the largest of the home islands of Japan

HOTARU • firefly, a nickname for the short-lived tokkō

ICHI/NI/SAN • one/two/three

IIE • no

ITAI • ouch; it hurts

JI • a bridge that supports a string on a koto; traditionally made of ivory. (There are thirteen bridges in all.)

JISEI • death poems, a Buddhist tradition in a variety of poetic styles, meant to convey the last thoughts of a person before death. Many jisei and final words are on display at the Chiran Peace Museum.

JIZO • Buddhist deity, protector of travelers and children, who leads the innocent across the Sanzu River to the land of the dead

KABUKI SEWAMONO • a type of play in the Kabuki style of theater, known for contemporary romances among other themes

KAGOSHIMA • a large city on the coast near Chiran

KAIMONDAKE • a mountain in Kyushu that resembles Mount Fuji

KAITEN • manned torpedoes used in kamikaze missions

KAMI • Shinto deities

KAMIFUSEN • paper balloon balls

KAMIKAZE • "divine wind"; also a name for tokkō pilots

KAMISHIBAI • "paper drama," a form of storytelling using illustrations accompanied by a live, spoken narrative

KANNON • Buddhist goddess of mercy

KEMPEITAI • military police

KENDO • a martial art that typically uses bamboo or wooden swords

KIMONO • a traditional ankle-length robe with long sleeves

KINSHA • a type of silk

KIRI • a type of wood used for making kotos

KONNICHIWA • "good day," a greeting typically used midday to early evening

KOTO • a stringed musical instrument

KUROBUTA-TONKOTSU • a local dish for which the famous Kagoshima pork meat, on the bone, is boiled for several hours with ingredients such as daikon radish, brown sugar, Kagoshima miso, and shōchū

KUROMATSU • a type of pine tree

KYUSHU • the southernmost of the four home islands of Japan

MANCHUKUO • a wartime puppet state created in China by Japan, which occupied a large part of Manchuria

MENKO • a card game

MISO • a seasoning made from fermented soybeans; a soup made with the same seasoning

MITAMA MATSURI • festival for the war dead at Yasukuni Shrine in Tokyo

MOMO • peach

MOMOTARO • literally "Peach Boy," the hero of a traditional Japanese folktale

MONO NO AWARE • the concept of sadness in beauty because it fades

MONPÉ • loose trousers, traditional work pants that are wide at the hips and thighs, and gathered at the ankles

MURA • a rural region supervised by local government, similar to a county

NADESHIKO • a flower from the dianthus family (pronounced *na-desh-ko*)

NAGAJUBAN • a robe, often made of cotton, worn beneath a kimono

NATTO • fermented soybeans

NIGARI • a type of salt

NINGYO • a mermaid-like creature

O- • a prefix used to show respect for daily items in life (for example, o-cha for tea, o-mizu for water)

OBI • a wide sash worn with a kimono

OBON • an annual Buddhist festival to honor ancestral spirits

OCHA • green tea

OJI-SAN • uncle (middle-aged man)

OJII-SAN • grandfather or old man (over sixty)

OKARA • soy pulp that remains after making tofu

OKĀ-SAN • mother (not as formal as "haha-ue")

OKAYU • rice porridge

OKINAWA • an island cluster south of the home islands of Japan; also the largest island in that cluster

OKONOMIYAKI • a popular local dish in Hiroshima featuring a savory layered pancake of noodles, vegetables, and meat, topped with a sauce

ONI • a demon in Japanese folklore

ONSEN • hot springs; spas or inns with hot springs

ŌTEMIZUSHA • large purification basin

OTŌ-SAN • father

SAKÉ • an alcoholic beverage made from fermented rice

SAKURA • cherry blossom

SAKURAJIMA • an active volcano overlooking Kagoshima Bay in Kyushu, Japan

-SAMA • a formal honorific suffix

SAMURAI • warrior nobility in early and medieval Japan

-SAN • a suffix added to a proper name to show respect

SANZU-NO-KAWA • "The River of Three Crossings"; the river into the afterlife in Japanese folklore, similar to the Greek River Styx

SATSUMAIMO • sweet potato

SAYOUNARA • goodbye

SENNINBARI • a thousand-person-stitch belt

SENSEI • teacher

SHAMISEN • a stringed instrument similar to a lute or mandolin

SHINMON • Main Gate

SHŌCHŪ • a local liquor made from sweet potatoes

SHŌJI • a traditional door or room divider made of translucent paper with a wooden or bamboo frame

SHOKUDO • a type of casual dining restaurant

SHŌNEN HIKŌHEI • Youth Pilot School

SHŌWA ERA • "the Period of Bright Peace"; the reign of Emperor Hirohito, from December 25, 1926, to his death on January 7, 1989

SODZU-BABA • an old woman who demands the clothes or skins of the dead once they've crossed the River of Three Crossings in Japanese folklore

SURIBACHI • a mortar, used with a surikogi for grinding food

SURIKOGI • a pestle, used with a suribachi for grinding food

TABI • traditional Japanese socks worn with thonged footwear, featuring a split between the big and second toe

TAI • unit

TANKA • a form of poetry based on haiku

TARO • boy

TATAMI • woven floor mats

TOKKŌ • special attack pilots, also known as kamikaze

TOKUBETSU KŌGEKI • "special attack," the term from which the tōkko take their name

TONARI-GUMI • a neighborhood association, comprised of nine households, that handles civic duties

TORII • a gateway to a Shinto shrine

TOYOTAMA-HIME • a goddess, daughter of the sea god in Japanese folklore, descendant of the sun goddess, and grandmother of the first emperor of Japan

TSUBURAJII • a type of evergreen tree

-UE • meaning "upper" or "above"; a suffix to show extreme respect

"UMI YUKABA" • "If I Go Away to Sea," a popular wartime anthem about the honor of dying for the Emperor

UNOHANA • sautéed okara with vegetables

YAMATO • an ancient name for Japan

YAMATO-DAMASHII • Japanese spirit

YAMATO NADESHIKO • the idealized Japanese woman

YASUKUNI SHRINE • an Imperial Shinto shrine in Tokyo dedicated to those who died in military service for Japan

YUKATA • a casual, lightweight kimono, often made of cotton

SELECTED BIBLIOGRAPHY

There is so much more history to share about the Tokkō Tai and Nadeshiko Tai. I fit what I could into the story. If, like me, you love a good rabbit hole, I suggest the following books (as well as Bill Gordon's website, kamikazeimages.net). They were invaluable to me in approaching Japanese history, culture, and in piecing together the imagined love story of Hana and Taro.

Cook, Haruko, and Theodore F. Cook, *Japan at War: An Oral History*

Davies, Roger J., and Osamu Ikeno (editors), *The Japanese Mind: Understanding Contemporary Japanese Culture*

Embree, John F., *Suye Mura: A Japanese Village*

Hashimoto, Akiko, *The Long Defeat: Cultural Trauma, Memory, and Identity in Japan*

Jowett, Phillip, and Stephen Andrew, *The Japanese Army 1931–1945*, volumes 1 and 2

Kawatoko, Takeshi, *The Mind of the Kamikaze*

King, Dan, *The Last Zero Fighter: Firsthand Accounts from WWII Japanese Naval Pilots*

Marsh, Don, and Peter Starkings, *Imperial Japanese Army Flying Schools 1912–1945*

Sheftall, M. G., *Blossoms in the Wind: Human Legacies of the Kamikaze*

Yamanouchi, Midori, and Joseph L. Quinn (translators), *Listen to the Voices from the Sea: Writings of the Fallen Japanese Students*

Yamashita, Samuel Hideo, *Daily Life in Wartime Japan, 1940–1945*

Yamashita, Samuel Hideo, *Leaves from an Autumn of Emergencies: Selections from the Wartime Diaries of Ordinary Japanese*

Zaloga, Stephen J., and Ian Palmer, *Kamikaze: Japanese Special Attack Weapons 1944–45*

ACKNOWLEDGMENTS

No book is written alone. This is especially true for historical fiction, where the lives of real people intersect with imagination. What reads true is because of the help I received. Any errors in these pages are my own. My deepest gratitude to everyone who helped me uncover and tell this story: authors Dan King and Samuel Hideo Yamashita for their books, their suggestions, and particularly Dan for his introduction to Takeshi Kawatoko. Kawatoko-san was my gracious guide through the Chiran Peace Museum. His book, *The Mind of the Kamikaze*, was full of details I could not find anywhere else. An exuberant thanks to Reiko Yoshimura, my intrepid guide across Kyushu. From Kagoshima to Chiran and beyond, she hunted down rivers and bunkers, and initiated conversations with every resident we met over the age of eighty. Without her help, I would never have found the tiny river where the Nadeshiko washed clothes, nor met the kind priest at the temple who could not recall ever seeing cherry blossoms there in his youth.

To the entire city of Chiran—from the women who served tea at the Samurai Gardens, to the kind people at the Chamber of Commerce, with their collection of photographs, and the little boy sitting cross-legged outside the old junior high school who pointed the way to the temple down the street, I was made to feel welcome. To the attentive, smiling staff at Tomiya Inn (and to the chef of the amazing multicourse meals!), I give gratitude. When I was introduced to the young woman behind the counter as the great-granddaughter of Tome Tomihara herself, I felt as though I'd fallen through the looking glass with wonders to be seen. A special thanks to Toshio Oba and his wife—two of the most genteel people I've ever had the pleasure of meeting in my travels.

Stateside, I owe many thanks to author Rahna Reiko Rizzuto, whose own deep research into World War II Japan has served as an inspiration and an education for my own. And thanks to koto player Reiko Obata, who answered my bizarre questions with kindness and insight (Can hair be turned into a koto or violin string? No), and introduced me to "Haru no Umi." I found Reiko online and knew I'd struck gold when she mentioned her daughter is a violinist. The conversation my inquiries sparked was just the support I needed at the start of this book. I would also like to thank Los Angeles Philharmonic concertmaster Martin Chalifour and Metzler Violin Shop in Glendale, California. It was at a Metzler exhibition that I had the pleasure of listening to Mr. Chalifour play fifty different violins and discuss their various traits. It was from watching him that I shaped Taro's own performances . . . and learned how easy it is to develop a crush on a violinist.

A long-overdue thanks to the two people who continue to keep me online (and in bookmarks!) in style—Torrey Douglass and Karen Bates. Your friendship, graphic design eye, tech savvy, and massive generosity overwhelm me.

I also owe thanks to Yasunari Kawabata for his masterful novels *Snow Country* and *The Sound of the Mountain*. I first read them in a Japanese Literature in Translation class as an undergrad at New York University. It wasn't until many years later that I came to better understand the story structure known as kishōtenketsu. The earliest versions of this book were modeled on that Eastern style of storytelling. Forgive the alterations here and there, as I adjusted the shape to more Western tastes.

This book would not exist without my editor, Stephanie Pitts, or my agent, Kirby Kim. My copy editors, Ana Deboo and Yoko Oikawa, worked diligently to correct my errors—grammatical, historical, and linguistic. Any remaining flubs are all mine. Kristin Boyle and Maggie Edkins designed several covers, reimagining the face of the book until it shined. My thanks to G. P. Putnam's Sons for wanting me to return to the Second World War. As our Greatest Generation passes on, it's up to us to remember the history they lived.

I am forever grateful to my husband, Kelvin, for putting up with dozens of Japanese words stickered around the house as I practiced the language, and for reminding me to give people hope.

To the people who fought and died on all sides of this terrible war. May we learn from your sacrifice to never tread that way again.

There are more people to thank, but I cannot list them all. Let me just say this book is a culmination of years of friendship, study, one very deep rabbit hole, and a hope for lasting peace.

READ ON FOR MORE
FROM SHERRI L. SMITH

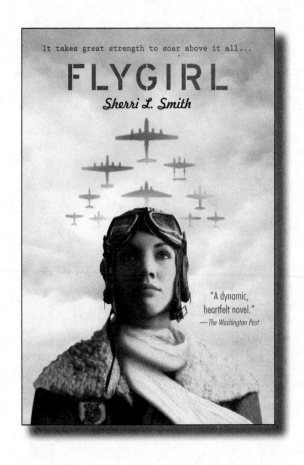

Chapter 1

It's Sunday afternoon, and the phonograph player is jumping like a clown in a parade the way Jolene and I are dancing. We're cleaning the Wilson house and Nat King Cole's singing on the record. It sounds fine. This is one of the best places to clean because they have a big yard and no neighbors close enough to hear our ruckus. Otherwise, working on a Sunday would be a real drag. But the Wilsons are gone for the weekend and Mr. Wilson said he'd pay extra for a clean house when he gets back. With Christmas just a few weeks away, the money will come in handy.

I am knee-deep in Murphy Oil Soap, washing Otis Wilson's sticky fingerprints off his mama's fine oak banister, when Jolene comes waltzing down the stairs with the laundry.

"I swear, these people must change their clothes every hour on the hour, every day. I've never seen such a mess of laundry in my life. Ida Mae Jones, hurry up with that polishing and come help me."

"I am hurrying. If they'd stop giving Otis jam for breakfast, I wouldn't be cleaning this railing every week."

"If they stopped giving Otis jam for breakfast, he'd cry for a week," she says.

Otis Wilson is the most spoiled white boy in New Orleans. Just a year younger than Jolene and me, but at seventeen, he's still a slobbering mess. Jolene says it's because he's soft in the head. I think it has more to do with being spoiled.

"You think he'd enlist if we ever join this war?"

Jolene laughs her big horse laugh. "Girl, can you see that little jam jar in a uniform? I mean he's big enough, for a white boy, and not bad looking, either, if you like the pasty type, but taking orders and holding a gun—we'd be better off surrendering than sending him to fight."

"Too true, too true." I laugh, thinking about Otis's broad-bellied self in a uniform. "Think they've got maids in the army to wipe the jam off his rifle?"

It's Jolene's turn to chuckle. "Now stop making me laugh and get to work. We're going to have to clean this house a hundred more times if you're going to get the money to go to Chicago."

"Don't I know it." I sigh. At home, we get by running our little berry farm, but getting by is far from getting rich. Even with cleaning houses full-time since Jolene and I graduated high school in June, the saving is coming slow. Sometimes it seems like my purse is nothing but a sieve with money running through it like water. "The way I see it, another month of solid work and I'll be set. Then all I have to do is find a way to get my mother to let me go to Chicago by myself."

"Or work another six months and take her with you."

"Oh, I can see that now," I say, rolling my eyes. "'Mama, you wait right here, I'm gonna go take my pilot's test.' She only lets me fly now because Grandy's with me. She hates to fly."

"Girl, I know better than to tell you to give it up. You've got the flying bug just as sure as your daddy did, but some days I think it's more trouble than it's worth. More money than it's worth, too."

"Bessie Coleman had to go all the way to France to learn

how to fly just because she was colored." She was one of my idols—the Negro Amelia Earhart. "She was nothing more than a hairdresser, but she did it. So why can't I? I already know how to fly, Jolene. If I can't get my license in Tuskegee, at least Chicago's closer than Paris."

Jolene shrugs over her armful of dirty shirts. "If you say so."

"I do."

Just remembering my first time in a plane, in my daddy's old Curtiss JN-4 "Jenny," I get goose bumps. Nothing else on God's green earth does that to me. Of course it's worth it.

Last year, just before I turned seventeen, Mama's daddy, Grandy, convinced her to let me go to Tuskegee to take my pilot's test. I'd taken over Daddy's side business of dusting crops, but I needed my license. Daddy would have taken me, had he lived. I'd already flown over forty hours with him, and I had passed the written exam by mail just before he died. All I needed to do was go up in a real plane with a certified instructor. Mama kept Daddy's promise by letting me go.

Grandy and I showed up real early at the airfield. I was so excited I thought I'd have to run to the restroom and pee every five minutes. Grandy was as calm as could be, though, and that helped me a lot. The instructor, a Mr. Anderson, showed up, and he was a white man, with blue eyes and a firm jawline. I'd heard he had passed other colored pilots at the base, and I thought he looked tough, but fair.

Well, I said a little prayer asking Daddy for help, and I took that instructor up in the test plane. It was a Jenny, like Daddy had taught me on, easy as slipping into an old sweater. We did rolls, and loops, and landings, and I could hardly stop smiling because I knew I'd done good.

3

But when we climbed out of that plane, Mr. Anderson looked at me and said, "You can fly, no doubt about it. But no woman's gonna get a license out of me. Go home, Miss Jones. You've failed."

I stood there, staring at his strong jawline and his blue eyes, and if looks could set a fire, he'd have been a three-alarm blaze by the time I was done. Grandy, who's seen more than his share of wrongness, just took my arm and said, "S'all right, honey. We've got better places to go."

That better place is Chicago, the Coffey School of Aeronautics. Owned and run by colored people, like me. Teaching men and women alike. No matter how long it takes me, that's what I'm working toward.

"Stop daydreaming, Ida," Jolene says, disappearing into the washing room. "Hurry down here so we can talk." Her voice carries from the back of the house. I finish scrubbing the banister, still trying to figure out how to get to Chicago without letting Mama catch on. She doesn't like the idea of me flying. She only lets me dust crops because it pays a little and Grandy comes with me. Daddy is the only person who could convince her that I'd be okay by myself. But since he's gone, I'm on my own. As far as Mama is concerned, going to the big city by myself is crazy enough. She'd call me a damn fool if she knew it was because I wanted to fly.

"Finally," Jolene says as I round the corner to the washing room. "Grab a tub—this is old-fashioned dirt in these socks. It'll take a washboard to clean them."

She pours boiling water from a kettle into the washer and runs those socks through about a hundred times each. Mr. Wilson fancies himself a golfer, but you'd think he was a go-pher with all the dirt he brings home with him from the course. The socks are a hopeless cause. Still, I put them in a galvanized tub with bleach to get them white and bluing to get them even whiter. Laundry is my least favorite part of housekeeping. The smell of the soap and chemicals stays in your skin for a week. Sometimes, on a hot day, I feel like I sweat bleach.

"Now, about Chicago," Jolene says, sounding just like her mother. Miss Tara is a math teacher, and whenever she puts herself to any sort of problem, math or otherwise, you just know she'll solve it. Jolene isn't as reliable as her mama, but it is comforting to have her on my side, just the same.

"Here's what to do. Tell your ma that you're visiting my mama's sister in Natchez, with me. I'll even go see my old aunt to keep your story straight."

"You make it sound like a sacrifice," I say, "when everybody knows your aunt lives across the river from the city. And that she falls asleep early every single night, Miss I'll Be Back Before She Knows I'm Gone."

"Why should I suffer for you?" Jolene raises an eyebrow and laughs. "Besides, we can't all fly airplanes. Some of us have got to keep both feet on the ground. New Orleans is a good place to do just that."

"On the ground, Jolene? On the dance floor of a jazz club is more like it."

Jolene grins, the gap showing in her smile. She pats her Marcel curls beneath the gray scarf that is part of our cleaning uniform. "Don't I know it, don't I know it." Jolene has a fantasy of leaving Slidell to sing in a New Orleans nightclub. Trouble is, she has no voice for it. So she spends her days in the city with me, washing clothes and cleaning houses.

"Jolene, you are nothing but trouble." I reach over her head

5

and turn on the radio we have stashed on the laundry room shelf. There's a ball game on, so I fiddle with the knobs.

"Put some music on. *Sammy Kaye's Sunday Serenade* should be on."

"You've already got the record going, and every radio station's starting up with Christmas carols. Besides, I just want to hear the news."

I twist the dial until the news comes in good and strong. The news is much the same as it was last night. The Germans and Russians are fighting in subzero temperatures, and Japan's moving troops in the Far East despite our peace talks. Jolene sighs and goes back to scrubbing the laundry. I turn the volume down so we can talk over the news and the phonograph playing upstairs.

"Did you know the Russians let their women fly military planes?" I say. "In England, too. Ferrying planes for the air force. Isn't that a kick?"

"Loony's more like it. What girl in her right mind wants to be flying around in a war zone?" Jolene rolls her eyes at me and my face goes hot. "Baby, you're not only fly crazy, you're war crazy, too. That's a bad combination."

I cut off the radio to keep the peace, and Jolene starts singing along with the record. It's nearly four o'clock by the time we're finished with the Wilsons'. We yank off our head scarves and shake out our hair on the back steps of the house. We button up our sweaters against the slight December chill. Jolene pulls her copy of the house key from her pocket and locks the place up tight.

"I sure hope Mr. Wilson is grateful for the Sunday cleaning," Jolene says, dropping the key into her bag. "I need a new pair of stockings."

6

"Why do you waste your money, Jolene? Silk is for show-girls and debutantes."

"And young ladies who hope to catch a man someday. You'd do well to get yourself a pair, or you'll end up an old maid."

"Takes one to know one."

"Speak for yourself," she says. I turn to see her smiling her prettiest little smile at some city road worker across the street. The boy can't be much older than we are, and he sure looks all right in his overalls and cap. It takes me a minute to rec-ognize him as Danny Taylor from our elementary school.

"Danny Taylor, is that you?" I call out.

Jolene frowns and drops the able-Grable sexy act. "Aw, heck, Dan. What you doing, looking all grown up like that?"

We wait for a break in the traffic and jog across the cobble-stones. Poydras Street is a leafy place, sheltered by live oaks with crepe myrtle trees growing in between. Danny Taylor smiles at us when we get closer. He's got a nice smile, broad with teeth as white as milk in a strong brown face.

"Ida Mae Jones, I thought you was a white woman walking over there with that fine light skin and pretty brown hair."

My hand goes instantly to my curls, loose and smooth, like my daddy's. The kind of curls Jolene calls "good hair." Not tight and hard to handle, like hers.

"What about my hair?" Jolene asks, eyebrows arched. "And my fine *brown* skin?"

Danny grins, unaware he's offended her or me, for that matter. I'm shy of my fair looks, and Jolene's more than a little jealous. "Well, that's how I knew she wasn't white. You're dressed the same, and Jolene, you're as black as a good cup of coffee."

7

"Best coffee you'll never have," she says, and turns her nose up in the air.

"Well, it was good to see you, Danny," I say, anxious to leave.

"What's your rush? I haven't seen either of you two since the eighth grade."

"Well, some of us stuck around and graduated," Jolene snaps. She's decided not to like Danny Taylor.

"Well, some of us had to work," Danny says right back. At school, I had known Danny mostly through my brother. I remember when Thomas came home one day and told us his friend had to quit school to help his family pay the bills. Jolene knows it, too.

"How's your mama?" I ask.

"Fine, fine. Doctor says she has a sugar problem, but she's doing all right."

"Glad to hear it," I say.

Jolene's folded up her arms now. She looks at me and frowns.

"Well, Danny, like I said, it was nice seeing you, but we've got to get the trolley and all before the buses shut down. Sundays are always awful tight."

"Say hi to your brother for me."

"I will." Jolene is dragging me away now. I stumble on the pavement, catch myself, and wave goodbye.

"You just keep waving goodbye to Joe Corn over there," she says in a clipped voice. "Girl, you can do better than smiling up in his face like that."

"Jolene, I was being polite. You could take a lesson or two. What's wrong with you?"

Jolene stops in her tracks and screws up her face so tight,

8

I think she's going to cry. "I don't know," she says unhappily. "It's just . . . am I pretty at all? He didn't even look at me. Just Little Miss Pretty Hair and Her Creamy White Skin. I love you, Ida, but he just made me so mad."

"Me, too." I put an arm around her. We stand there, half hugging, with nothing left to say. Daddy once told me color didn't matter as much to folks up north. Light-skinned like me and him or dark like Mama and Jolene, up there he said they'd treat all colored folks the same, like we were all white. I'd sure like to see that, 'cause down here, color seems to be the only place it's at.

The trolley down St. Charles Avenue is empty of colored folks. Jolene and I sit to the back and watch the big houses roll by. St. Charles Avenue is the prettiest place on earth, a green tunnel of live oak trees arching across two paved roads, the trolley running down the middle on its cables. Only the richest, whitest folks live up here. We trundle past Audubon Park and the university, same as always, but inside this trolley car something is different. Jolene nudges me with her foot.

"It's like a funeral in here," she says. It's true. Usually, the trolley is buzzing with laughter, chatter, and just plain noise. But now, it's like a storm is coming. The few people on board are deadly quiet.

"Sooner we get home, the better," I tell her. The trip up Carrollton Avenue is just as slow. At the last stop, we hop off and run across the wide street to catch the bus back to Slidell.

There's more folks sitting in the back of the bus. One of them, a dignified-looking, coffee-colored gentleman in a neatly pressed suit, has a newspaper.

"Excuse me, sir. What's the news?" I ask him.

He looks up at me, startled, and starts to stand. There are plenty of seats, though. Jolene has saved me one.

"Ma'am, I'm sorry," he says, rising.

"Oh, no, no. I just noticed you had the paper. Does it say what's going on? Everyone seems so . . ."

He looks at me a moment longer and settles back into his seat, seeing that I'm colored, too.

"Ah, sorry, baby girl. You haven't heard? We've been attacked by the Japanese."